EVERNIGHT PUBLISHING ®

www.evernightpublishing.com

Copyright© 2019

Kory Steed

Editor: Karyn White

Cover Art: Jay Aheer

ISBN: 978-0-3695-0036-6

LIGHTNING'S HIDDEN MENACE

DEDICATION

For Mark, for believing in me.

LIGHTNING'S HIDDEN MENACE

LIGHTNING'S HIDDEN MENACE

The Lightning Series, 2

Kory Steed

Copyright © 2017

Section One
No longer alone

Chapter One
Reunited

December 21, 2009, 8:45 AM, MST
Homestead

  Jason led Aaron by the hand, as they ran up the hill *towards* the stockade under the bright morning sunlight of the winter solstice while the two men from Pacific North Air Transport watched from the helipad above. It was all Aaron could do to keep up. He'd only recently started to walk again, let alone run and on top of that, he'd sprained his right ankle, his good ankle, five days earlier on the day he'd been discharged from rehab. When they reached the open gate, Jason stopped to let Aaron catch his breath. Aaron bent over to massage his ankle. "Jason, I'm not quite used to this yet. The uneven, rocky terrain and tall grass are tough to get through with my ankle, and I only got out of rehab last week."

"Oh, Aaron, I'm sorry. What happened to your ankle?"

"No, really … it's okay. I just need a minute. I'm a little winded, that's all. I sprained it last week."

"How'd you do that?"

"Later. I'll tell you all about it later."

Jason bent down and hugged Aaron from behind. "I can't believe you're really here. I just can't believe it."

Aaron stood back up.

"Tell me, Aaron," Jason said, "Tell me what happened. Tell me all about it."

"I will, I will and in detail. I promise," Aaron said, still wincing a little, "but first, let me have a few minutes to just take all this in. Let me take you in, Jason. I've missed you so much, I can't even begin to tell you."

"Oh, Aaron, I've missed you, too, more than I can say."

After another minute, Aaron let out a big breath. "Okay, I'm better now, but can we just walk? I'm still getting used to using this cane."

"Yes, yes, of course. I still can't get over how tall you are." Jason stood on his toes and pulled Aaron's mouth to his. Aaron wrapped his arms around Jason and kissed him deeply, then hugged him tight to his chest. "Jason, I need to ask you something."

"Of course, Aaron. Anything. What is it?"

"Jason, can I stay? Can I live here with you?"

"Are you kidding, Aaron? Of course you can stay. It's been my dream, but I hope you're not asking because you feel like you owe me something."

"Am I kidding? You're the one who's kidding? God no, Jason. I love you! You're all I've thought about, coming back here and making a life with you, just like we planned. You are right about one thing though, I will always feel like I owe you. Yes, you saved my life, but please know this, my love for you is stronger than any debt I could ever feel. These months we've been apart have been the most difficult time of my life."

"Then all I can say, Aaron, is welcome home."

Again, they embraced and kissed. Jason wouldn't let Aaron go for the longest time.

"So tell me all about this place," Aaron said as he swept his hand across the view in front of him. "Remember, I only saw it for a brief moment, and that was when I was flat on my back when you and Jack and Rod carried me out of here on the stretcher."

Jason put his arm around Aaron's waist and led him towards the open gate. "Okay. Okay. Sure. There's three acres inside the stockade. It's electrified by those solar panels." Jason pointed to the small panels that were fastened to the tops of every fourth main, telephone pole-thick post around the stockade. "There's three control panels, one here," he pointed to an enclosed, weatherproof box mounted on the stockade wall just outside the gate, "another one just like it, mounted inside the gate, and a third next to the front door of the cabin on the porch."

As they walked, Jason continued. "The panels house the controls for two independent system that work simultaneously, so if one goes down..."

Aaron stopped walking and faced Jason. With a nearly imperceptible nod of his head, he crossed his arms in front of him. His entire face lit up as he smiled broadly, and his eyes glistened.

"Oh, sorry, Aaron. I'm overwhelming you with too much stupid information. It's not important right now. I'll tell you how it all works later."

"Baby, nothing's stupid." He pulled Jason into a hug and kissed his cheek. "You can tell me anything you want. It's just that I like hearing the sound of your voice. Is it okay that I call you that, again? Baby, I mean?"

"Oh, Aaron, I love it!"

"So that's the barn over there?" Aaron asked, pointing.

"Yes."

"Well, there's a certain young lady I've been dying to meet. Can you take me to meet Heather?"

"Sure thing."

As they walked arm in arm through the dry grass up to the barn, Jason took the time to explain how best to meet the livestock. "Remember, none of them know you. They only know me. We should walk in together and then you should sit down in the chair next to the work table while I go over and talk to them. They'll be able to see you, but they'll probably be a little wary of you, at least initially.

"You may remember me telling you that Nellie and Sarah are standard sized donkeys. As a billy, Jasper still has his horns, so be careful around them. He doesn't usually mean to hit you with them, but if he gets excited he might knock you over by accident. Heather's were removed when she was still a kid, before I got her. They've all gotten used to Rod and Jack over the years because they come in here to get the wagon to haul the supplies up from the helipad, and Nellie and Sarah will let them collar and harness them to it."

"Okay. I'll follow your lead. What about the chickens?"

"Hmmm. I didn't think of them. The only one who might be a problem is Big John, 'coz of his spurs. I know some roosters are territorial about their hens, but he's never given me any problems. We'll just have to play it by ear. Too bad I just fed everyone. If you had food they'd probably take to you a lot better."

"So can't they have a snack?"

Jason smiled. "Of course they can."

Chapter Two
Introductions

When Jason opened the barn door, Nellie and Sarah immediately began to bray, and Heather and Jasper started to bleat in the hopes that he'd feed them again, but when he led Aaron to the chair, they all quieted down. Always cautious since her mother had been killed by a rogue male cougar, Nellie eyed Aaron as she walked to the far corner of her and Sarah's stall and leaned against the wall.

Sarah, her daughter, had no such memories. She was still young and full of curiosity. She lifted her head and sniffed the air in Aaron's direction. Heather and Jasper stood on their hind legs at the gate, flicking out their tongues, begging for food.

Jason walked over to the stalls and spoke in a low, soothing voice. Then Nellie picked up her head and began to sniff the air. She pointed her nose towards Aaron and began to swish her tail as she took a few tentative steps towards the gate. "Aaron, I think she smells you."

"Maybe she knows my smell from off of you. You probably carried my scent on you from back when I was injured."

"Here, give me your shirt," Jason said excitedly.

"Baby," Aaron said with a smirk. "There's a lot better lines you could use if you want to see me out of my clothes."

It was all Jason could do to not laugh out loud. "Oh, just you wait, Mister. You don't want to get my juices flowing. Not yet anyway."

"I can only hope," Aaron said coyly.

Jason watched Aaron stand up and then seductively unzip his coat and slowly unbutton his shirt.

The sheer masculinity of Aaron's broad, towering shoulders, his bulging biceps, his massive pecs with their prominent nipples, covered by his thick, trimmed, dark blond body hair, and his rippling six-pack abdomen made Jason's breath quicken. He stood there, motionless, with his mouth agape.

"Um, you said you wanted this," Aaron said with a less than innocent smile as he reached out with his shirt. "You seem to be distracted by something. Anything wrong?"

Jason shook himself. "I see you've been working out. You certainly didn't slack off in working your upper body, that's for sure, and it's paid off well, Aaron, really well," he said running a finger across Aaron's chest and down his six-pack. "You've put some pounds back on, too."

Jason raised up on his toes and kissed Aaron. "Oh, and thank you for this," he said with a smile as he stepped back and brought Aaron's shirt to his face, inhaling deeply. When he breathed in Aaron's scent, he began to shake. Then he started to cry. "I didn't think I'd ever smell you again, Aaron."

Aaron stepped in to him and wrapped him in his arms. "I think that shirt was meant for Nellie, but I'm right here, Jason. Breathe me in, baby. Breathe me in all you want. I'm not going anywhere. Not now. Not ever again." They stood like that for over a minute until Nellie broke the silence when she began to bray.

"Oh, I'm sorry, girl," Jason said as he pulled himself away. When he held Aaron's shirt just over the top of the stall, Nellie walked over and sniffed it for a moment while Sarah approached it and sniffed it, too. Then they both lifted their heads up and down and brayed, loudly. "They know you Aaron. Come say hello."

As Aaron walked toward them, Nellie and Sarah put their heads over the top rails, reaching out for him. When he was close enough, they nibbled his arms with their lips and then rested their necks over them. "I think they both want hugs, Aaron. Like this."

As Jason leaned forward over the rail, Nellie laid her neck over his shoulder, resting her chin on his back. "This is how donkeys hug," Jason whispered.

When Aaron leaned over next to Jason, Sarah moved her chin to his back and began to nibble him again. "It tickles," he said.

"Those are donkey kisses, Aaron. She knows you're family." Nellie lifted her head from Jason and brayed at Sarah. When Sarah backed away, Nellie moved in for her own hug with Aaron. Then Heather and Jasper skirted over to the rails between the stalls and hopped back up on their hind legs again as they reached their necks towards Aaron. "Now everyone wants to meet you. Come say hello to Heather and Jasper."

Jason put some oats in a wooden bucket and took down some sweet grass from the ceiling and handed it all to Aaron. "Pour the oats into the trough and hold out the grass to them. You'll be friends for life."

Not wanting to miss out, Nellie and Sarah came over and joined in.

****

"Um, sorry, guys. Are we interrupting anything?" Rod, the owner of Pacific North Air Transport said, as he and his foreman, Jack, walked in on Jason and a half-naked Aaron embraced in a passionate kiss. "It's just that we've got a lot of stuff to unload, and we should get to it ASAP if we're going to leave you two alone to get reacquainted. We're gonna need Nellie and Sarah's help with the wagon."

"Stuff?" Jason said as he broke away from Aaron,

"What stuff? I didn't order anything."

"No, you didn't, but I did!" Aaron bounced up and down on his toes. "Ow! Ankle!" Aaron grimaced, but then smiled. "Wait 'til you see what I've brought with me!"

When Jack sniggered, Rod elbowed him in the ribs. "Let's just get this done, Jack, so we can leave these two lovebirds in peace."

Jason blushed. "Hold on, Rod. You can at least stay for lunch. I just took a loaf of bread out of the oven, and I've made chicken salad again."

"If you insist," Rod said, as he removed his hat and made a fanciful bow.

When Nellie and Sarah had finished with their treats, Rod and Jack opened the gate so they could hook them up to the wagon, but Jason stopped them. "Just a minute, guys. They still need their Aaron hugs."

"What do you mean, Jason?" Aaron asked in confusion. "They already gave me hugs."

"That right, Aaron, but you didn't give them hugs." Jason took Aaron by the hand and led him into the stall.

"Is this safe?" Aaron asked. "They really don't know me yet."

"Aaron, if they gave you hugs, they've already accepted you. Just be mindful of their hooves. They might forget themselves in the excitement and step on your feet by accident."

"Then show me what to do."

"Like this." As Jason walked into the stall, Nellie and Sarah came up to him, one on each side. He reached his arms around Nellie's neck, leaned against her, and rested his chest and head over her shoulder. After a moment, he did the same thing with Sarah, and then he stepped away.

When Aaron walked towards them, Nellie and Sarah moved forward and took up a place on each side of him. Then they began to gently nuzzle his face and head. He reached his arms around Nellie's neck, and as he leaned into her, she leaned into him and began to shiver. As he rested his head across her shoulder, Sarah lifted her head and rested her neck across his back.

"That's a donkey sandwich," Jason said with amusement in his voice. "There's no doubt in my mind that they've really accepted you now, Aaron."

When Aaron released Nellie, he turned to Sarah and repeated the hug. Nellie turned her head and with her big donkey lips, began to kiss him up and down his back and neck and then finished by pulling against the hair on the top of his head.

As Aaron turned away, Jason handed him some chicken feed and scratch. "Here, throw this around for the chickens. You need to make friends with them, too." As soon as Big John saw Aaron toss the food, he flew down from his perch and strutted and clucked as he picked against the ground.

****

For twenty minutes, Jason walked Aaron around the barn and then to the other structures within the stockade. By the time he'd finished his tour and brought Aaron to the cabin, Rod and Jack were leading Nellie and Sarah into the stockade with the first load of supplies and some of the new things Aaron had bought. As the storm door banged shut behind Jason, Jack said to Rod with a wink, "Bet they've got some catching up to do."

"It's always sex with you, Jack. Can't you see they're in love? Aren't you happy for Jason?"

"Of course I am. It's just…"

"Just nothing. Leave them be!"

You can be a real asshole sometimes, Jack, Jack

thought to himself.

Chapter Three
I Come Bearing Gifts

10:00 AM

"So show me around. I really only know the place from the view from the bed," Aaron said.

"Why don't you take the lead and walk around?" Jason offered, "Are you okay to walk around this much on your leg, and what about your ankle? You've already been on them for nearly forty-five minutes."

"Yeah, sure. The ankle's fine, now that I'm on level ground, and Doc said you did a real good job of setting my left tibia, considering you had to do it here, in the cabin, but they opened it up and re-broke it and then put in plates and screws to get it in perfect alignment. Did the same thing with my throwing arm. See." Aaron extended his right arm and pointed out the surgical scars. Then he lifted his left pant leg and did the same.

Jason ran his hands over the scars. "I didn't know if you were going to make it, Aaron. When I found you dangling from that tree, twenty feet off the ground below your shredded parachute and then found all those wounds and that huge gash in the back of your head, I was afraid you weren't going to make it through the night."

"I know, the doc told me you did an incredible job. Like you said back then, it was a good thing I was unconscious for two days. Otherwise I'd have never been able to take you stitching me up and setting my arm and leg."

"I know."

"So about the tour?"

"Right. Just walk around, open doors, cabinets, peek into things, you know, pick stuff up, and I'll answer any questions you have."

"Good idea, but first, I need the use the

bathroom."

"It's right down here," Jason said, pointing down the center hall.

As they passed the bed, Aaron stopped and began to tear up. "This was my whole world for those five weeks, Jason. It's where I fell in love with you. This will always be a sacred place for me."

"And this is where you saved me, Aaron, from myself." Jason pulled Aaron to his lips.

There was a knock at the storm door.

"Ah, sorry, guys, but where do you want all this stuff?" Rod said from the threshold.

"Wherever you can find room for it," Jason answered, turning his head to look over his shoulder. "Just put it down on the floor in the common area or leave it out on the porch."

"Some of this stuff needs to be assembled, Jason," Rod answered.

"Assembled?" Jason turned to Aaron with a puzzled look on his face.

"Well, baby," Aaron said with a wry smile, "I've brought quite a bit with me, and some of it is to add to your *toy collection*. I'd like to put that into use as soon as possible." Aaron leaned down and drew Jason's tongue into his mouth, wrapping his own tongue around it.

"Aaron?" Jason pulled away. "What have you brought, and why do Rod and Jack know about it?"

"Well, Jason they don't 'know' know about it. Just that it needs to be assembled. Relax. We're all adults here. You once told me you trusted me. Do you still?"

"Um, yes, but I'm still at a complete loss."

"Good."

"Good? Good to what, that I trust you or that I'm at a loss?"

"Both," Aaron said with a smirk and a wink.

After using the bathroom, Jason followed Aaron through the cabin as he learned his way around. While Jason pointed out the different rooms and features to Aaron, Rod and Jack continued to haul in the supplies. After half an hour Aaron stopped and leaned against the table.

"Do you need to rest?" Jason asked.

"Yeah, sorry. The ankle's still not up to standing for long periods of time, but it's getting better."

Jason pulled a second chair to his table and they sat down.

"Thanks," Aaron said. "Jason, I have some things I'd like to talk to you about."

"Sure."

"First, and before anything else, I brought this for you to see."

"What is it?"

"It's the results of my HIV test. I had it drawn last week. I know that's important to you, and I wanted you to be sure about me."

"Thank you for this, Aaron," Jason said as he took the paper, leaving it folded. "But you didn't have to do this. I trust you completely."

"No, Jason, I wanted to be sure there was no question in your mind. Now please look at it right now so I know that you know. I've been with no one since you in October. You're my only love."

"Okay," Jason said as he read the form. "I appreciate it, Aaron, really I do. That you thought enough of me to do this means a lot. Now, what did you want to talk to me about?"

"Those three empty rooms at the back of the cabin, do the wood stoves in them work?"

"They do, but I've only actually used them a few times. The architect suggested that I divide that area into guest rooms in case I ever had visitors, so I just went along with him."

"That's good to know. If it's okay with you, I'll have Rod and Jack set up some of what I've brought in one of them, and I'd like to ask that you allow them to stay overnight in the other rooms until tomorrow or the next day. There's so much I need to discuss with you, and if you're interested in even a part of it, Rod and Jack are going to play a role in some, if not most of it, maybe even a big role."

"Aaron, this is all moving so fast. I don't know what to think."

"You said you trust me."

"I do, I do."

"Then please do just that for the next … however long this is going to take. We're going to need Rod and Jack's help, even if it's just getting me moved in here."

"Okay, I trust you, Aaron, completely. If you say it's important to you then it's important to me."

"Good. If they end up staying, we should light fires in all the stoves to get the rooms warmed up well before they go to bed."

"Will do. I'll take care of it," Jason answered.

Aaron spent a long time laying out his hopes and dreams for the future. Jason was not only in agreement with all of it, he was also excited by it and proud of Aaron for conceiving it.

As Aaron talked about the days to come and his desire to do something for gay athletes who required physical therapy after sustaining injuries, maybe even building a rehabilitation center specifically for them, Jason realized why Aaron wanted to include Rod and Jack because the more they talked, the more they realized they were going to need a lot of help to achieve it all. Their lives were going to change dramatically over the coming year, and the stockade and surrounding land on the mountain were going to receive some dramatic face lifts.

When they finished, Jason laid both his hands over Aaron's. "There's something you need to know about me."

"What's that?"

"I know I told you before that I was a multimillionaire, but I've recently learned that I'm nearly a billionaire, and what's mine is yours."

"Jason, that's a hell of a lot of money! You should think this through."

"I've had nothing but time to think about it. Months. It's been months that you've been gone. Please believe me when I say what's mine is yours."

"But, Jason?"

"Aaron, it's only money. What can I do with a billion dollars? All those construction plans I drew up for us months ago, they were just the beginning of what I had dreamed for us. What you've just proposed only helps me to focus on how I can help others, like I wrote in my letter to you in the hospital. Did you ever get my letter?"

"Oh, yes, Jason, I did, and I read it every day. It's what kept me going. Knowing how you felt about me, because that's exactly how I felt about you, kept me pushing myself whenever I felt overwhelmed. You'll never know how much your words meant to me and sustained me."

"I meant every word of it, Aaron, but can we hold off on talking for a bit? It's getting close to lunchtime. Why don't you supervise Rod and Jack as they bring things in, and I'll start to get lunch ready?"

"Okay, we'll pick this up later, but I think we should first talk with Rod and Jack over lunch to see whether they want to be a part of all this."

"It will certainly change their lives dramatically, so yes, we really do need to ask them before we start to bring in other people."

"Agreed. Oh, by the way, I'm glad to see there was a lot of empty room in the fridge 'coz you won't need to worry about dinner. I've brought it and all the food we could possibly need for another several days. All that will need to be done is to heat up what needs to be heated up."

"That's great, Aaron. I was beginning to wonder what kind of meals I should start to prepare."

Aaron turned towards Rod. "Rod, that one big box we talked about. When you've unloaded everything, can you get it set up in the empty room on the left at the back of the cabin?"

"Will do, Aaron," Rod answered with a salute.

"And all the coolers with perishable food, please put what you can in the refrigerator. The rest of the frozen stuff will keep because of the dry ice."

"I'll take care of it."

"Why don't we plan to break for lunch at noon?" Jason said.

There was agreement all around.

****

11:15 AM

While Rod and Jack continued to unload Big Daddy under Aaron's direction, Jason returned to the kitchen and mixed up a double batch of sourdough for the next day and set it on the counter in an oiled and covered bowl for a slow rise until morning. Then he prepared lunch. In addition to the chicken salad he'd already made, he went through the new foodstuffs Aaron had brought and took out a mixed salad, dressing, croutons, and a chocolate cake. He sliced a loaf of bread he'd baked that morning, took out a pound of Heather's butter from the fridge, and put down a tablecloth and set the table. After pulling up two benches from along the wall, he was ready.

Once Jason had finished preparing lunch, Aaron asked him to teach him how to start the wood stoves in the back rooms. Jason showed him how to take some coals from the kitchen's wood stove, and then carry them in an ash can, along with several split logs and tinder, to the back of the cabin.

****

12:15 PM
Lunch

"Okay, guys. Why don't you stop and sit down for lunch?" Jason called out onto the porch as he began to set out the food. "You can wash up at the kitchen sink."

After everyone sat down and began to eat, Aaron cleared his throat. "Jason, I ran a few things past Rod when I met with him in his office last week, and we've talked on the phone a few times and then again this morning before we left the hangar so I could get a feel for his operation. Rod, have you briefed Jack at all?"

"Not really. Based on what we discussed I wasn't sure in what direction things might be headed, so all I told him was to pack some extra clothes because we might stay a day or two to help get stuff set up and you get settled in."

"Okay, so … first I need to be sure everyone's on the same page." There were nods all around. "Jason and I are going to be making a life together here on the mountain, and I think you know we're both gay. I hope that won't be a problem for either of you."

Both Rod and Jack smiled at Jason. "Can I tell him?" Rod asked as he looked between Jason and Jack.

Jason blushed at what he thought Rod was about to reveal, but he realized that Aaron should know everything. "Yeah, go ahead, Rod."

"Yeah, Rod. Go ahead," Jack added.

"Aaron, we're, me and Jack, that is, are gay, too."

"I ... I had no idea, Rod," Aaron stumbled. "Sorry, I just assumed..."

"It's okay, Aaron," Jack chimed in. "Most people don't know."

"Um, Aaron," Jason spoke up. "How do I say this? Ah, Rod and Jack and I, um ... well, we used to..."

"Oh, Christ, Jason, just say it," Jack said, slapping the table. "Ah, hell! I'll just tell him. Aaron, we were butt buddies, but that was way in the past. Way long before you came into the picture."

"Oh," was all Aaron could say. Jason put his hand over Aaron's and squeezed it.

"Well, color me stupid," Aaron said after a long moment.

Everyone laughed.

"Okay, well that puts a different perspective on things," Aaron continued. "I guess that sort of makes you family, so I'm very comfortable talking to you both about this. Should I go on?" Everyone nodded. "We're going to be making some changes around here, big changes, but we don't know how far reaching this is all going to go. Not yet anyway.

"You know that my trainer, Nathan Taggart, died in the plane crash that I survived." Rod and Jack nodded their heads solemnly. "You should know that Nathan and I were a couple, and we were in love. Nathan saved my life by putting my parachute on me and pushing me out of the plane before himself. He never made it out because the plane exploded before he could get to the door, and he died." Aaron closed his eyes and paused for a moment. Then he went on.

"So, I've talked with Jason about this. We want to build a rehabilitation center for LGBT athletes in Nathan's name. That means lesbian, gay, bisexual, and transgender."

"We know," Jack said with a smile.

"Oh, right," Aaron said with an embarrassed look on his face. "It'll also have short-term housing for the families and significant others of the athletes while they're going through therapy, and there will be a separate center that will serve as a retreat and a spa for the families and for LGBT athletes who aren't patients, but just need to get away for some downtime and want a safe place to do it. Everyone will be welcome."

"Hold on a minute, Aaron," Jason said. "Someone had better start taking notes."

Chapter Four
A Menace in the Making

December 21, 2009, 12:22 PM MST
Hinnen Valley, Local noontime news broadcast
"Coming up after the commercial break, we'll be bringing you breaking news on the career of Aaron Jaeger, the injured quarterback for the Nevada Bighorns."

****

Dive Bar, Hinnen Valley
"Damn shame about Jaeger," the bartender said, tilting his head towards the TV at the end of the bar. "I heard they're letting him go. That plane crash did in his career."

"Ah, he was a pretty boy," said a stocky patron sitting on a stool as he sipped his drink. "Guys like him have it too easy, if you ask me. Everything's just handed to 'em. I'd like to see him try and do a real man's day's work." He downed his drink then smacked his glass down on the bar. "Give me another."

As the bartender poured his drink, the news returned.

****

12:25 PM
"We end our broadcast this afternoon with the final chapter in Aaron Jaeger's career. As you may recall, Jaeger was signed to the Nevada Bighorns as their quarterback before the beginning of the season. Jaeger was rescued this past October, five weeks after the plane crash that killed his trainer, Nathan Taggart and the pilot.

"The footage you see on your screen was shot at Hinnen Valley Medical Center when he was unloaded from a helicopter by the three men who rescued him."

****

The stocky customer froze in place as he watched the TV. He stood up so abruptly, he knocked over his stool.

****

"In a statement today, John Forester, the team's general manager announced that the damage from Jaeger's injuries prevented him from regaining the function and flexibility he would need to play. Regrettably, it was determined that Jaeger would not be able to return to the team in any capacity, and he was released from his contract.

"Calls to Jaeger and his agent have yet to be returned."

****

"So, Corpsman Ackerman, that's what happened to you," the customer said under his breath as he noticed the company name on the side of the helicopter. "Now I know how to find you."

He downed the last of his drink and quickly shrugged on his worn-out, army-green, camo-coat. "I always knew the day would come when I'd find you. We've got some unfinished business to take care of, faggot," he growled through clenched teeth. "And I'm comin' to see you. Me and Baby, that is."

He pushed his way through the bar's other patrons and headed out into the midday sun towards his rusted sedan. He opened the trunk and lifted a tarp. Baby, his M16A2, was secure.

Chapter Five
LGBTQ(S)

12:39 PM
Homestead

Jason went into the supply room and returned with four yellow, lined pads and pens, and a pair of sneakers. He placed the sneakers on the table next to Aaron. "I thought you might want these back."

"Jason! My sneakers! Where'd you find them?"

"You were wearing them the day I cut you down from the tree. I forgot all about them until I saw them just now on the shelf."

"Wow, Jason, thanks. Oh look, that's my blood on them, isn't it?" Aaron began to pick at the blood and mud.

"I guess so."

"Thanks again, but I don't think I'll wear them anymore. That was the absolute worst day of my life, but really, thinking about it now, it was also the best day of my life, 'coz that's the day you came into it. Can I keep them just the same?"

"Of course you can. They're yours. I'll just put them back on the shelf for now."

"Please don't. The last time I wore them I was with Nathan." Aaron's eyes began to tear up. He stopped picking at the bloodstained sneakers. "It's like he's here right now, and that's important."

"You're right," Jason whispered. "I'll leave it to you."

The table got quiet for a minute as everyone waited for Aaron to collect himself.

"Okay, I'm better now," Aaron said.

"Are you sure, Aaron? We can do this later."

"No, I'm ready. Thanks, everyone."

"Aaron?" Jason placed his hand on the sneaker that Aaron had been picking on. "That's your name!"

"Yeah. I got an endorsement deal from the company. This pair was a pre-production sample. I think it's the only pair that was ever released." Aaron was silent for another moment. "Okay, enough of my trip down memory lane. Let's move on."

"I'll take notes," Jason began. "If I'm talking, Rod would you take notes?"

"Sure thing." Rod nodded.

Jason went on. "Please, everyone, write down any ideas or questions that come to mind so we don't miss anything."

"Great, Jason. Thanks," Aaron said. "So, where was I? Oh yeah. It'll be dedicated to the memory of Nathan. I'm thinking of calling it Nathan's Promise, and it'll be for kids, too. I mean, you know, LGBT high-school athletes."

"What about people who still have questions about who they really are?" Jason asked, "I know I did when I joined the army."

"Okay, then it'll be for LGBTQ athletes."

"What about Native Americans?" Jack added. "They call them Two Sprit people. They're members of the tribe who are believed to possess both male and female sprits. They're highly regarded and honored."

"I guess I never considered them separately, Jack," Jason said, "Leave it to Native Americans to get it right. There were a couple GIs on the bases I was stationed at during the war who were Native American and gay. I just thought of them as soldiers, but yeah, of course, Two Sprit people, too."

"Do we need to make a separate designation for them, Jack?" Aaron asked.

"I don't think so, Aaron. They've got their shit

together about that."

"Then what about straights?" Jason added. "You said it wouldn't discriminate against anyone?"

"Then it'll be for LGBTQS athletes. It won't even discriminate against straights." Everyone laughed. "But, I really don't think any would ever come. Okay, before I go on, are there any other people we need to add a letter for?" Everyone shook their heads.

"I had a thought just now," Jason said. "Would it be all right if we included military veterans? And what about law enforcement? I know there's a lot of gay people in the military, and I have to believe that law enforcement isn't any different."

"You're right, Jason. I'm sorry I didn't offer that when we talked earlier. I should have thought of them, too."

"It's all right, Aaron. I'm sure there's going to be a lot we think of in the coming days and weeks that will cause us to change our plans more than a few times. There's also a few points I've thought of that need to be made. Can I speak for a minute, Aaron?"

"Of course."

"Here are my thoughts, guys. We need to assemble a team, because Aaron and I can't do this alone. If we want to do it right, we're gonna need all kinds of specialists and construction crews and all the staff who will work at the center. That's gonna include housing, dietary, laundry, waste and sewer management, and trash facilities. I'll have to find out if a bigger, deeper well can even be dug up here to supply all the water it'll require."

"Not only that," Rod added, "where are all the staff who will work at the center going to live? You're in the middle of nowhere. Will housing be built for them up here as well? Can it even be done? Or do you need to look to build the whole thing somewhere else? And don't forget about legal and finance."

"Shit, guys," Aaron said with a mouth full of sandwich. "I never thought of any of that. Can we do this? Do you guys really think we could pull something like this off?"

"Of course we can, Aaron," Jason said. "All we need to do is find the right people."

"Damn straight!" Jack shouted as he pounded the table with his fist. "Gays unite! We're gonna take over this mountain!"

"Whoa, Jack. Calm down there," Rod said. "Aaron. Jason. You've got a great and noble idea here, but it's like Jason said, there's a lot to consider. What do you want from me, Aaron?"

"Well, now I don't know. I really don't. It's all become a little overwhelming to me."

Rod spread his hands across the table in front of him. "Can I offer up a few things?"

"Yes, please do," Aaron answered, and Jason nodded.

"First things first. I assume you'll want me or Jack and me to handle the transportation of people and supplies. Is that right?"

"Yes, of course," Jason answered.

"Well, let's start with people. Before such an undertaking can get off the ground, you've got to have a committee of some kind to spearhead this, that is if you're serious about bringing in the right people. You've got to get them involved right from the start." Both Jason and Aaron nodded. "Second, Jason, you can't leave the animals for more than a half day, right?"

"Yes."

"So whatever you do will have to be done together as a group, either here in person, or over the internet. I'd suggest in person. How many people do you think you can house up here for a couple days at a time?"

"I don't know, Rod," Jason answered. "Maybe three, one in each of the extra rooms, or six if they wouldn't mind doubling up. We'll have to get some beds."

Rod continued. "Do you have bathroom facilities, eating and meeting space enough for eight people, including yourselves? Can you cook for eight people on your wood stove? Can your septic system handle that kind of sudden influx? Also, winter's here. How are six people going to get up here, let alone get back down to the valley? What if my chopper is grounded due to ice or the weather?"

"Shit!" Jason shook his head. "We're going to have to add bathrooms, get tables and chairs, maybe even a secretary."

"Also, ground's nearly frozen. I don't know if it's even possible to put up temporary structures right now. I don't want to rain on your parade, but could this possibly wait until the spring?"

"Aaron?" Jason asked.

Aaron looked dejected. "Fuck! Sorry, guys, but I never took any of this into consideration. Are you in, Rod? Jack?"

"Definitely!" Rod answered.

"Me, too!" Jack chimed in.

"Good," Aaron went on. "'Coz now I realize I've bitten off way more that I can chew."

"We both did," Jason said, sympathetically.

"Jason?" Aaron asked.

"Yes?"

"I hate to ask you this right now—hell, we haven't even had one night together. Sorry, guys." Aaron looked at Rod and Jack. "Let's lay all our cards on the table. Jason, what you told me just a little while ago about your situation…"

"You don't have worry about Rod and Jack. They're aware of my wealth."

"Okay. Were you serious about what you said a little while ago, about money?"

"Absolutely."

"Good, because I'm not completely sure about my finances any more. I thought I could handle the expenses for this whole project, but now that we're talking, it's gonna cost way more than I ever imagined. And even if I do get to keep my signing bonus, it's gonna be way more than even that."

"What do you mean *if* you get to keep your bonus?" Jason asked. "Not that money was ever an issue, but what's going on?"

"I think the team is trying to renege on my signing bonus as well as my contract. I haven't gotten in to it with you, Jason, but I believe the real reason I was let go from the team was because they found out I'm gay."

"What!" An incredulous look came over Jason's face.

"I don't want to spend a lot of time on this, but I was told by Matt Anderson—he's the head trainer for the Bighorns—that they were going to put me back on the lineup as soon as I was discharged from rehab 'coz I was doing so well. The very next day Coach Thompson visited me. I was asleep when he came in, and I had been reading your letter. It was on my lap.

"When I woke up, he was acting real weird like he was in shock or something. I didn't think anything of it at the time, but the next day, one of the therapists told me she was out in the parking lot the day before. That's when she saw the coach get into his SUV. She said he looked real mad. The next thing she knew he was shouting into his phone. She could hear him shouting right through the window glass. He yelled the name 'John,' several times, and she heard him say, 'He's a fucking fag'.

"I was discharged from rehab the following week. When I got home, my agent called me. He said he'd just gotten a call from John Forester, probably *the John*. He's the General Manager for the team. Anyway, and I don't know all the technicalities about contracts, but he said they were releasing me from my contract because of the uncertainty surrounding my physical abilities.

"Apparently, there's a clause in the contract to that effect. He, my agent that is, is trying to get them to honor the four million signing bonus, but there's some kind of complication because I never actually played in a game. They've already paid it to me, but apparently, they want it all back.

"It's all up in the air right now, and I don't know where I stand. I've already spent a small chunk of it, so good luck to them. Regardless, they're gonna have to sue me before I give it up.

"Then my agent told me the sneaker company called. They'd put my endorsement deal on hold while I was in the hospital and rehab, but the moment they learned I was off the team, they cancelled it. That's when I sprained my ankle. I was so pissed off that I kicked the wall and tripped and then landed wrong on the ankle. I called Matt after a couple of hours. He came over and iced it and wrapped it for me. He said it didn't look too bad, but if it wasn't feeling better in a few days I should go and get it X-rayed. What upset me the most was that he told me he couldn't be seen seeing me any more 'coz he'd get in trouble with the team. Management's told them all to cut all ties with me."

Jason was seething. "Don't worry, Aaron. I've got a crackerjack lawyer. I don't know if she can do anything about the endorsement deal, but if she can't handle the team I'm sure she knows someone who can. By the time she gets done with the Nevada Bighorns, you'll probably end up with more than your whole contract was originally worth. And anyway, I've got you covered. Don't you worry one bit."

"Thanks, Jason." Aaron paused for a moment to collect himself. "Okay, guys, how can we start getting this off the ground right away? I've got physical therapy contacts. Who do you guys know in finance, legal, construction, architecture who we can meet with and how will we meet with them with the weather restrictions that we're going to face?"

Rod cleared his throat. "Can I start?" Everyone nodded. "First, let's be realistic. Christmas is in four days. Then there's New Year the following week. We shouldn't expect to get started until after then because you probably won't be able to get anyone to come out now. Agreed?"

Everyone nodded.

"Good. Then here's what we'll do. Jason, I'm going to give you priority on one of my choppers, either Big Daddy or Big Mama, whoever's free at the time. Both of 'em can handle just about anything you can throw at 'em. You just give me twelve hours' notice for anything, people or supplies, and I'll see to it that it gets done."

"Thanks, Rod."

"Second," Rod went on, "Jason, your internet is working, and you have the satellite phone so you've got two independent communication systems that can be used simultaneously. Right?"

"Right."

"Good. Here's what I propose. Jack and I will fly back tonight and return tomorrow to bring up the rest of Aaron's cargo, just like we had originally planned before Aaron asked about staying over a couple nights. Aaron, you said you might need us for a couple of days. Is that still the case?"

"I think so."

"Well I don't have to be anywhere until Christmas Day. I have to go visit with my sister and her husband and their kids. Uncle Rod is a big part of my nieces and nephews' lives, but that's it. Jack, do you have any plans?"

"No, not really, you know I'm Jewish anyway, right? Abraham? Jewish? Family name? So, no, I don't celebrate Christmas."

"Yeah, I knew, but I was just checking. Okay, then we'll plan that you can have us until Christmas Eve. I've always got my satellite phone with me so after we've got all of Aaron's stuff settled in, and we've done everything you need us to do, we can start making some preliminary calls and try to get the ball rolling."

"That's a great idea, Rod," Jason said, "and I'll get my legal and financial people on it, too."

"Thanks, guys," Aaron added. "It's obvious to me now that this is going to be a way bigger project than I ever imagined."

"So, Jason," Rod asked, "where do you want the chest freezer?"

"Chest freezer? What chest freezer?"

"The thirty-cubic-foot chest freezer I bought," Aaron answered. "Rod pulled the order for your industrial kitchen refrigerator-freezer from his files, so I ordered enough stuff to fill it and the new freezer. He also knew how big your storeroom and pantry are and how full they were after they brought your last order. We figured it all out, and I've brought enough stuff to fill everything."

"This is unbelievable, Aaron. Thank you. The only thing I don't know is whether my battery bank will be enough to power it," Jason said. "Do you know, Rod?"

"It doesn't take that much power once everything's cold, Jason, but remember, it'll draw much more current when it's working to freeze things. Fortunately, everything's already frozen. From what I remember, you've got electricity to spare and then some. Your system has so many redundancies, it's never been even close to stressed. Fact is, if you were hooked up to the grid, you could probably be selling electricity back to the power company."

"Good," Jason said, "but I'm a little overwhelmed right now. I guess, put the freezer next to the refrigerator."

"Great. We'll get it plugged in right away. Remember, it should run for twenty-four hours before you start putting food in it."

"That'll work out, Rod," Aaron said. "All the frozen stuff is packed in dry ice that'll last at least seventy-two hours."

"Regardless, we better start getting non-frozen perishables put away," Jason said. "I really don't know what you've brought, Aaron. I haven't seen most of it yet. Jack, do you have any idea what you've unloaded so far in the kitchen?"

"Nope, except what I put into the refrigerator, and that was just salads and fresh vegetables."

"Well, then why don't you guys unload the freezer and install it and then if you have time, come in with me to the pantry and storeroom. We can go through everything and put away what still needs to be put away."

Rod stood up. "Um, Aaron … wasn't there something you wanted us to set up?"

"Yes, there was." Aaron smiled. "Um, Jason, I'll help you with the unpacking while Rod and Jack take care of that."

"Okay … whatever *it* is. Just don't push yourself, I mean, your ankle."

"Then we'll take off. Okay?" Rod asked.

"Would you mind putting Nellie and Sarah back in the barn?" Jason said. "Since you're finished with them for now there's no need for them to stay out in the cold."

"I already did," Jack said. "I figured since we'd finished unloading Big Daddy, there wasn't any sense in them standing out in the cold."

"That's great, Jack. Thanks."

Chapter Six
Longitude and Latitude

2:30 PM
Headquarters, Pacific North Air Transport
  With a flashlight gripped between his teeth, a stocky figure lifted an order form from a file cabinet in the darkened office. It revealed the longitude and latitude of the former Corpsman Jason Ackerman's home.

  "So this is why I couldn't find you, Ackerman. Well, if I can't get to you some other way, at least now I've got the coordinates of where you been hiding, but first I gotta find me some warm duds."

  He slid the form back into place, closed the cabinet drawer and slithered from the office, making his way up and over the perimeter fence at the airport.

    ****

Homestead
  Jason and Aaron began to unload the coolers while Rod and Jack brought in the chest freezer off the wagon and installed it in the kitchen. Then they disappeared to the back of the cabin.

  "Oh, wow, Aaron, you said you brought enough food for a couple of days, but the four of us could eat off of just the heat and eat food for several weeks. And look at this! There's over a dozen frozen steaks, and they're huge. What else? Look, twenty filets, twenty pounds of country ribs, three smoked hams, two turkeys! Two turkeys! Wow! And what's all this?" Jason exclaimed as he began to open four cardboard boxes. "Good grief! There must be four months' worth of dried and canned goods in these!"

  "Jason, we're out in the middle of nowhere, and it's gotta get damn cold at this altitude. The last time we talked about it, you said you could get snowed in for months. I figured if you ordered supplies to last for just yourself until spring, I'm now adding another mouth to feed, so we'd need at least double, but this isn't all of it. There's still more coming tomorrow."

Jason scratched his head. "Holy, moly, where am I going to put it all?"

"Don't worry, baby," Aaron hugged him. "It'll all work out. Oh, I forgot to tell you. I bought a new restaurant size microwave oven, too."

****

3:00 PM

Outside the fence at the headquarters of Pacific North Air Transport

The shabbily dressed, stocky figure drummed his fingers against the steering wheel of his rusted-out sedan, while he sat, thinking.

"So how do I go about getting them to take me up to visit the Corpsman? I've got no fucking money, so what can I use as an excuse? I know, I'll tell them we're old army buddies. That I ran into him at the hospital where I work as an orderly when he was there back in October. He told me that I could come up for a visit and that he'd pay for them to fly me up. *Me and Baby*, that is! Now for them duds, and I know just the place."

Chapter Seven
One Hell of a Ride

4:00 PM
Homestead

"Hey, Aaron," Rod called from the back of the cabin. "You want to come check this thing out?"

"Be right there," Aaron called out as he leaned away from the dresser where he'd started to put away his clothes. He put his muddied and bloodstained high-priced sneakers in a box and then placed the box in the bottom drawer and closed it.

Jason walked out of the pantry. "What needs to be checked out?"

"Um, wait here," Aaron asked.

"What is it?"

"Please, Jason. Wait here."

"All right."

Aaron made his way to the back of the cabin where he found Rod and Jack admiring the sex sling he'd asked them to assemble in the playroom. As he walked through the door, Jack whistled with admiration as he pushed the black leather sling with adjustable stirrups and triangular trapeze and watched it swing back and forth from four heavy-duty bicycle chain-like chains that ran through spoked gears just below welded brackets that were bolted around the rafters. The chains were attached to the four corners of the sling and would allow its pitch to be adjusted.

"That's some top-of-the-line piece of equipment you got there, Aaron," Jack said. "Some piece. You guys are gonna have a lot of fun with this. One hell of a ride, that's for sure!"

Aaron blushed. "Well, in all honesty, it's custom made."

"Leave him alone, Jack," Rod ordered.

A moment later, Jason walked in. "What's all the shouting about? Oh. Um, wow! Um, … that's sure something, Aaron. And with a trapeze and a sitting stool." Jason blushed.

A two-tone whistle escaped Jack's lips.

"Don't you remember what it was like to be young once, Jack?" Rod asked.

"Sure do," Jack continued, "but we didn't have anything like this back then. Took a bit of engineering, that's for sure. I take my hat off to you, Aaron. Boy oh boy, with something like this, you could go on and on for hours and hours. No back cramps. No leg cramps. No slipping out. No…"

"For Christ's sake, Jack! Shut up!" Rod yelled. "And no asking to try it out either!"

"Spoilsport," Jack answered in a dejected tone.

"Out!" Rod ordered as he pulled Jack from the room by the arm.

Aaron turned to Jason and hugged him. "I'm sorry about that, baby."

"It's okay, Aaron," Jason whispered as he inched up for a kiss. "I've always wanted to try one of these, and besides, now you can fuck me proper."

"Really?" Aaron exclaimed.

"Yes, really, and then I can repay the favor," Jason said as he nibbled on Aaron's earlobe. "Definitely repay the favor," he whispered.

"Oh, Jason. I love you," Aaron said as he picked him up around the waist and swung him around in a circle.

"Careful! Your ankle."

"I don't feel it any more, not now anyway."

"I love you, too, Aaron. I love you, too."

"We'll try it out after Jack and Rod leave. Huh?"

"Definitely! Now, I better start putting some kind of dinner together. Any requests?"

"How about lasagna and garlic bread?" Aaron suggested. "The lasagna's cold, but it isn't frozen."

"Sounds good to me, but let me ask Rod and Jack if they want to stay and eat. They are our guests after all, and they're really helping us out."

"Fine with me, Jason. The garlic bread's already cut and buttered. All it needs is to be warmed up."

They walked out together with their arms around each other's waists. Jason left Aaron by the dresser to finish unpacking and headed to meet up with Rod and Jack by the front door. "Would you guys like to stay for dinner?"

"You know, that's real nice of you, Jason, but we should start thinking about heading home," Rod answered. "I'd like to be back to the hangar before sunset. We'll finish bringing in the last crates and boxes and then we'll say our goodbyes and be off."

****

Fifteen minutes later, Rod called, "Okay, guys, we're gonna head out."

"Thanks so much, Rod, for everything," Jason said as he gave Rod a big hug, and then so did Aaron.

"Hey, where's mine?" Jack said as he walked in from the porch.

"Oh, you too, Jack," Aaron answered.

After hugs were exchanged, Jack said, "I'll see you tomorrow. Oh, and there's a surprise for you both on the porch."

As Jason and Aaron followed them out the door they found two wicker rockers set up with a small table between them. "That's your housewarming present from me," Jack called over his shoulder as he headed down the porch steps and began to walk across the yard. "Now you can watch the sun set. I wish you both all the happiness in the world!"

"Thanks, Jack," they called in unison as they sat down in the rockers.

"Hey, hold on a minute," Jason called. "Rod, what time do you think you'll get back up here tomorrow?"

"Oh, early to mid-morning, if that's all right with you?" Rod answered.

"That would be great, but if you're early enough, I'll have breakfast waiting for you."

"It's a date then, but if we're later, don't worry about it."

"Tell you what, regardless, I'll have everything ready to go. That way I can just put it into the pan and have it ready in a few minutes."

"That's good for me. I like breakfast any time of the day."

"Me too, Rod," Aaron chimed in.

"Then it's settled," Jason decided. "There'll be breakfast ready to go whenever you want it."

****

Shortly after Rod and Jack disappeared beyond the stockade's gate, they heard Big Daddy's engine come to life. After the rotors reached full speed, it lumbered into the sky and then disappeared over the ridge.

"Well, my big stud," Jason said as he reached across the table and took Aaron's hand, "should we break in the sling before or after dinner?"

"After. That way, we'll have the whole night."

"Good. Dinner will be ready in fifteen minutes."

Chapter Eight
Foreplay

6:00 PM

After the dishes were washed and put away, Jason kneaded additional flour into the sourdough sponge for the following day and returned it to the oiled bowl on the counter. With Rod and Jack staying for a few days, he'd need more fresh bread.

Aaron took a shower while Jason went out to milk Heather, feed the animals, and give them fresh water. After putting the milk away, he found Aaron lying seductively on the bed wearing a robe with it opened just enough for Jason to see his goods.

"Oh, how I've missed them," Jason said as he reached down and lifted Aaron's semi-erect cock in one hand and caressed it while he fondled his balls with the other. "I'm going to take a shower, baby, and then I'll be ready for you."

"I was hoping you were going to say that, but first, I have a request."

"What's that?'

"I want you to make love to me."

"Really, Aaron? Are you sure? I'm not that experienced in topping, and I've never topped you. I don't want you to be disappointed."

"Yes, I'm sure, and you could never disappoint me, Jason, never. I've been dreaming of it since the day you left me in the hospital. I want to know what it feels like to have you deep inside me, to shoot your load into me while you pound my prostate."

"Then I'll do my best to give all of myself to you."

"I can't wait, baby. I can't wait. I've turned on the propane heater so you'll have plenty of hot water."

"I'll be sure to make good use of it."

"And the room is all set up. I put a sheet down, and I raided your toy box. I've laid out a few of them for you to try on me. I've also brought poppers for me to use so that I can open up easily and take all of you."

"You won't need poppers, Aaron. If you trust me, I think I can prepare you to receive me without them."

"I trust you, Jason. I trust you completely."

"Good."

****

Jason cleaned himself out, just in case Aaron was up to reciprocating, and returned to the shower. No sooner had he put his head under the stream of water than he felt two hands reach from behind and begin to caress his cock and tug on his sack. Aaron nuzzled his neck and leaned firmly into Jason's back until he had him pressed against the tiles.

He picked up the bar of soap and began to lather Jason's growing erection with one hand and then moved it to the other so he could soap his buttocks and crack. Jason began to moan and gyrate his hips, thrusting his growing erection through Aaron's tightening grip while Aaron worked a soaped-up finger against the outer recesses of Jason's hole.

"Oh! Oh, Aaron," he moaned. "How I've missed your touch. And your body. My God, it's rock hard, and your arms are so … oh my God, what are you doing to me?"

Aaron slowly worked his soapy finger into Jason's hole.

"And your arms are so strong. Good Lord, I can feel the ripples in the muscles of your thighs."

Aaron forced his legs between Jason's, then spread them apart as he wiggled his finger deep inside him and alternated stroking his now eight-inch stiff erection while caressing his tightening ball sack. He swung Jason around and brought his lips down, sucking Jason's tongue deep into his mouth, as he pulled his head towards him until their mouths became merged into one. His raging, thick, ten-inch hard-on pressed up against Jason's cock as he began to thrust his hips up and down, forcing pre-cum to spill from Jason's slit.

As quickly as Aaron pulled his mouth away and sucked deeply against Jason's throat, then moved down to his chest and nibbled his nipples between his teeth, threatening to draw blood. Jason's body began to shudder and spasm. He moved down further and drove his tongue into Jason's navel then traveled further still until his mouth engulfed Jason's cock. He sucked with abandon, stimulating Jason's juices deep within his loins, as Jason's nectar-filled balls pulled tight up against his shaft.

As quickly as Aaron started, he stopped. He stood up and pulled Jason to him, caressing his back and massaging his buttocks with his thick, meaty, athletic hands. Jason melted into him and began to falter, but Aaron caught him and lifted him, until Jason wrapped his legs around his hips, locking his ankles behind.

"Aaron, your ankle."

"Fuck my ankle. I took eight-hundred milligrams of ibuprofen before dinner. Now shut up."

Jason's cock began to thrust against Aaron's rippled abdomen uncontrollably as Aaron's cock searched out Jason's crack and then found it. Jason squeezed his cheeks tightly around the shaft while Aaron began to thrust his manhood back and forth between them.

As fatigue began to overpower him, Aaron's thighs began to tremble. He reached around to the shower knobs and changed the setting to a gentle rain then lowered himself to the tiled floor, cradling Jason's body against his own. With Jason sitting in his lap, Aaron began to work the soap into a lather over his skin, covering every inch of his body, while showering his face and mouth with kisses.

He held Jason tightly and called his name again and again, professing his love, until the soap had washed away. "My Jason. My Jason. I can't live without you."

"Oh, my Aaron. My Aaron," Jason whispered, "how did I survive before you?"

"I'll never leave you again. I love you, Jason. I love you."

"Before you came to me my life was so empty."

"You are my life and my breath, Jason, and I am yours."

"Now that you've returned, I don't think I could live without you again."

"Me neither, Jason, me neither."

"Don't ever leave me. Aaron. Please don't ever leave me."

"I won't. Never. Now please, make love to me."

They looked into each other's eyes. Jason nodded, and then they stood together. Aaron turned off the water and guided Jason from the shower where together they gently blotted the water from each other's bodies. Then Jason took his hand and led a limping Aaron down the hall.

Chapter Nine
Make Me Your Man

Aaron raised his eyebrows in question as he reached for the bottle of poppers, sitting with the dildos, dilators, and anal speculum on the table, but Jason moved his hand away, shaking his head and mouthing, "No."

Aaron nodded, then leaned back into the sling and pulled himself up with the trapeze. He lifted his legs, and Jason guided his feet into the stirrups and then he lay back.

"Make love to me, my love," Aaron whispered. "Fill me with your seed. Whatever you desire, take it from me."

"Yes, Aaron. Yes, I promise."

Jason leaned his hips against the large, firm globes of Aaron's meaty buttocks. The head of his erection lifted Aaron's plum-sized balls until they parted and slid back down along the top of Jason's shaft. He raked his fingernails beneath Aaron's shaved sack and then massaged each of the globes between his palms and fingers, enticing them to release their man seed.

He traced his fingers around and across the contoured, athletic, short wedge of Aaron's pubic hair and then leaned in, forcing his cock to grind against Aaron's shaft. He forcefully grasped their shafts and squeezed them together while he pumped his hands up and down their lengths.

"Yes! Yes, my Jason, my love."

Jason released their cocks and pressed his shaft into the recesses of Aaron's meaty buttocks as it searched for his opening while he trailed his fingertips up Aaron's treasure trail into the thick, trimmed, and contoured hair that rose above the raised ridges of his six-pack abdomen. When the tip of his cock pressed against

Aaron's hole, Aaron gasped. Jason moved his hands further across Aaron's massive pecs, then around and around his rising, swelling nipples, pinching and pulling them slowly upwards.

Aaron began to lick his tongue across his lips and pant deeply as he reached up to grab the trapeze and used it to rock back and forth, tapping his hole against Jason's cockhead as it probed and tried to enter. When Aaron increased his pace, Jason's balls began to slap against the back of Aaron's butt cheeks while his cock alternated entering the outer recesses of Aaron's hole with sliding up and down across his P-spot.

As Aaron lay back, Jason dragged his fingers down across his abdomen, down around his shaft and balls, down further still until he reached the muscular globes of Aaron's buttocks. He used them to part Aaron's crack while he lowered himself to the stool and leaned his face in to sample the muskiness of Aaron's puckering hole.

Aaron squealed when Jason's tongue drilled past his outer sphincter, and then he convulsed when Jason began to suck and burrow in deeper and deeper while his fingers pried their way in to hold Aaron open until the last barrier had been breached, while drop after precious drop of Jason's pre-cum dripped from his slit onto the floor, forming a slick, growing stain on the sheet in front of the stool.

"Oh, my, God!" Aaron yelled, as his cock began to spasm. His thick, honey-like nectar began to leak from the tip of his cock and cling to the thick, cropped hair that covered his abdomen until it pooled in his navel. "God! Yes!"

"Yes."

"Yes."

"Yes, Jason."

"Oh, Jason, yes!"

Jason dipped into the jar of lube to remove a large glob and began to spread it around Aaron's subdued hole to coat its edges. Then he slid two fingers into the inner depths and began to wiggle them around like a caterpillar working its way in to devour an opening rosebud. Gently, he advanced them to their hilt, as they sought out Aaron's quivering orb. Once found, Jason began to stroke up and down, round and round, up and down, round and round, over and over again.

A stream of thick pre-cum was ejected from Aaron's slit and pooled between his navel and breastbone as his prostate contracted in response to Jason's touch. More pre-cum flowed out as Jason's fingers worked their magic and ran across Aaron's tensed six-pack and down onto the leather sling.

"Oh my God! My God! Jason. Jason, you're … you're going to make … make me come! You're going … to make … me come!"

"Not yet, baby. Not yet."

Jason eased his fingers back until their tips locked inside Aaron's inner sphincter, then added more lube with the first and second fingers of his other hand to open Aaron up even wider while he massaged the sphincter muscles between his fingers and thumbs to relax them.

"I need you, Jason. I need you! I need you, inside me."

"Inside me, Jason. Inside me, now."

"Now, Jason, now!"

Jason inserted the tips of all four of the fingers and thumb of his left hand into Aaron's now tamed hole to hold it open, then reached his right hand down to the open jar of lube and scooped out a generous amount, then smeared it into Aaron. He grasped his own shaft and slathered the remaining lube along its length, milking out his own pre-cum and added it to the mix. He smiled as he noted the unneeded, unopened bottle of poppers sitting on the table.

"Aaron, my love. I won't need any of the other things you've laid out. You've opened yourself up for me beautifully. You're ready to receive me now."

"Yes, Jason. Yes. Make me your own."

"I'm going to go slow, Aaron. I don't want to hurt you."

"You could never hurt me, Jason. Never."

"But, you'll let me know if you feel pain immediately, right?"

"Jesus Christ, Jason! Stop being so kind, so gentle. Just fuck me, Jason! Fuck me! Make me your man!"

Jason stood and removed his left hand while he leaned forward and pushed his shaft downward until the tip touched Aaron's outer sphincter. Aaron sucked in his breath. Jason advanced slowly as the shrinking sphincters readily parted once again and welcomed him in.

"Oh, Jason. Oh, Jason!"

Jason leaned in further and watched his glans disappear into Aaron's depths, then the first inch of his shaft, then the second and the third. Aaron moaned and moaned as he turned his head from side to side.

"More, Jason. Give me more!"

"I will, Aaron. I promise."

"I want all of you. All of you!"

"Yes, Aaron. Here it comes!"

"Fill me, Jason. Fill me with your cock!"

Jason pulled back until the edge of his glans exposed itself then leaned in, driving himself just a little bit deeper then back out and back in further.

A rumble began to rise from deep within Aaron's chest and mix with his moans. His moans turned to groans when Jason's glans brushed his prostate. "That's the money spot, Jason. The money spot!"

Jason advanced further and further until his cock was buried to the hilt, well past the depths of Aaron's prostate. "That's all of me, my love. You've taken in all of me, Aaron."

"Yes, Jason. Yes. It's amazing." Aaron's body began to tremble as the words left his mouth in a staccato rhythm. It's ... wonderful. I feel so full, Jason. So ... so full."

"Are you ready, Aaron?"

"Yes, forget ... forget making ... love to me! Fu-fuck me, Jason! Fuck my ... fuck my brains out! Fuck my brains out!"

Jason withdrew slowly, so that Aaron would barely feel it. Then he lunged forward with such force, it caused his heavy, sperm-laden balls to strike the meaty globes of Aaron's buttocks with a *thwack*! The rumbling in Aaron's chest turned to growls. Then grunts and groans began to escape his mouth.

"It's been so long!" Aaron moaned. "So long! Pound me! Pound my ass!"

Thwack!

"Oh!" The sling rocked back and forth.

Thwack!

"My!" The sling rocked further.

Thwack!

Rocked faster. "God! Oh, my God! Harder, Jason, harder!"

Thwack!

"Harder!"

Thwack!

"Harder!"

Jason picked up the pace.

Thwack — Thwack — Thwack!

"Oh! My! God!"

The slapping of Jason's ball sack echoed down the hall and throughout the cabin.

"Make me come, Jason. Make me come!"

"Not yet, my love." Jason pulled out halfway. The head of his cock lay in wait just within reach of Aaron's spasming prostate. He advanced just enough to caress it, then pulled back just enough to caress it again. He advanced and pulled back, advanced and pulled back over and over again, as his cock struck glancing blows across Aaron's gland, causing it to clench in spasms.

As Jason quickened his pace, he lowered his hips, slightly changing the angle until it was hitting Aaron's prostate full on. His cockhead's taps turned to strikes.

Aaron's shaft strained against the pressure of blood being driven into it as the veins snaked round and round, just beneath the surface of the shaft, threatening to burst open.

Jason gripped Aaron's cock and began to pump it in rhythm with the thrust of his hips as he hammered into Aaron with his pelvis, impaling his rectum with the shaft of his cock as if it were a cudgel. Aaron's prostate tightened and tightened.

For the next fifteen minutes Jason slowed his pace and slowed it some more until the head of his cock barely grazed Aaron's spasming orb. Then he thrust forcefully into the recesses of Aaron's depths. Back and forth, back and forth he went until Aaron could take no more.

"You bastard! You bastard, Jason!" Aaron's head was swimming. "Fuck me! Fuck me raw! Make me come!" he pleaded. "Please, make me come!"

Jason slowly picked up the pace again and leaned over until his mouth was within reach of Aaron's purpled, massive cockhead. He waited and waited some more for the moment. His timing had to be just right.

"I can't take it anymore! I can't take it," Aaron pleaded. Then he began to whimper.

The sounds of Aaron's pleas were more than Jason could withstand. He bent down and grazed Aaron's slit with his tongue, then sucked in and swallowing the stream of nectar that flowed from the depths of Aaron's loins. Aaron screamed.

Jason lowered his mouth over the first several inches of Aaron's shaft. As his hips pounded into Aaron, Aaron's cock was driven in and out of his mouth while Jason sucked with all his might. Aaron's shaft swelled as it advanced deeper and deeper until it nearly became wedged at the back of Jason's throat, making it difficult for him to breathe. Jason locked his lips around the shaft and pummeled Aaron's ass, threatening to drive Aaron's shaft even further down his throat.

Aaron rose up on the sling and grabbed the back of Jason's head, forcing it up and down along the entire ten-inch length of his cock. Jason grasped Aaron's shaft with both hands and pumped them up and down to the rhythm that Aaron had set.

With one final lunge, Jason drove Aaron's prostate beyond the point of no return. It clamped down, and his flood gates opened. When he felt Aaron's urethra pulsate against his tongue, Jason reached the precipice of release himself. As stream after stream of hot cum forced its way up and out to the back of his throat, Jason swallowed as much of the thick cream as he could, but half of it poured from his mouth.

Jason's vision began to dim. He couldn't breathe. As the room closed in around him, his loins released. The intensity of his fucking Aaron combined with his near suffocation created the most intense orgasm Jason had ever experienced as load after load of his jism pumped into Aaron's depths.

Aaron's hands tightened around Jason's head, driving him down against his shaft just as the last wave of his cum shot past Jason's tonsils. Aaron lifted Jason up, pulling him from his shaft, until their mouths met. He sucked in hard, pulling his own musky cream right out of Jason's mouth, then rolled it across his tongue. Then he shoved Jason's mouth down around his shaft once again, pummeling his cock with Jason's throat.

Jason's vision grayed. HIs body began to spasm as he struggled to free his mouth from Aaron's grip while his own cock continued to spew thick ribbons of cum into Aaron's colon. His legs finally buckled, pulling his cock from Aaron's hole, but Aaron sat up in the sling and grabbed him under the arms, causing the last of Jason's several loads to shoot against the backs of Aaron's thighs or between his legs, landing on Aaron's chest and chin.

Aaron wrapped an arm around Jason's chest and rolled his head away, releasing Jason's mouth so that he could scoop Jason's cum from his chest into his hand. He brought it to his lips and sucked Jason's cum into his mouth and mixed it with his own cum before he swallowed it all, together.

Jason's head rocked back and forth as he gasped for air. Aaron lifted him up and then pulled him to his chest and held him tight. Their sweat mixed with the traces of their combined cum and dripped from their bodies, pooling into the recesses of the sling or sliding down their legs to be absorbed into the sheet on the floor.

Aaron nuzzled Jason's neck and kissed it while whispering his name. "Oh, Jason, my Jason. Thank you. Thank you, my love. I needed to feel you inside me. You were like an animal, ravaging me, conquering me." He shouted, "I feel so alive, so very alive!"

Jason managed, "Can't talk," as he continued to

gasp for breath.

Aaron caressed Jason's face and his back, kissed his eyelids and his cheeks, and continued to murmur loving words into his ear until he had recovered.

Chapter Ten
Afterglow

After many minutes, Jason was finally able to push up and slide off the sling. Aaron slowly followed, and together they shuffled to the shower where they spent a half-hour kissing under unlimited, warm, gentle rain while lathering the sweat and spunk from each other's bodies.

"You were so intense, so beast-like, so savage, Jason. To experience you. To be taken with such passion and such force was the most intense sexual experience I have ever known. Oh, my Jason. My Jason."

"Thank you, Aaron. Thank you for asking me to do that. I guess I do know what I'm doing, huh?"

"More than you know, Jason. More than you know."

Jason began to laugh, and Aaron joined him.

Finally, Jason turned off the water. "I'm starving. My blood sugar has bottomed out. If I don't sit down, I'm gonna fall down."

"I'm not quite that bad off, Jason, but I am feeling weak, too. I sure have some work to do to regain my stamina, but what a way to begin! How about a big piece of chocolate cake and a tall glass of milk?"

"Sounds great, Aaron."

"You go lie down in bed. I'll bring it to you."

Several minutes later, Aaron carried in his old bed tray with two pieces of cake and two glasses of Heather's milk. He raised the head of Jason's side of the king-size bed and placed the tray over his legs. While Jason ate off the tray, Aaron sat cross-legged next to him with his plate on his lap.

When Jason finished, Aaron carried the dishes to the kitchen where he washed them and put them in the drainboard to dry.

"Thanks, Aaron," Jason said when he returned.

Aaron climbed into bed. "It's the least I could do after your weeks and weeks of caring for me and then fucking me like I've never been fucked before. It was weird though, me sitting next to you while you ate off the tray. It was like we reversed roles for a minute. I know I can never repay you for all you did for me, but I want you to know that I realized how difficult it must have been for you. You did it all by yourself. You did what it took an entire team of doctors, nurses, therapists, and dietary and housekeeping staff to do for me while I was in the hospital, and you did it for five whole weeks. I was in the hospital for only two. And on top of that, you took care of this home and the animals to boot. I so admire you, Jason, and I respect you. I can only hope that someday I can prove to you that I was worth all your efforts. I hope one day I can make you proud. I have so much to learn from you."

"Aaron, I am proud of you, and I love you. There's nothing more to it."

Aaron reached over to turn off the lamp and then scooted over next to Jason and pulled him into his muscular arms.

"It's awful quiet," Aaron said.

"I like the quiet."

"Ever think of turning the chimes back on the grandfather clock?"

"No, do you want them on?"

"Maybe. What do they sound like?"

"You know, I'm not sure I remember. After we get settled in I'll play around with them. There's a few tunes they can play on the hour. I'll let you hear them and then you can decide, but we should keep them low. Otherwise they'll wake us up in the middle of the night."

"Whatever you think is best, Jason."

They lay there in the moonlight until they drifted off to sleep.

Chapter Eleven
Biding Time

December 22, 2009, 1:30 AM
Headquarters, Pacific North Air Transport
  The stocky figure, now dressed in brand new outdoor survival gear, couldn't believe his luck when he returned to the fence outside the headquarters of Pacific North Air Transport. There in front of him, illuminated by a spotlight, sat a large helicopter that hadn't been there the prior afternoon.
  "That must be the bird they've been using," he said to himself. "Change of plans. Now I won't have to try to convince them to take me up."
  After getting out of the car, he went to the trunk and lifted out his duffel bag, survival gear, and Baby. He threw the duffel and gear over the fence and then climbed it with Baby slung over his back. After he'd cleared the fence, he made his way round to the office door and picked the lock for the second time in less than a day. He hid his gear behind a stack of pallets in a back corner of the bay and unrolled his sleeping bag. He would wait for morning and then make his move.

Section Two
Thunderstruck

Chapter Twelve
We're Going to Need a Place in the Valley

6:30 AM
Homestead

Jason had showered well before sunrise, well before Big John announced morning had arrived. By the time the rooster had crowed his greeting to the dawn, Jason had mixed pancake batter, scrambled eggs, and cut thick slices from a smoked side of bacon. As he finished, Aaron called to him from their bed.

"Good morning, Jason. Good morning, my amazing lover."

"Good morning to you, my big, manly stud," Jason answered. "Are you hungry? You must be after last night. Want some breakfast?"

"It's you who's the stud. You really worked me over last night. It was amazing. Amazing! I've only bottomed a couple of times, but with you, I'm not the least bit sore. It's like my entire region down there, my cock, my balls, my ass, and my prostate are so alive. I'm so aware of every nuance of what I'm feeling. I can still feel you, deep inside me. You're a wonderful, wonderful lover, Jason."

"Now don't make me blush," Jason said as he turned away to conceal the red rising in his face.

"Look what you've done to me," Aaron said as he walked into the kitchen, naked, pointing to his ten-inch cock standing at attention, high above his pendulous balls, swaying in their hairless sack. "He wants more!"

"Oh, he'll get more, but not for a little while. I need to recharge a bit. Last night drained every last bit of

63

not only my sexual energy, but *all* my energy. I'm running on reserves right now."

"Then recharge them, baby, recharge them! And quick! You've ruined me, Jason. I could never look at another man. Not after what you did to me last night."

"I'll take that as a compliment. Now what do you want to eat?'

"Changing the subject so soon?"

"Yes. Rod and Jack are coming, and we've got a busy day ahead of us."

"Okay, okay, you win," Aaron said as he scooped Jason up in his arms and swung him around. "I love you, Jason."

"I love you, too, Aaron," he answered as he moved in for a kiss.

"So what can I help you with?" Aaron asked as he put Jason back down.

"To start," he said, as he punched down the dough sponge from the day before, "I have no idea what else you've got coming up here, so I only hope there's room for it all. Can you tell me? Anything?"

"All the rest of my clothes, some furniture that I didn't want to have to give up, some personal stuff, trophies and awards and the like, and their cases, and a surprise or two for you. That's all. The rest I'm giving away to charity."

"Aaron, what else could there be?" Jason said as he worked and divided the dough into three loaves and put them into greased pans. "I have every tangible thing I could ever need, and now that I have you, I'm doubly blessed."

"Oh, Jason, I'm actually here. We're actually together!"

"And we're going to be together, forever and ever, Aaron. This is all still so surreal to me. To think that this is actually happening, I can't wrap my mind around it." Jason's voice caught for a moment, but he pressed on. "I love you more than I could ever show you, but I'm going to spend the rest of my life trying."

"How'd I get so lucky, Jason?" You don't have to prove a thing to me. What did I ever do to deserve you?"

"You loved me, Aaron, completely, and you trusted me. What's more, you believed in me. What else could there be?"

"I don't know, Jason. I'm not deep like you are, but I hope you can teach me. You're so wise and so grounded. I only hope I can learn."

"Oh, baby, thank you for saying that, but half the time, I'm just reacting to whatever life throws at me." Jason put the loaf pans into the proofing box. "And don't cut yourself short. You made a career for yourself, a quarterback for a major football team no less, and the youngest quarterback to ever be signed as the starter. That's no small accomplishment. You should be proud of that. And anyway, most of what I know, I've learned by trial and error. Trust me, I've made more mistakes than I've had successes."

"Then I hope you'll teach me so I don't have to learn the hard way."

"It's a deal, but I'm sure I'm going to learn as much from you if not more. So how about some breakfast?"

"When are you going to eat?"

"I figured after I took care of the animals."

"Then I'll wait to eat with you."

"Okay. Why don't you go take a shower while I go out to the barn? We'll eat after we're both done."

"You got it." Aaron kissed Jason again and sauntered away, emphasizing the lobes of his, naked buttocks as he walked.

Jason watched Aaron's muscular physique move through the common area of the cabin until he disappeared around the corner into the bathroom. "No, my Adonis, I'm the lucky one," he whispered.

****

7:00 AM

"Good morning, ladies and gentlemen," Jason announced as he opened the barn's back door from the woodshed. "It's gonna be a beautiful day!"

As he poured feed into the trough between Nellie and Sarah's, and Heather and Jasper's stalls and scattered seed and scratch on the barn's dirt floor for the chickens, Jason realized he was whistling again. He just couldn't help himself.

At the sight of the seed, Big John flew down from the front barn window and strutted around picking out the choicest pieces like he owned the place.

Once Jason had portioned out some oats, Heather walked to the gate as he opened it and dipped her head into the wooden bucket for a mouthful before hopping up on her milking table. She continued to munch while he washed her teats and collected a good two quarts in the stainless steel pail.

No sooner had he finished than she hopped back down and walked into her stall to finish her breakfast. He gathered eight eggs from the hens' nesting boxes, a generous number, and before heading back to the cabin, he leaned into Nellie and Sarah's stall and scratched Nellie behind her ears.

"Well, girl, our lives are going to change around here. The love of my life has returned, and we're gonna to make a life together. I know you'll come to love him as much as I do. I'm so happy, Nellie. I'm so very happy."

When Nellie nuzzled the right side of Jason's

neck with her big donkey lips, Sarah began to bray and hung her head over his left shoulder for a hug. Then Nellie lifted her head over his shoulder and rested her chin against his back while he reached up with both arms and patted their necks. "Thanks, girls, and thanks for being so welcoming to him yesterday. He's family now. We're all going to be one big happy family."

****

When Jason returned from the barn, he found Aaron in the kitchen making coffee. He poured Heather's milk into a bottle and put it in the fridge. Then he added a log to the oven.

"How is everyone this morning?" Aaron asked as he finished pouring boiling water over grounds in the porcelain, European-cone, coffee filter.

"Heather gave us a little over two quarts, and the girls laid eight eggs," Jason answered as he washed the milk pail and then the eggs and then added them to a bowl in the fridge. "That almost breaks the record of nine, but there were more hens back then, and I see you figured out the coffee."

"No figuring needed. This is the exact same way my German grandmother used to make it. The only difference between her coffee maker and mine is electricity and an automatic timer. The principle is the same. Hey, Jason, I wanted to ask you something." Aaron added water from the tap to the kettle and put it back on the stove.

"What's that?"

"Now that I'm going to be living here, would it be easier if we had Rod deliver supplies more often? That way you wouldn't have to hunt as much, and you wouldn't have to milk Heather every day and gather the chickens' eggs."

"I would never want to give those things up,

Aaron," Jason said as he took the loaves from the proof box and put them in the oven. "And besides, I can't milk Heather any less than twice a day or her milk will dry up and it would be really, really painful for her while that happened. I wouldn't want to put her through that. And besides, if she keeps to her schedule, she's going to be going into heat soon, and I want her to have another kid."

"Well then, good. I'm glad to hear you say that, because I was thinking, maybe we could expand the flock of chickens and get more goats since there's going to be two mouths to feed. We'll probably need more than what they can produce right now, and I want to learn how to do those things, you know, learn how to care for the animals. You've got three acres inside the stockade and…"

"No, Aaron, *we've* got three acres inside the stockade."

"Oh, Jason. Thanks. You really mean that. Don't you?"

"Of course I do. It's only right. This is *our* home now." Jason emphasized the word "our".

"Well what do you think? Should we expand?"

"I think it's a good idea to get another nanny goat if you want more milk to drink, but she'll have to be pregnant and birth the kid here. I would never want to separate a milk producing nanny from her baby. We can either keep the baby, give it away after it grows up, or sell it. Heather actually produces much more than I need. I've been making butter with her extra milk and freezing it. I use what's left over in my bread or I drink it. The liquid is buttermilk, but it's sweet, not like what you buy in the store. When Rod comes up, I give him the extra butter to donate to a homeless shelter in the city. There's about fifty pounds every six months or so.

"I've been thinking along those lines you since

you suggested it yesterday, and I thought about it briefly when you were here back in September, but there was too much else going on. I couldn't handle any more than I was doing, and besides, I had no way of even contacting anyone on the outside to buy any more animals.

"I think we should wait though to decide until after we know what's going to happen with Nathan's Promise. If we wind up building up here, there's going to be a lot going on. We may not be able to handle too many changes at once."

"I'm not so sure, Jason, but before I forget, I'd like to see how you make butter from Heather's milk."

"That's it right there," Jason said pointing to the wooden churn at the end of the counter. "It's a very simple motorized system that I have hooked up to the battery grid. It'll hold a gallon of cream at a time, and it runs slowly and at a low wattage so it doesn't put a strain on the system or use up a lot of electricity."

"That's so cool, Jason. The next time you do it, please show me how."

"I will, but it takes time. You have to allow the cream to separate from the milk for at least half a day before you start, and it's quicker if you do it with fresh, room temperature milk that hasn't been refrigerated. I pasteurize the cream for the butter I give away and then chill it before I start. Making goat butter is different than butter from cows' milk."

"I look forward to it. Now back to what we were talking about before. Do you think it's possible that you're thinking a little small?"

"What do you mean, Aaron?"

"Well, if we do end up building it all up here, aren't we going to have to hire staff for everything? Why can't we get a few people to help out here in our home?"

"Good grief, Aaron, that never occurred to me. I *have* been thinking too small. Way too small."

"And even if we don't build up here, aren't we going to be involved in the running of Nathan's Promise? I know I'm planning on it."

"You're absolutely right."

"So if we're going to be doing that," Aaron continued, "our lives are going to dramatically change anyway. Even if we're only overseeing the operation, we're still going to have to spend a lot of hours on it every day, even if it's just in the beginning. If you still want to get milk and eggs from animals you raise, someone's going to have to look after them, even if it's only part of the time. Otherwise our milk and eggs are going to have to come from someplace else."

"That's a great idea, Aaron, and to build on it, what would you think about starting a farm? We're going to need a place in the valley where we can grow a lot if not most of the food for the athletes while they're going through therapy, and their families for that matter. It should be the freshest and healthiest food possible, and what could be fresher than right from our own farm every day?"

"Why down in the valley?" Aaron asked

"The growing season up here wouldn't be good for leafy vegetables because of the altitude. That makes it cooler, and the growing season is shorter. If not in the valley, we could buy a farm or build a farm somewhere where it's better suited for vegetables. Where did I put my tablet? I should write all this down so that we can discuss it with Rod and Jack."

As if on cue, the whop-whop-whop of Big Daddy's rotors reached their ears as he cleared the ridge and settled on the helipad.

Chapter Thirteen
Salads and Greens

8:45 AM
Homestead, helipad

Once the rotors came to a stop, Rod and Jack climbed down from the hold and headed down the hill towards the stockade's gate.

****

When Rod and Jack were out of sight, a stocky figure slithered from behind crates and tarps at the rear of the chopper's hold, pulling his duffel and the gear behind him. He stealthily exited the cargo doors and headed into the forest where he'd bide his time.

****

Homestead

Jason called to Rod and Jack once they were half way into the yard. "Good morning, you two. Breakfast is ready to go. Why don't you come in?"

"We were going to try to get a jump on unloading Big Daddy," Rod called back. "We can eat later."

"No, come in now. We'll eat together."

"Well, I don't have to be asked twice," Jack shouted as he jumped ahead of Rod.

"You mean you waited for us?" Rod called.

"Not really, I only got back in from the barn a little while ago," Jason said as he met them just off the porch with a hug to each.

"Good," Rod said as he climbed the steps. "I'd feel real bad if you held up your breakfast just for us."

"Mmmm, I smell coffee," Jack said as he rubbed his hands together against the morning chill, after they walked inside.

"Here, I'll pour you a cup," Aaron said. "I just made it ten minutes ago. How do you take it?"

"Black is just fine."

"And you, Rod?"

"Milk and one sugar. Thanks, Aaron."

"Pancakes, scrambled eggs, and country smoked bacon will be ready in a few minutes," Jason said. "I added cornmeal to the pancakes, just like you like them, Rod."

Rod took off his coat and gloves and then headed for the table. "That's great, Jason,"

"Me, too," Jack chimed in. "That's exactly how I like 'em."

"Oh, Jack. I've got your grapefruit juice, too."

"Thanks, Jason," Jack took a seat opposite Rod.

"What's all this?" Rod asked as he began to read the new notes Jason had just written down.

"Just a few things we talked about this morning." Jason took down three large serving platters from the cupboard and put them in the warming bin over the oven. "We'll discuss it later, after you've finished unloading. You did bring some changes of clothes with you, right?"

"Yup," Jack answered. A couple days' worth."

"Good," Jason stirred the eggs in the pan.

"I'll make some more coffee." Aaron threw out the grounds and started pouring the simmering water over a fresh filter. Then he helped Jason at the stove.

****

"Sure smells good, guys," Jack said. "I'm starving."

Jason looked over his shoulder towards the table. "It's nearly ready. Aaron, would you take out the platters from the warming bin and put them on the counter?"

A few minutes later they carried in breakfast. "Don't be shy. Everybody dig in," Jason began to pass around the platters.

For the next few minutes, everyone concentrated

on their stomachs. Then Rod got up and pulled a folded-over, brown paper bag from his coat pocket and handed it to Aaron. "These should be right. They were delivered to the hangar yesterday. I've kept them from freezing, just like you asked."

"Thanks, Jack. I'm sure they're okay. The man from the company promised me they'd all be good."

"What's that?" Jason asked.

"Part of your surprise."

"Okay, how long are you guys going to keep me in the dark?"

"Go ahead and show him, Aaron." Jack said, "What difference is an hour going to make?"

"You're right." Aaron turned to Jason. "Here, baby. These are for you."

Jason unfolded the bag and shook out two dozen packs of seeds. "I don't get it. What are these for?"

"Vegetables, for your greenhouse, baby. You said you wanted one."

"I still don't get it."

Jack chuckled. "Jason, are you dense?"

"Huh?"

"A greenhouse," Jack went on. "A friggin' greenhouse, dummy!"

"But I don't have a greenhouse."

"Um, Jason," Aaron said with a smile, "you do now."

"A greenhouse! Where?"

"It's in Big Daddy's hold," Rod said, laughing. "We'll have it set up today or tomorrow, depending on how much we can get done today."

"Where would we put a greenhouse?"

"It can go on the porch or even in here, maybe in one of the spare rooms," Aaron answered. "It's self-contained, and it has its own solar powered heating and lighting system. It's for starting seedlings and for growing plants. I figured once you have your big greenhouse built, the plants and seedlings can be moved in there. In the meantime, you can have vegetables until the permanent greenhouse is up and running. Then we can donate it to an organization that needs one."

"A greenhouse. I'm going to have my own greenhouse!" Jason exclaimed as he jumped up and moved to kiss Aaron.

Aaron smiled up at him. "I remember how you said you missed salads and greens."

****

After breakfast, Rod and Jack went to the barn and hitched Nellie and Sarah up to the wagon again. They'd made two trips between Big Daddy and the cabin and had them unloaded by lunch time when Jason made them stop to eat. Before everyone sat down, Rod returned the girls to the barn for a rest and to get out of the cold. Jason served a loaf of fresh, sliced sourdough bread he'd baked, along with a platter of cold cuts, mayonnaise, mustard, pickles, fresh sliced tomatoes and lettuce, all courtesy of Aaron.

Once lunch was over, Rod and Jack went back for the girls and returned to Big Daddy for two more loads of Aaron's things. When they returned with the second load, Jason made them stop and take a break.

"If we're going to stop working, why don't we pick up with our discussion where we left off yesterday?" Rod suggested.

"No," Jason answered as he carried in a pot of coffee, a pitcher of Heather's milk, and the remaining chocolate cake from the day before to the table, "When I told you guys I wanted you to take a break, I meant take a break, not do some other kind of work. Now have some cake and coffee. You've more than earned it."

"If we're taking a break then Nellie and Sarah are gonna take a break, too," Jack said. "They've been hauling a lot, and it's close to freezing out there."

"You're right, Jack," Jason said as he sliced cake. "You guys sit down. I'll take care of them."

After Jason led Nellie and Sarah into the barn, he took turns rubbing each of their shoulders and scratching their necks before he rubbed them down with dry hay and put their blankets over their backs. "Thanks, girls, I don't know what I'd do without you. You're done for the night. You rest up now, okay."

****

Camouflaged hideout, beyond the homestead

Peering over the stockade through a pair of military grade binoculars from a rise beyond the tree line, former Corporal Calvin Garrison, though cleanly outfitted, still presented a stocky and bedraggled appearance. He was heavily camouflaged among the remnants of fallen leaves and vegetation on the forest floor by his recently acquired, high-end sleeping bag. Motionless, he sat with Baby across his lap, an ill-gotten M16A2 remnant from his army days. She was locked and loaded and just itching to see action again. He waited patiently for his chance to meet with Corpsman Jason Ackerman one last time. They had unfinished business to attend to.

****

Homestead

Before Rod and Jack left the table, Jason asked, "Hey, guys, are you okay with lasagna, garlic bread, and salad for dinner?"

"Sounds great!" they both said in unison.

"Good, 'coz there's a ton of it. I don't know what you were thinking, Aaron, but those are foodservice sized pans of heat and eat food you brought. I figured it out. Each of them can serve twenty people."

"Well good. That way you won't have to cook so much. I can cook a few things, but my repertoire is very limited."

"Hell," Jack chimed in, "I could eat lasagna for a week. I won't mind at all."

"No, Jack. I've already started to defrost one of Aaron's smoked hams and a macaroni and cheese pan. I'll serve them with green beans tomorrow night if everyone's okay with that. And there's a couple of frozen pies. You guys let me know what you prefer."

"Um, Jason." Aaron raised his hand. "Sorry, but you said ham. Jack is Jewish."

"Oh, shit! I'm sorry, Jack, I completely forgot."

"No worries, Jason. I don't keep kosher. Ham is one of my favorite gentile foods. I'm looking forward to it."

"Are you sure, Jack? There's so much other stuff I've brought," Aaron asked.

"I'm sure. I'm sure. Now don't give it a second thought."

****

By the time, Jack and Rod had finished moving all of Aaron's things from the porch into the cabin, it was nearly dark. "That's it, guys. You're done for the night," Jason ordered.

"There's another half load of supplies to bring in from Big Daddy's hold that we couldn't fit in the wagon the last trip," Rod protested. "It won't take long, really.

"Sorry, no, we're done. You can unload it in the morning. I've already told the girls they're done for the day, and besides, I've already put them to bed, blankets and all. By the time you finish setting up Aaron's furniture and trophy cases, stocking the pantry and cupboards, and filling the freezer, it'll be dinner time."

"Yeah, guys, you've done great," Aaron said. "I'm gonna go get your wood stoves going so your rooms will be nice and toasty by the time you turn in. I'm sure they've gone cold since yesterday."

"I can get that, Aaron."

"No, Jason. I've watched you. I know what to do."

Aaron scooped out some coals from the kitchen's stove into the ash can and carried an armload of split logs and kindling back to the two empty rooms Rod and Jack would sleep in. After he got the stoves started he loaded up with firewood from the porch and made several more trips, stacking it in the bins in all three of the back rooms.

****

While Aaron took care of the guest bedrooms, Jason returned to the barn to feed all the animals and put an extra portion of sweet grass in the trough for Nellie and Sarah, but Heather and Jasper pitched in and helped them eat it.

"Thanks, girls," he told them. "I was afraid they'd insist on keeping going, but now it's settled. You rest up for tomorrow." Then he reached in to Heather and scratched her behind her ears. "I'll be back to milk you after dinner, Little Miss. Eat up now."

It still wasn't cold enough to fire up the barn's wood stove, but Jason checked the thermostat's thermometer just the same, then turned it up a notch. He was glad he'd had the solar powered hot water heating system put in the barn when it was built. It sure made early and late winters easier on the animals and himself. Fortunately, tonight wasn't going to go down too far below freezing. Though the solar system couldn't handle the deep freeze of winter, tonight wouldn't be any problem. Heather certainly didn't appreciate cold hands on her teats when he milked her, and it helped the hens with their egg laying over the winter, too.

****

When Jason returned to the cabin, he cut plenty of lasagna from the pan for the four of them and put it and a fresh loaf of garlic bread wrapped up in foil that Aaron had brought into the oven to heat up. Then he took out the mixed salad and set the table for dinner. While the food was warming up, he went to help Rod and Jack put the dry and canned goods away in the pantry.

Once the food was hot, Jason ordered everyone to the dinner table where they sat down for a long relaxing meal loaded with carbohydrates.

****

Camouflaged hideout, beyond homestead

"That's right, Corpsman Ackerman," Calvin said as he peered into the cabin through his binoculars from his hideout on the bluff. "Enjoy your big, fancy dinner. It just may be your last." He ripped off a chunk of beef jerky with his teeth and chewed it slowly as his breath steamed and drifted upward every time he opened his mouth.

It would soon be time to make his move.

Chapter Fourteen
A Menace Made Known

December 22, 2009, 5:45 PM, MST
The Regular Evening News Broadcast
"So it appears that retail theft is on the rise once again during this holiday season all across the region. This is Brent McMaster coming to you live from police headquarters in Hinnen Valley. Back to you in the studio, John."

"Thanks, Brent. In a related news story, there was a break-in at Sportsman's Haven in downtown Hinnen Valley last night. Security camera footage revealed a lone, stocky male figure making off with multiple items including ammunition, outdoor survival gear, survival food, hiking boots, wool socks, several pairs of lined denim jeans, a camouflage-print sleeping bag, and heavy, quilted flannel shirts totaling in value over seven hundred dollars. Police say it appears the thief was aware of the security camera positions because he turned away whenever he came into their field of view.

"Police ask that anyone with information should contact them at the number appearing at the bottom of your television screens."

****

After dinner
Homestead
While Rod scraped, Jason washed and handed dishes to Jack to dry, who then handed them to Aaron to put away in the cupboard.

"Hey, guys, it's been a long day, and I'm pooped. I still have to milk Heather and then close everyone up for the night. Why don't we just stop and pick up again tomorrow?"

"Nah," Rod said, "we'll keep going. There isn't

that much more to put away, and I think we can get that last half load in from Big Daddy's hold."

"No, as I already said, it's dark outside, and it's down to…" Jason looked at the base of the kitchen window to see the temperature on the digital thermometer. "What in the world is that?"

Then the yard exploded in a blinding light as a tremendous lightning bolt struck a tree just outside the stockade. Its crack rattled the windows and shook the cabin. The rumble of thunder sounded like a herd of buffalo racing by.

"I felt that in my bones!" Jack exclaimed.

"What is what?" Aaron asked as he and Jack moved to look out the window.

"For a moment I thought … Rod, you closed up the gate, right?"

"Yes, I did, Jason, and locked it. Why?"

"What did you see?" Aaron asked.

"It must have been nothing. For a moment, I thought I saw something moving out in the yard right before the lightning struck, but it couldn't have been anything. It was probably the lightning bolt playing tricks with the light as it came down, just before it hit. Okay, look, it's twenty-nine degrees outside," he said, pointing to the thermometer, "and there's a freezing rain coming down right now. If there was ever any question, Mother Nature's answered it for us. No one's going anywhere."

Jack started to speak. "We really don't mind…"

"No, everyone's staying in for the night. I don't know what predators are lurking out there in the dark, and you guys don't know the place at night. We're staying in. Period."

"We've got flashlights," Rod said. "We'll be just fine."

"No, Rod. End of discussion. Like I said, I've

already put the girls to bed for the night. I don't want them to have to go out when it's this cold outside and with freezing rain falling."

"Okay, okay, we'll stay in. Good thing we already unloaded all the perishables. They'd be ruined."

"Thank you. I'm glad that's settled now," Jason said. "Aaron, would you check the wood stoves in the guest rooms and make sure there's at least one new log burning in each? Oh, crap. I just realized I don't have beds for you guys. What do I have that you can sleep on?"

"Already taken care of, Jason," Jack said. "We brought inflatable camping mattresses and there's a compressor to fill them. We'll be just fine."

"Good. That's a relief."

****

7:15 PM

After dinner was cleaned up, Jason put on his coat to go out to the barn. "Guys, I should be back in about fifteen minutes, after I finish milking Heather. I sure am glad I put the woodshed between the cabin and the barn. It makes getting to my nighttime chores so much easier in the winter."

"Do you want some help?" Aaron asked.

"Thanks, but no, I'll be fine, and you should stay off your ankle as much as possible. The woodshed's nothing more than a roof over bare ground and there's still rocks and roots, so it's not very level. You could trip over them and re-injure yourself. Two rows of split logs, stacked in rows up to the roof, make up the other two walls that run between the cabin and the barn."

Aaron smiled and leaned down to kiss him. "Okay, love, but I'm not feeling it as much after nearly a week of ibuprofen and keeping it wrapped. See," he said, walking around the kitchen without his cane and bouncing. "No pain."

"Don't push it, Aaron and use your cane. I'll be back in a few."

"And I'll be here, waiting impatiently. Hey, just think, we're going to be sleeping in the same bed tonight, again, and I can move around all I want."

"That's right, buddy boy, and we're still going to be using a sling, but a different one and in a different way. Just not when Rod and Jack are here. Last night wasn't a one time thing," Jason said teasingly.

"You are so bad." Aaron slapped Jason's butt.

"You have no idea."

****

Rod had changed into his union suit and was coming out of the guest room as Jason headed out through the back door to the woodshed. "Just going out for a nightcap," he said as they passed. "Be back in in a few."

Rod put on his coat, hat, and gloves and carried a bottle of scotch and a glass out to the porch. He poured himself a respectable portion, lit a big, fat cigar and leaned back in one of the rockers.

****

Barn

When Jason opened the door to the barn, he flicked on the light switch, but the bulb didn't come on. "That's strange."

Something didn't feel right. He reached into his pocket and found his mini flashlight and twisted it on. Nellie, Sarah, Heather, and Jasper were pacing in their stalls, and Jasper was snorting. None of them came to greet him, and the chickens were clucking loudly instead of cooing. He assumed they were acting funny because of his flashlight or the earlier lightning bolt.

"It's okay, babies. It's only me. I just have to get

to the other switch to turn on the rest of the lights. Then we'll be back in business."

As he made his way into the barn, he heard the door hinges creak and then the door latch click. Then there was a click and all the lights came on, temporarily blinding him.

"Hello there, Corpsman. Long time no see."

Jason spun around as Corporal Calvin Garrison jumped down from the rafters near the circuit breakers by the door. As Jason began to raise his arms, he was met by the butt end of a rifle.

"What the fuck?" he shouted, grasping his jaw.

"Shut your mouth, boy!" Garrison pointed Baby's barrel directly at Jason's gut. "Don't make a sound or your friends won't live to see the sunrise. I'm just here for you."

"Who the hell are you?" Jason mouthed around his swelling tongue as he spit out blood. "What do you want?"

"Oh, you hurt my feelings, Corpsman, especially after that intimate moment we almost shared, what, some nineteen years ago? I sure remember you."

"What? What are you talking about? Who are you?"

"Take a good look, Ackerman! You better remember me! You're the one who ruined my life and my career!"

Jason couldn't think. He tried to remember the face. Then... "Oh, my God! Garrison? Corporal Garrison?"

"Bingo!"

"How'd you get here?"

"Caught a ride up in the back of that chopper. Plenty of room—"

"Rod would've never—"

"Plenty of room to hide."

"What do you want with me? I haven't done anything—"

"Shut up, faggot! Yes, you did! Yes, you did! Because of you, every move I made was scrutinized. Next thing I knew I was accused of being a queer, and then they gave me a dishonorable discharge, and it's all your fault!"

"Look, Garrison, I didn't do anything. I didn't say a word. I didn't even testify at my hearing." Jason spit out more blood. "I'm the one who was accused of sexual assault, not you!"

"I said shut up! Shut the fuck up! I'll do the talking! I'm no fag! I don't let guys fuck me up the ass. I don't suck other guy's dicks. Guys see my cock, and they want it. They can't get enough of it. They come after me, not the other way around, and believe me, I get made passes at all the time. Hell, they offer up a tight little ass or a warm mouth, who am I to turn down a good nut bust?"

Jason slowly looked around the barn for a weapon. He inched towards the sickle he used to cut the sweetgrass for the animals, hanging from a peg on the wall next to the table and chair.

Garrison saw it, too.

"Don't even try it, Ackerman. I can take out all your babies," Garrison spit, "Ha, babies my ass. You're pathetic. I can end them with one squeeze of the trigger. Now back away."

"Garrison, I wasn't trying anything. I was going to sit down, that's all."

"Liar! I hate liars. You, sitting in judgment of me. You, lying about me. You could go to jail for telling lies on the stand."

"Garrison, I never took the stand, and I never

judged you. It doesn't matter to me what you do with your life. Go on, live it however you want."

"I don't need your approval, faggot, but come to think of it now, maybe I will sample what you've got."

Jason's eyes opened wide as the color drained from his face. He put up his hands. "Please Garrison, no. Don't do that. You don't want to do that. That would be rape. You said…"

"What the fuck does it matter what I said? You're gonna be dead in a few minutes anyway, but I'll tell you what. Let's make a little deal. If you don't put up a fuss, I'll leave your friends alone. I'll leave your animals alone. Hell, maybe I'll even let you live, that is, if you make it worth my while. Come on, Ackerman, show me a good time. Show me a good time while I'm pounding your sweet, tight little ass."

"Please, Garrison. No."

"You willing or not?" Garrison said as he reached down and unzipped his fly. "It's tougher when they squirm. Take a look at this monster, Ackerman." Garrison said waving eight inches of semi-erect penis in the air. "You want it, don't you, boy? You want it. Don't you!" he shouted as he pointed the barrel at Jason's head. "It's not even fully hard yet. Come on, show my nine inches of prime beef a good time while I'm pounding your ass!"

Oh, Aaron, forgive me, Jason thought.

＊＊＊＊

When Aaron opened the barn door, he called out.

"Hey, Jason? See, I made it all by myself and without my cane. Now what's been keeping you?"

"What the fuck!" Garrison yelled. His pants were down below his knees. He had a hold of Jason's waist with both hands and was just about to shove his cock into his ass. Jason was bent over and tied down to the worktable with a coil of rope. He'd been stripped completely naked and his legs were spread wide apart with his ankles fastened to the table legs with more rope.

Aaron screamed, "Jason!"

When Garrison reached for his rifle on the table, Jason shoved his butt backward into Garrison's groin with all his strength, moving the table in the process. Garrison groaned and then screamed in pain.

"My cock! My cock! What did you do to my cock? It's bent! It's bent! You fucking faggot! You broke my cock!"

Garrison gripped his rifle in his right hand as he buckled over, grabbing at himself in pain with the other. His finger was on the trigger.

"You son of a bitch!" Aaron yelled as he dove towards Garrison to tackle him. "That's my man!"

Garrison raised the barrel, pointed it towards Aaron, and squeezed the trigger. There was a deafening repetition of concussive cracks as Baby flew upward in a wide arc. Wood split and glass shattered until the bullets found dirt.

At the sound of the gunfire, Big John flew into a rage and launched towards Garrison. He struck out at Garrison's face with his spurs leaving gashes across his forehead and holes in his cheeks and his hands as he raised them to protect himself. The next thing Garrison felt was a tremendous thud to his legs as Aaron plowed into him, then a bone-crushing blow to his flank. Then he was airborne. There was a sharp pain at his collar bone, then at his temple. Then there was an instant flash of light behind his eyes.

Those were the last things Corporal Calvin Garrison felt and saw. When his head struck a heavy supporting post that reached to the roof, he crumpled into a heap on the barn's dirt floor.

"Aaron! Aaron! Aaron!" Jason screamed his name over and over again.

Aaron was on the ground. He wasn't moving.

Chapter Fifteen
There's Blood

Homestead

"What the fuck?" Rod shouted as he lurched back in the rocking chair, tipping it so far it crashed to the porch floor, breaking its back and one of the rockers. His glass of scotch flew from his hand and shattered when it bounced from the porch floor and struck on a rock in the yard. His head landed with a thud. "Jesus Christ! Jack! Jack! That was military!"

"I heard it! I heard it!" Jack called out from the kitchen.

"Where's my .45?" Rod yelled back as he struggled to get to his feet. "Grab my Colt out of my holster! It's over the back of the chair!

"Where's Aaron?" Jack shouted as he retrieved the revolver.

"I don't know!"

"He went out to the barn to check on Jason just a minute ago!" Jack yelled.

"Oh, fuck! Hand me my .45 and get behind me."

****

Barn

As Rod and Jack circled around and approached the main barn door from the yard, they heard Jason yelling Aaron's name. His voice was nearly drowned out by the sound of Nellie and Sarah braying. It sounded like they were screaming.

When they burst into the barn the first thing they saw was Jason trying to undo his bindings. He was naked and bent over the table, bound by rope crisscrossing his back. His ankles were bleeding as he struggled and yanked to break free of the ropes that tied them to the table's legs.

"What the fuck!" Rod yelled.

"Get me untied!" Jason yelled. "Rod, help Aaron. He's been shot! God damn it, Jack, get me untied! Get these fucking ropes off me!"

Jasper seemed to appear of nowhere. Blood was pouring from his right horn, just above his skull. He reared up and charged at Rod, but Rod jumped up onto a crate and then grabbed a rafter and pulled himself up just as Jasper shattered the crate. Jasper immediately turned his attention to Jack and charged, chasing him out of the barn, but Jack grabbed ahold of the door and swung himself up and over the top. He jumped down and pulled the door shut, bolting it from the inside.

There were more than a dozen loud crashes while the door shook and dust fell from the rafters as Jasper hammered it from the other side, trying to break through to save his friend, Jason.

"Jack! Jack! Look at me!" Jason ordered. "Look at me, Jack!"

At the sight of the body on the floor, Jack bent over and hurled up his dinner. "You can puke later, Jack! Untie me! Untie me, now! Rod, the barn door is strong. There's no way that Jasper can break through it. Don't worry. Go check Aaron. He's been shot, Rod! He's been shot!"

Nellie and Sarah continued their bloodcurdling brays while Heather bleated her little heart out. Jason tried to speak calmly, but failed.

"Nellie, it's okay, girl!" he shouted. "Sarah, it's okay, baby. Calm down. You're both fine. Nellie, please, you're safe. No one's going to hurt you. You're fine, girls. Heather, my sweet, you're fine. You're fine, baby girl. All of you are fine!"

"What the fuck!" Rod yelled as he stepped over a body on his way to Aaron. "Who the hell is that?"

"He's a killer, Rod! He tried to rape me. Then Aaron came in," Jason yelled. "He's a killer! He's killed my Aaron! He's killed my Aaron!"

"What the hell happened?" Jack asked as he wiped the back of his hand across his mouth.

"Later!" Jason shouted. "Later! Hurry, Jack! Get these fucking ropes off me!"

The moment Jason was free, he ran to Aaron, nearly pushing Rod out of the way, but Rod held his ground. He was holding a towel against Aaron's left temple.

"Oh, God," Jason exclaimed, "there's blood!" He shook his head to clear it. "Jack," he shouted over his shoulder. "Run to the storage closet. There's a bright orange trauma kit on a shelf straight back from the door at chest height. Aaron! Baby! Open your eyes for me! Open your eyes, Aaron!

"Jack, you can't miss it. It's got TRAUMA written in big reflective letters across the top," Jason continued to shout as he felt Aaron's neck for a pulse. "Bring it to me and grab two clean bath towels. I'm gonna have to make a cervical collar for him. Then get on the phone and call somebody, the state police, the Forest Service, I don't know, and call 911."

Jason lifted Aaron's eyelids and checked his pupils. "And tell them we need to airlift a twenty-three-year-old male with a GSW—that's gunshot wound—to the head. Now, Jack! Now! Run! Rod, move to the top of Aaron's head, but don't let go of that towel. Place one hand on each side of his head and keep it still. Don't let it turn or roll. He might have a cervical spine injury.

"Aaron! Baby! Wake up for me Aaron! Please, Aaron! Please wake up for me! Oh, my God! I can't feel a pulse. I can't feel a pulse, Rod. Oh, baby, I can't lose you now! I can't! I've only just gotten you back!"

"He's gonna be okay, Jason." Rod said, "He's gonna be okay."

"How can you know that, Rod? Aaron! Wake up! Please, Aaron! Please!"

"Because his blood is still flowing, Jason," Rod said calmly, "and it's red. He's still breathing, Jason. He's breathing. You're shaking too much to feel his pulse."

Jack made the round trip to the storage room and back to the barn in less than forty-five seconds.

"What took you so long, Jack?" Jason yelled.

Rod spoke in a steady voice. "Whoa, Jason. Jack was back lickety-split. Calm down, buddy. You're not going to do Aaron any good all worked up like this."

Jason shook his head to clear it. "Jack, I'm sorry."

Jack knelt down in the dirt, placing the trauma kit beside Aaron's head. "It's okay, Jason. Don't worry about it. Now what can I do to help?"

"Make those calls, Jack. Make those calls. Rod," Jason said as he began to roll the two towels together. "I'm going to slide these under his neck and tape them. Don't let his neck move while I'm doing it."

"Will do, Jason."

After Jason had secured Aaron's neck, he began ripping open dressings and pulled out a penlight from the kit. "Rod, when I say to, ease your fingers off that towel, but don't let go of his head and don't let it move."

"Will do."

****

"Yes, operator. I've got an emergency," Jack said into the satellite phone as he walked back towards the barn. "There's been a shooting, and a death, and a sexual assault. Yes, thank you. Yes. We're in the Bear River Mountains. Our coordinates are…"

****

Jason shined the light into Aaron's eyes. His pupils reacted quickly and were equal in size. "Good. He hasn't blown a pupil. No sign of increased intracranial pressure, yet."

As Jason moved in with a dressing, Rod moved his fingers off the towel. "Please don't let there be any brain matter. Please," Jason said as he lifted the towel. "Oh, thank God. There's skull showing, but I don't see any fractures."

"Jason," Rod said in a low voice, "you can tell me to shut up if you want. I'll understand, but isn't this two head injuries for Aaron in like four months?"

"Yes, Rod, I know, and he was unconscious with the first one and now with this one."

Jack returned through the barn's back door. "Jason, sorry to interrupt, but I talked to the 911 operator. There's no medical choppers available right now because of the freezing rain. She said she'd contact the state police and the forest rangers' office, but she has no idea when they can get here. It might not be until tomorrow."

"It's all my fault." Jason began to shake and cry. "It's all my fault!"

"Jason," Rod said calmly, "nothing is your fault. You didn't cause any of this." Then he turned to Jack. "Jack, go get some blankets. Jason is starting to shiver. It's fucking freezing out here."

"If I didn't live all the way out here," Jason said, "Aaron wouldn't be so far away from a hospital. If I hadn't joined the army, I would have never even met Garrison and Garrison wouldn't have shot Aaron. It is my fault, Rod. It is."

"Jason, listen to me. Aaron wouldn't even be alive if it wasn't for you. You rescued him and nursed him back to health. You saved his life. You—"

"Whoa, what the hell happened?"

Both men looked down at Aaron, startled.

"Aaron! You're awake! Oh, Aaron! Oh, baby! You're awake!" Jason covered Aaron's face with kisses.

"Jason what the hell were you doing naked and tied to a table with some dude about to butt fuck you? I didn't know you were into bondage."

Everyone started to laugh. "What? What's so funny?" Aaron asked. "What the hell is so funny? That guy had a machine gun. Jason, you owe me an explanation."

****

Homestead

After they carried Aaron into the center of the cabin on the same old army stretcher that Jason had carried him into the cabin on back in September, Jason began to cut away his clothes, much to Aaron's objection. Jack had already re-stoked all the wood stoves, and Rod pulled some extra blankets from the linen closet in the hallway to keep him warm. There were bullet holes under the left sleeve of his sweatshirt at the armpit and through the shoulder on the right.

Jason inspected the corresponding areas of Aaron's body closely, but he couldn't find even a scratch or a bruise. After anesthetizing the wound with xylocaine, Jason pulled out a large chunk of wood from under Aaron's scalp at his temple where his skull was exposed and scrubbed the wound out for all it was worth with hydrogen peroxide and providone iodine. Then he sutured a drain into place and sutured the skin around it. He applied triple antibiotic ointment and then covered it with a sterile dressing. When he pulled out the syringe and bottle of penicillin G, Aaron scrunched up his face.

"I know what that is," Aaron said, "and I'm not too happy about it. I remember how sore I was the last time you hit me in the ass with that stuff."

"Well your ass is safe," Jason said as he wiped Aaron's left thigh with an alcohol swab and injected the medication.

"You son of a bitch!" Aaron exclaimed. "That fucking hurt!"

"I know, baby," Jason said, "and I'm sorry, but you need it." Then he leaned over and kissed Aaron's thigh. "See, all better now," he said with a smile.

Rod and Jack sat quietly nearby in case Jason needed anything as he continued to assess Aaron's entire body for injuries.

"What you're witnessing right now, Jack," Rod whispered, "is a master at his craft. Just look at that boy work."

"Good God!" Jack whispered back. "Fuck the craft. Look at what a piece of ass Jason's got his hands on."

"That boy sure knows how to pick them," Rod whispered. "Now I can understand why he'd pass up on someone like me. I'd do the same thing in a heartbeat."

                              ****

After another fifteen minutes, Jason had finished inspecting Aaron's body.

"Aaron, you can't go to sleep tonight. You've had another head injury, and we're gonna have to keep you awake until tomorrow. I've already talked it over with Rod and Jack, and we're going to take shifts to sit with you."

"Okay, Jason. Whatever you say. Now can I please sit up?"

"How do you feel?

"I feel fine, but I need some clothes. I know I wasn't shot. I ducked my head when I saw him raise the rifle at me, just before I tackled him. Then something with hooves and fur flew over top of me, and I hit my head on something. That's the last thing I remember."

"You're right. It wasn't a bullet that made that hole in your scalp. It was something wooden, 'coz I took out a splinter about an inch long."

"Ew. That's gross! I think I hit a corner post of Heather and Jasper's stall. That's the last thing I saw before I blacked out."

"Is your tetanus up to date?"

"Yeah, I got one when I was in training for the team in the summer."

"Okay, I'll let you up, but you're getting right into bed, Mister. Right into your PJ's."

"Yes, sir!" Aaron saluted.

"Rod, you'll stay with him?"

"Of course."

"Okay, if you need me, I'm headed to the barn. I have to check on Jasper. He took a bullet to his horn. It should have been treated right away, but I couldn't leave Aaron. I hope he's all right. Goats can die from hemorrhage from a horn, and I still have to get Heather milked. Boy, they're all going to be so upset. You know, it was Nellie who finished Garrison off."

"Really?" Aaron and Jack said at the same time.

"She's my girl. Jasper charged him and rammed him in the flank with his horns, just as Aaron tackled his legs, like a one-two punch. Sent him airborne right to Sarah. She reared up and shattered his clavicle with her front hoof as Nellie spun around and kicked her hind legs up and connected with his head with her left hoof. I saw blood and brain splatter into the air at the same time."

"Wow," was all Rod could say.

Chapter Sixteen
Collateral Damage

Barn

No sooner had Jason left the cabin, he yelled in from the barn. "Jack! Hurry! I need your help!"

Jack went running. When he got to the barn, he found Jason dragging a half dead Jasper in through the front barn door. "Jack, open the cabinet and get out a bottle of powder called Blood Arrestor and the roll of paper towels and duct tape! He's lost a lot of blood. He can't die on me now. I owe him my life, Aaron's, too. I can't let go of him 'coz he'll try to get up."

"Here it is, Jason. What do I do?"

"Shake the powder down into the hole in his horn. Good. Good. No, more. More! Fill it. Now wad up some of the paper towels to fit in the hole and pack it tight. Good. That's great. Now pour on more of the powder and then wrap it with the duct tape to hold it in place. We're gonna have to get him into the cabin. It's too cold out here for him. He's lost a lot of blood, Jack, a lot of blood, and he could die easily from hypothermia or shock or both."

****

Homestead

Jason and Jack carried Jasper into the playroom and made a bed for him near the wood stove. At Jason's request, Jack took down the sex sling and packed it, the stool, and all the toys away. Jason returned to the barn to milk Heather and then returned to the cabin. Throughout the night, Jason, Jack, and Rod all took turns sitting with Aaron and Jasper.

Jason took first shift with Aaron. While he sat with him, he made phone calls to his attorney and financial manager to give them instructions. Both said they'd keep themselves available around the clock. He promised to call them the moment he knew when Aaron was going to be flown to the hospital so they could meet him there.

After he hung up with them, the attorney and financial manager got the ball rolling in their particular areas of expertise. There were big changes coming to the cabin, to Jason's estate, and to his portfolio. Jason wasn't messing around anymore. Things had gotten real serious, and he was going to deal with them head on. As a matter of fact, things were going to be taken care of so well that Jason wouldn't have to worry about anything except Aaron, and Aaron wouldn't have to ever worry about anything ever again.

Jason also spoke privately with Rod and Jack, out of Aaron's earshot, and they made some phone calls of their own. Rod told Jason about his brother-in-law, Lars, who was a farmer. When Lars was told how much Jason was willing to pay, he agreed to fly up with Rod to take care of the animals himself and have his foreman watch over his own farm. He'd stay at the cabin with Jack, who was going to remain behind to watch over everything and deal with the police, medical examiner, and anyone else who came to investigate the crimes that had been committed by the late Corporal Calvin Garrison.

Lars placed a call to Jason's veterinarian, Dr. Naomi Weston, and explained the situation about Jasper to her. She agreed to fly up with one of her technicians to attend to Jasper and stay to attend to him if he needed it, for as long as he would need them.

Section Three
Hinnen Valley Medical Center

Chapter Seventeen
An Assignment of Assets

December 23, 2009, Daybreak
At the first hint of light Jason explained to Aaron that he couldn't eat yet. Then he went into the kitchen and made coffee and toast.

At 7:00 AM, he checked on Jasper, who he found resting quietly with his head in Jack's lap while Jack sat stroking his neck. Then Jason went in and woke up Rod and returned to the kitchen to butter the toast.

By 7:45 AM, Rod and Jack had showered and put on clean clothes, and Jason had milked Heather once again. No sooner had they gotten dressed than the distant whop-whop-whop sound of helicopter rotors began to grow in intensity. At 7:50 AM it set down in the middle of the yard. Two paramedics, a nurse, and a physician made their way to the cabin's porch carrying several bags of medical equipment and a stretcher. Then there was a soft knock at the door.

They were professional and listened carefully to Jason's report of his initial assessment, his findings, and his treatment of Aaron as well as what his neurological status had been overnight. They treated Aaron like he was royalty.

While the medical crew was taking care of Aaron, Jason called his attorney and financial manager. They assured him all the wheels were turning, all arrangements had been made with the hospital, and that they would be waiting for him on the helipad when he landed.

At 8:30 AM, the medical team began to carry Aaron out on the stretcher. Aaron stopped them so he could give Rod and Jack each a hug. As the medics carried Aaron down from the porch, Jason gave Rod and Jack some last-minute instructions, hugged them, too, and then ran to catch up to Aaron.

After the medical chopper took off, Rod headed out to Big Daddy to get him deiced and fired up. Jack waved from the porch as Rod took off and then went back to sit with Jasper while he waited for the police, forest service, and anyone else to start arriving.

****

December 23, 2009, 9:10 AM
Hinnen Valley Medical Center

As the medical helicopter set down at Hinnen Valley Medical Center, Jason could see a medical team begin to approach. Behind them stood Claudia Duncan, his attorney, Winston Tanner, his financial manager, and another woman whom he immediately recognized. Jason kissed Aaron before they lifted him from the helicopter's hold and waited until the medical crews had departed. As he climbed down from the helicopter, the three approached him on the pad. He shook hands and hugged Claudia and Winston. Then Claudia introduced him to Penelope Whitley, one of the hospital administrators.

After her elaborate and flattering greeting, Jason pulled Penelope close and whispered in her ear. When she leaned away, her face was stone cold. She apologized, turned, and walked back in through the doors.

"So she's the one?" Claudia asked.

"Yes, the very one. And thanks for making sure she was the one who met us. Maybe I'm being a prick," Jason said, "but I don't have time for a bitch like her. I'll not allow her to have anything to do with Aaron's care or with me for that matter."

"What happened, Jason?" Winston asked.

"She wouldn't let me see Aaron after I brought him here back in October and spewed spittle in my face when she shouted at me, 'You're not family,' and never informed me that he'd been moved from the Emergency Department to his room even though she knew I was the one who brought him in.

"I could forgive all those things if she had been kind, or considerate, or even professional, in denying me access to him, or if she had at least cited HIPPA regulations, but she was a real bitch, not only to me but also to the entire ED staff. I simply won't tolerate her being anywhere near Aaron while he's here. Now, who's above her?"

"Well, that's Ms. Simone Jones," Claudia answered, "She's the hospital CEO."

"Does she know I'm here or anything about Aaron?"

"Not from us," Claudia answered.

"But, I'll betcha she's hearing about you both right now," Winston added.

"Good. Winston, did you bring my portfolio?"

"Yes, Jason, I have it right here. Would you like to see it?"

"No, not right now, but make sure that Ms. Jones somehow gets a glimpse of it. I'm not fuckin' around. I may be nobody, but my money is at least something. I've never used my wealth as leverage, but this is about Aaron now. Where does the portfolio stand this morning?"

"Well, Jason, as of the end of the trading day, last Friday your assets stood at $999,865,724.47. Since then you've made a little bit more. At yesterday's closing, you were at $1,003,252,839.55."

"Good. Make sure Ms. Jones gets a glimpse of that number as well. We're going to chip off a little of it over the next few days, and I'm going to be dipping into it significantly over the coming year, so we're going to have to change our investment strategy a bit. I'll leave it to you to determine how aggressive we need to get, Winston, but please know that right now, the goal is to build up assets and liquidity as rapidly as possible. Be careful not to risk too much in any one field, and keep the risk to a minimum whenever you can."

"Yes, Jason. Those instructions conflict, but I understand."

"Claudia, did you bring the documents I asked for?"

"Yes, Jason, I have them right here."

"Good. I'll sign them after we get inside. Is there a notary available?"

"Yes. She's waiting in the hospital lobby for my call."

"Thanks for taking care of that. Now, I've told you both about Rod and Jack. Whatever they tell you, take as gold. Whatever they ask for, get them or whomever they designate, paid right away. Also, Winston, you brought your checkbook?"

"Yes, Jason, just as you instructed."

Good, I want you to make out a check for $100,000 to Claudia as soon as we get inside."

"Jason, no! I can't take that!" Claudia pleaded.

"Oh yes, you can, my dear Claudia, and you will. You're going to be working your tail off for the next year, and that little sum is going to be just the beginning."

"Jason, I don't know what to say."

"You don't have to say anything and, please, not another word about it. The fact that you're here right now, with almost no notice, is proof enough to me that you deserve it. You dropped everything for me, Claudia, and I won't forget that."

"Winston?"

"Yes, Jason."

"Make out a check to yourself for the same amount."

"B-but ..."

"Uh, uh, uh, no buts," Jason said wagging his finger. "Everything I just said to Claudia, I'm saying the same to you. Please have those checks ready for me to sign as soon as you can."

From behind Claudia and Winston, Jason noticed a tall, African-American woman dressed in a smart business suit approaching from the hospital doors. "Ah, I'll bet you both a thousand dollars," he nodded towards the helipad doors, "that Ms. Jones approaches."

Chapter Eighteen
An Exchange of Pleasantries

12:15 PM

Jason made small talk with Ms. Jones in the Department of Medicine's conference room where Aaron's team of healthcare providers would assemble for a lunch meeting about Aaron's care. Claudia came in and stepped behind him and whispered in his ear while he was speaking with Ms. Jones.

"Please excuse me for a moment, Ms. Jones."

"Jason," Claudia began, "Winston and I met with Ms. Jones to convey your wishes for Aaron's hospitalization immediately after you left us at the helipad to head to the ER. She's been told that you would cover his hospital bill and was most appreciative of your desire to donate a significant sum to the hospital on behalf of Aaron following his discharge. She also assured me that Aaron would not be approached by the hospital's finance department to inform him that you are paying for his stay. I checked, and you were right about your suspicions. His health insurance was cancelled by the Bighorns the day they dropped him. Miss Jones and I both agreed it was best if Aaron isn't made aware of that right away."

"And the papers?"

"Aaron has signed the documents that authorize you to make any and all treatment decisions on his behalf and that you're to have unrestricted access to his medical records and any and all hospital staff that will be involved in his care."

"Thanks, Claudia."

"This is Miss Guthrie," Claudia said. "She's the notary public. Please step over here to this table and sign these documents. I've given her your ID already."

"Hello, Miss Guthrie. Thank you for coming," Jason said as he signed the papers. Miss Guthrie nodded and smiled. "Thanks, Claudia. What's next?"

Winston then stepped to his side. "Jason, as you predicted, Ms. Jones accepted your $50,000 check towards any extraneous expenses that may arise spontaneously on your or Aaron's behalf during Aaron's stay with great enthusiasm. I told her that more would come if the need arose."

"Okay, guys, thanks. Now let's huddle up. What's the status on the police, Forest Service, Jasper and the veterinarian, care of the animals, security modifications and personnel, the temporary housing, catering, laundry, organization facilities and staff for our steering committee meetings?" Jason asked.

"Jason, you wouldn't believe how much Rod and Jack have already put into motion," Winston said. "Suffice it to say, everything's moving quickly."

"What about Dr. Tolbert? Have you been able to reach him?"

"No, not yet," Claudia answered. "The recording on his voicemail says he's away for the holidays, but I've left several messages for him. Do you have an email address for him?"

"Yes, but it's on my laptop at home. I'll see if I can get Rod to get it for you the next time I talk to him."

"Okay," Claudia continued. "The state police and Forest Service were supposed to head up to the cabin sometime today, but I haven't heard anything yet from Jack. I'll let you know as soon as he calls me. Just prepare yourself. I'm sure they're going to want to interview both you and Aaron as well as Rod and Jack. At your request, I've also talked to a colleague of mine, a criminal attorney. He's going to fly up to the cabin with Rod so he can be with Jack, hopefully before the police get there."

"Let me borrow your phone for a minute, Claudia," Jason asked.

Chapter Nineteen
Setting It All in Motion

As Jason was finishing up the call, he put his hand over the mouthpiece and turned to Claudia and Winston. "Here's the rundown. Jasper is very bad. The vet says he's going to need intensive care. Your attorney friend Joshua Bergmann is there. I've hired him to handle the police investigation.

"Rod has already spoken with the architect and builder. It appears the house can handle a lot more than I thought so we won't need to modify any of the plumbing. They're going to put in six pre-fab housing units to start to handle the new staff. He's hired a security firm. They're going to occupy one or more of the units, and they've already made recommendations on perimeter lighting around the stockade, a wired surveillance system, and an armory.

"Claudia, can you be sure Rod has both your and Winston's cell numbers? He's going to need them so he can give you both information about costs and who to cut checks to as it becomes available. He's also going to give you the contact information for my old friend Dr. Conrad Tolbert off my laptop. I'm going to get back to Ms. Jones. Thanks."

Jason handed Claudia's phone back to her and then returned to Ms. Jones just as Aaron's care team started to arrive. He made a point of greeting each team member he already knew by name as they entered the room and was introduced to those he didn't by Ms. Jones. He made a special point of welcoming and praising Dr. Yvonne Spencer, the hospitalist who was so kind to him, and Braden Darby, RN, Aaron's nurse, from when Aaron was admitted in October.

"I hope my request for you to care for Aaron

while he's here," he said to Braden, but looked over Braden's shoulder at Ms. Jones, "hasn't upset the applecart."

"Oh, no, Jason," Braden answered. "I'm only too happy to help out in any way I can."

"I can assure you, Mr. Ackerman," Ms. Jones emphasized, *Mr. Ackerman*, clearly for Braden's benefit as she firmly settled her hand on his shoulder, "that Braden is one of our best nurses."

"I already knew that, Ms. Jones. That's why I asked for him, and he already knows to call me Jason from when Aaron was here before. You, too, please. That's a ground rule while I'm here. I go by Jason. You're sure it wasn't a problem?"

"No, not in the least. Whatever we can do to make Mr. Jaeger's stay as comfortable as possible, we're only too happy to oblige."

"Yes," Jason added with a smile. "I'm sure I speak for Aaron when I tell you how much we appreciate the accommodation."

Chapter Twenty
Plan of Care

An elaborate luncheon had been provided, including china, silver, and crystal place settings. Everyone followed Jason's lead by taking a plate and standing in line to be served by the young men and women behind the hot and cold food tables before taking a seat. Once everyone was seated around the conference table, Ms. Jones opened the meeting.

"I'd like to thank you all for coming on such short notice. Mr. Ackerman, Jason to us all, has asked that we meet today to discuss Aaron Jaeger, Jason's partner, his case, and to plan his care."

"Thank you, Ms. Jones," Jason interjected, "but I'd like to ask that we wait to talk about Aaron until after everyone's finished eating. Please, everyone, really, eat your food. How often do you actually get to sit down for a few minutes for lunch? We can begin after everyone's gotten something from that lovely dessert table."

"Whatever you say, Jason," Ms. Jones smiled, "is fine with all of us. Everyone here has cleared their afternoon for as long as you need them."

"Oh, and my compliments to your Dietary Department, Ms. Jones. They've really accomplished a miracle here. And thank you to these young ladies and men for serving us today."

"I'll pass your gratitude along to the Dietary Director."

"You know what, Ms. Jones, now that I think about it, I'd like to go to the kitchen myself to thank the people who actually did the work, if that wouldn't be an inconvenience."

Ms. Jones shot a glance to her administrative assistant, Freda, who nodded back. "Of course, Jason.

I'm sure they would be honored by your visit."

Immediately, Freda was on her mobile phone, to the Dietary Director to advise him to expect a surprise visit.

****

After everyone had gone to the dessert table, Ms. Jones introduced Dr. Walter Scottsdale, Chief of Medicine.

"Thank you for coming everyone." Dr. Scottsdale began, "Jason, we have the results and images of all the diagnostic studies that Aaron received today, and during his prior hospitalization. If you direct your attention to the screen behind me," the lights in the room dimmed, "the first images are those of Aaron's CT scan of his brain and his skull X-rays. I'll turn this over now to Dr. Jarvis Emerson, our Chief of Radiology and Dr. Sylvia Gladstone, Director of Emergency Medicine."

"Hello, Jason," Dr. Gladstone began. "Aaron arrived in the Emergency Department today at 9:13 AM. He was awake, alert, and oriented to person, time, and place. His initial neurological exam was unremarkable except for a complaint of dizziness. He also complained of burning from the wound on his left temple and a sore right thigh from an antibiotic injection you gave to him. The report we received from the flight crew who brought him in was that he was unconscious for approximately ten minutes. Is that correct?"

"Yes, it is," Jason nodded as he answered. "He was also unconscious for an undetermined amount of time, probably over a day and a half back in September when I pulled him from a tree, some twenty feet in the air. I was with him from early in the morning until the following morning before he first regained consciousness. However, I don't know whether he came to while he was in the tree before I found him. He landed in the tree the night before, approximately thirty-seven hours prior to his regaining consciousness."

"Excuse me, please. I'm Dr. Phyllis Chandler, Chief of Neurology and Medical Director of the Neuro Intensive Care Unit. I'm here with Dr. Johann Richter, our Chief of Neurosurgery, who will be available should his services be required. I was not made aware of a prior loss of consciousness. This is very important. To be clear, he's had two episodes of unconsciousness in four months, one of which we know for sure was due to head trauma."

"That's likely two incidences of head trauma, Doctor," Jason added. "The first was after his fall from the plane. In addition to multiple orthopedic and soft tissue trauma with major blood loss, he sustained a twelve centimeter, full-thickness laceration to his occipital region with exposure of the skull. I had to put a drain in it for debris contamination from the tree as well when I sutured it. I lost count at one hundred and seventy sutures that I put in him in total and several more wounds required drains for debris from the tree."

"I'm sorry, Jason," Dr. Gladstone interjected. "Are you a physician?"

"No, ma'am, I was a medic for two tours in Iraq. I worked beside the trauma surgeons in the trauma bays and in the OR. We averaged twenty major trauma casualties over twenty-four hours that went to surgery. That doesn't include the dozens and dozens of minor traumas during the same time period. We had as many fatalities every day."

"Thank you, Jason," Dr. Chandler said. "This information is important to take into consideration as we plan his care. I'm sorry to interrupt, Dr. Gladstone."

"Not at all," Dr. Gladstone continued. "I'm going to turn this over now to Dr. Jarvis Emerson, Chief of

Radiology."

"Hello, Jason," Dr. Emerson began. "Aaron's ER CT scan and skull X-rays were also unremarkable for gross trauma, but there was evidence of mild cerebral edema. His CT was done with injectable contrast because we were aware of his prior head injury and the possibility that his recent loss of consciousness might have been due to a GSW. We could find no evidence of injury other than observational physical evidence of a superficial laceration that I believe you treated yourself. Is that correct?"

"Yes, sir. The bullet holes in his clothing revealed no corresponding soft tissue or penetrating trauma."

"What bullet holes?" Dr. Gladstone asked.

"One under the left armpit and the other through the shoulder of his sweatshirt. I did remove an approximately one-inch wooden splinter from the wound over his left temple. It appears to have come from a corner post from my animals' stalls. That's what Aaron told me, and I did notice a chunk missing from it later on. His skull was exposed by the trauma, but I really scrubbed it out before I sutured it with a drain in place. Also, he's up on his tetanus, and I administered 1.2 million units of Penicillin G, IM in his left thigh."

"Thank you for sharing that, Jason. I was not made aware of those bullet holes."

"That's probably my fault, ma'am. I may not have told the flight crew about them. I was operating on no sleep for twenty-four hours by that point. I think I'm now up to twenty-eight."

"I understand," Dr. Gladstone went on. "As for the remainder of his physical examination, Aaron is a well-developed twenty-three old male with a recent history of an ORIF of his right ulna and radius, and left tibia, as well as arthroscopic repair of left ankle tendons and ligaments and removal of bone, tendon, and ligament fragments, as evidenced by the presence of recent surgical scarring as documented in his prior medical record. In addition, he has multiple scars across just about every region of his body, though I must say, the suturing job that was done to them was impeccable. I doubt most of those scars will be visible except under the closest scrutiny in a few years. Have we missed anything?"

"That's everything that I know, ma'am."

"Do you want a job?" Dr. Gladstone asked in good humor. "We could use someone with your skill set." There was laughter around the table.

"So, ladies and gentlemen, where do we go from here?" Jason asked. "My greatest concern for Aaron is his long term neurological status."

"Yes, we agree," Dr. Chandler offered. "That's why we've admitted him to the Neuro ICU. We'll be closely monitoring his neurological status and doing neurological assessments around the clock. He's currently receiving oxygen therapy and IVs, and we're monitoring his vital signs every fifteen minutes.

"The head of his bed is being maintained at thirty degrees or higher, depending on his comfort level, to reduce his intracranial pressure and his cerebral venous pressure. He's also receiving Dexamethasone for his cerebral edema. Our present plan is to keep him in the Neuro ICU for at least four days. In view of what I assume was a wound contaminated from animal fecal matter from the splinter, we'll add additional antibiotics to his treatment regimen."

"I'll also take another look at his skull films," Dr. Emerson added, "to be sure there's no residual wood foreign body fragments in the wound, but none were noted on the initial review of his films."

"Will he have an EEG, and when will it be performed?"

"Yes. Tomorrow morning."

"Do you have any thoughts on his prognosis yet?"

"I'm afraid not at this time, Jason. It's too soon to say, but on the upside, he hasn't had any neurological events since his first trauma in September, right?"

"I don't know, ma'am. He only returned to me two mornings ago. We've been apart for nearly three months. You could check with the rehab center he was transferred to after he was discharged. I don't know where that was though."

"We can find that information very quickly, Jason," Ms. Jones offered, looking to Freda, "You'll have that information as soon as we get it."

"Does anyone else have anything to contribute?" Jason asked. Everyone shook their heads. "Then I'd like to thank you all for coming."

After the meeting broke up, Ms. Jones asked for a moment of Jason's time in her office.

Chapter Twenty-One
Extenuating Circumstances

2:10 PM
Administrative Wing, Office of the CEO

Simone Jones smiled from behind her desk. "I asked to speak with you about another matter, but before I begin, I want you to know how impressed I am with your medical knowledge and with what I've learned of the care you provided for Mr. Jaeger while he was with you in September. I've been told by several people who are familiar with the treatment Mr. Jaeger received here in October that had it not been for you, he would have never regained normal use of his limbs. Considering what you did accomplish, all by yourself in a cabin in the forest, it is nothing short of miraculous."

"Thank you, Ms. Jones. What did you want to speak with me about? I'd really like to get up to Aaron's room."

"I understand. I'll be quick. I would not normally broach this subject, but I believe you to be a very kind, compassionate, and intelligent man. I'm not just saying that. I truly believe it based on what I just witnessed during the conference.

"I received a call this morning from Penelope Whitley, one of the hospital administrators. She conveyed to me your brief meeting with her upon your arrival here today. I want you to know how sorry she is for her conduct in the Emergency Department this past October when Mr. Jaeger was brought to us and for her interaction with you. She is ashamed and devastated that she presented herself and our medical center to you in anything other than a professional manner."

"Thank you for telling me this, Ms. Jones, but I don't want to have to deal with her."

"I apologize, Jason. I would not normally continue, but there are extenuating circumstances surrounding Ms. Whitley's behavior on that day. May I go on?"

"Yes, certainly."

"Ms. Whitley's parents were killed in an automobile accident by a drunk driver, ten days before you encountered her in the ED. She was their only child, and she has no relatives close by. She buried them five days prior to her return to work on the same day that Mr. Jaeger was admitted. I've known Ms. Whitley for more than a decade, and I've always found her to be courteous and professional in her conduct as one of our administrators. I can only believe that the pain she suffered after the loss of her parents combined with the pressures of accommodating the degree of notoriety of someone like Mr. Jaeger and the overwhelming assault on our ED by the media and the football league on that day was simply too much for her and in a moment of weakness, she faltered."

"Oh, my God. What have I done? Ms. Jones, you don't have to say any more. It is I who must apologize to Miss Whitley. Can you arrange for her to meet with me sometime later today?"

"Yes. I'll have her find you in the Neuro ICU."

"Thank you, Ms. Jones, and thank you for having the courage to bring this to my attention. I know my team can be a little intimidating. I suffered the loss of both of my parents within a month of each other. I, too, had no one close by, and I was the only family member at their funerals. I was their only surviving child. I lost my brother and sister from a car accident when I was seventeen. I believe it was their deaths that caused the downward spiral in my parents' health. They simply lost the will to live. It's like they say, 'you never know the pain that another person might be carrying silently.'"

"Thank you, Jason. I'll stay in touch. If you need me for anything, anything at all, please call me immediately, day or night. When would you like to visit our Dietary Department?"

"Whenever it's convenient, but first, I need to check in on Aaron. You'll let me know a time to visit then?"

"Yes, I will."

Chapter Twenty-Two
I've Been Where You've Been

2:27 PM
Room N-615

"Hey, baby. How are they treating you?" Jason asked as he walked into Aaron's room.

"Jason! How did the meeting go?"

"I'll just give you guys some privacy," Braden said as he excused himself from the small desk in the corner.

"Great." Jason leaned over and kissed Aaron's forehead. "All the doctors and staff are on the same page, and I'm comfortable with their plan of care. Did anyone tell you about the EEG?"

"Yes, Dr. ... what's her name? Dr. Chandler was here a little while ago. She's a neurologist. She said it's scheduled for first thing in the morning, and I'm not supposed to get much sleep tonight."

"That's so you'll be tired and possibly sleep through most of it. They might have you do some things at different points during the test like read something or do simple math problems. Stuff like that."

"How come?"

"So they can see how your brain works while it's doing work."

"How come I need an EEG?"

"Because you've had a traumatic head injury with loss of consciousness and because it's your second one in four months. They want to be sure you don't have any injuries to your wiring."

"Oh, but I feel fine."

"I know, baby, but it's better to be on the safe side. You learned about concussions with football, didn't you?"

"Yeah. Oh, so it's like that. They want to see if I had a concussion then."

"Right."

"Well I guess if crashing into a tree and hitting a post were enough to knock me out then they've got the same impact as being hit by a defensive lineman."

"That's a good way to look at it. Do you need anything? Are you hungry? Thirsty?"

"The only thing I need is you, Jason. I was so looking forward to having you to myself last night and now this. Does the cosmos have something against us?"

"No, Aaron, we've just had some bad luck, that's all. And look, we've got plans for Nathan's Promise, right? That's what we should focus on."

"That's all well and good, Jason, but all I've been dreaming about for over three months is focusing on you."

"Well, baby, we'll just have to wait a little longer, that's all."

"I love you, Jason."

"I love you, too, Aaron."

****

December 23, 2009, 3:30 PM

Jason lay with his head on Aaron's hospital bed. A trickle of drool from the corner of his mouth had pooled into a wet spot on the sheet.

There was a knock at the door. "Excuse me. Mr. Ackerman?"

Braden jumped up from the desk and hurried to the door to shush the visitor. He pulled the curtain aside. "Oh, Miss Whitley, it's you. They're both asleep," he whispered.

"Yes, sorry. I dozed off," Jason called out softly.

"Huh? What is it?" Aaron snorted and shouted as he was startled awake.

Braden couldn't conceal the annoyed look on his face, but he recovered quickly.

Penelope smiled. "I'm sorry, gentlemen," she called from the other side of the curtain. "I can come back later."

"No. No, come in. Come in," Jason said as he pulled the curtain aside. "Oh, Miss Whitley, it's you. Thank you for stopping by." He looked at Braden. "Is there somewhere Miss Whitley and I can speak in private?"

"Sure is, Jason. You can use the staff lounge if you like. I'll just make sure no one is in there."

"Aaron?" Jason pulled the curtain back enough to see him. "I'll be right back."

"Okay. Love you!"

"Love you, too."

Jason left Aaron's room and followed Miss Whitley to the staff lounge.

****

After entering the lounge, Penelope turned to face Jason. She unclenched her hands and reached down to spread them across the front of her dress as if to smooth it. It was an act, used to give her a moment to collect her thoughts, but the anxiety she felt was obvious on her face.

"Mr. Ackerman," she said with a quiver in her voice. "I'd like to apologize for how I treated you in October. It was unprofessional of me, and I have no excuse for my behavior."

"Please, Miss Whitley, call me Jason."

"Yes, sir. I understand from Ms. Jones that you wanted to speak with me."

"Yes, I did. Miss Whitley, it is I who owe you an apology for what I said to you this morning when you came to meet me on the helipad. I was way out of line."

119

"Forgive me, but no, sir, you were not. You had every right to…"

"Miss Whitley. I lost my parents, too, and I was alone. I understand. I also lost my brother and sister from a car accident when I was seventeen. I understand how painful it all can be. I've been where you've been."

Try as she might, Penelope Whitley was unable to prevent the tears that began to stream down her face. She lifted her hands to cover her eyes as her body trembled with the memories that returned.

"Please forgive me," Jason said as he wrapped his arms around her shoulders.

Penelope could not hold back her deep sorrow any longer. She wept, openly, as her body began to shake with heavy sobs. After months of suffering alone, for the first time she was able to begin to break the chains she'd been burdened with. Finally, the pain she'd held at bay, deep inside, for so long, began to loosen its grip.

"I'm so sorry, Mr. Ackerman. I'm so sorry. This is so unprofessional of me."

"Jason. Please call me Jason. You have nothing to apologize for." Jason stood holding her for minutes.

****

Administrative Wing, Office of the CEO

From the vantage point of her office, Ms. Simone Jones, CEO of Hinnen Valley Medical Center witnessed the exchange in the staff lounge of the Neuro ICU on her feed from the security camera. Though she'd believed what she'd said to Jason earlier about his kindness was true, it had not been heartfelt. She made her mind up right then and there about Mr. Jason Ackerman. He was one of the good ones.

Chapter Twenty-Three
An Investigation

3:50 PM
Room N-615

"Jason?" Claudia said as she knocked.

"Yes. Come in."

"Hi, Aaron. How are you feeling?"

"I'm doing okay. Thanks, Claudia."

"Jason, I just got a call from Rod. The state police and Forest Service have been at the cabin for almost two hours. They've called in the coroner. He's due there any time now. Jack said he overheard the trooper on his radio say that the death of Calvin Garrison looks suspicious. An investigator and trooper are coming here to interview you and Aaron and should be here shortly. Are you up to meeting with them?"

"We don't have any choice, right?"

"No, not really, but I'll be there with you. I also heard from Joshua. He said the investigating trooper at the cabin was real tough on Rod and Jack and Lars, and he also interviewed the veterinarian and her technician. They didn't even know there was a body in the barn, and they were really freaked out about it."

"That's my fault," Jason said. "I didn't even think to tell them. Well, all I can say to the police is what happened."

"Yes, just tell them the truth."

"How's Jasper?"

"According to Rod, he's doing well. The veterinarian gave the trooper a slug of lead she pulled out of his horn when she was cleaning it out. After that his whole demeanor changed."

"For the better, I hope."

"That's what it sounded like from Rod."

Jason nodded his head. "Good. Rod called me earlier. He's going to fly the vet along with Jasper and her tech back to the city so she can admit him to the ICU in her animal hospital. With all her equipment and machines, she can care for him better there. Where are you staying right now?"

"The hospital has given Winston and myself suites on the seventh floor. They're fully furnished, and they each have a desk and internet connection so we've set up temporary offices in them."

"That's great. Should I call you when the state police get here?"

"Jason, I'm not leaving your side until they're well and gone."

****

4:05 PM

Simone Jones appeared in the doorway to Aaron's room.

"Jason, Aaron, I'm sorry to disturb you, but I just received word that there is an investigator and a trooper from the state police here in the Emergency Department looking for you. Miss Whitley is escorting them up here as we speak. Doctors Spencer, Chandler, Richter, and Scottsdale are all on their way in case medical opinions are required. Is there anything else I can do for you?"

"No, thank you, Ms. Jones," Jason answered. "You've been most helpful."

"Very well. If you need anything, anything at all, please don't hesitate to call me."

"Thank you, Miss Jones," Aaron said, "we will."

Chapter Twenty-Four
The Interrogation

4:15 PM

Penelope Whitley knocked on Aaron's door. "Mr. Ackerman, Mr. Jaeger, the state police are here to see you."

A woman walked in, followed by a man, both in uniforms. "Mr. Ackerman, Mr. Jaeger, I'm Chief Inspector Cassandra Addison with the Idaho State Police. This is Trooper Byron Stringer. We're here to talk to you about a homicide that occurred in your home last night."

Jason and Aaron both took in the immensity of the strapping six foot six, hazel-eyed trooper with the dark, short cropped hair and chiseled face. He was imposing indeed and towered over the five foot ten, beefy inspector who was, herself, impressive in her own right. Her green eyes and long auburn hair would have made her stunningly beautiful had she not worn her hair in a tightly pinned bun or presented a no-nonsense business expression on her face. Together they appeared formidable.

Behind the inspector, Penelope mouthed, "Good luck," and then left them.

Unruffled, Claudia stepped her five foot one frame forward, effectively creating a barrier between them and Jason and Aaron. "How do you do, Inspector, Trooper?" she said, extending her hand. "I'm Claudia Duncan, Mr. Ackerman and Mr. Jaeger's attorney."

"It was an accidental death brought on by the deceased himself," Jason answered before Claudia could stop him.

"We'll get to that in good time, sir," Inspector Addison said.

"Forgive me, inspector," Jason answered. "I

haven't really slept in thirty-two hours. Just a short nap a little while ago."

"Jason, please be quiet," Claudia ordered.

Chief Inspector Addison noted Jason's offered information about sleep deprivation and immediately began to formulate her approach to the interview she planned to conduct. So fatigued, it shouldn't be difficult to get the truth out of Ackerman.

"Excuse me."

There was a knock at Aaron's door.

"We're in the middle of an investigation," Chief Inspector Addison turned and said as Trooper Stringer moved to block the doorway with his body. "State Police business. Can this wait?"

"I'm sorry. I'm Dr. Phyllis Chandler, Mr. Jaeger's physician. I came to examine him."

"I say again, can this wait?"

After so many years at the bedside, Dr. Chandler was unfazed by the inspector. She abruptly stepped forward, startling Trooper Stringer into stepping back. "How long will you be?" she continued. "We're concerned about Mr. Jaeger. Mr. Jaeger, may I discuss your medical condition with these officers?"

"That's Chief Inspector and Trooper," Chief Inspector Addison said with authority.

"My apologies. And you are which?

"I'm Chief Inspector Cassandra Addison. This is Trooper Byron Stringer."

"Mr. Jaeger, may I have your permission?" Dr. Chandler repeated.

"Yes, of course, Doctor."

"Inspector, through no fault of his own, Mr. Jaeger has received two traumatic head injuries with an extended loss of consciousness during each occurrence in just a few short months. We must be cautious about traumatic brain injury. In addition to diagnostic testing, the best way to watch for progression of any damage is to conduct extensive neurological examinations on a regularly scheduled basis so that we can compare our findings from one examination to the next.

"To delay any one examination poses the threat of missing changes in the patient's neurological status which is the first indication of brain injury, thus delaying surgical intervention which would save a patient's life. The addition of psychological stress could only serve to aggravate any underlying pathology. Is that what you wish, to risk irreversible brain damage?"

"No, of course not!"

"Then I ask again, how long will you be?"

"We can begin with Mr. Ackerman," Inspector Addison said, her feathers now ruffled. "You may conduct your examination, Doctor. Is there someplace we can go where we'll have privacy?"

"You can use the staff lounge," Braden offered from his desk. "Just let me make sure no one's in there."

"Thank you, nurse. We'll wait here."

Braden returned after just a minute. "The room's free. You can go in there now."

"Stringer, you remain here with Mr. Jaeger. Mr. Ackerman, if you will please accompany me. Nurse, please lead the way."

Claudia began to follow Jason and the inspector. "You can wait here as well," Inspector Addison ordered Claudia.

"You are terribly mistaken, Inspector! I'm not some kid, fresh out of law school, and you don't intimidate me! I will accompany Mr. Ackerman and represent him during your inquiry! He has the right to legal representation during any interrogation, and you know that!"

"Very well."

****

4:30 PM
Administrative Wing, Office of the CEO
Simone Jones and Penelope Whitley sat silently in Simone's office watching the monitor.

****

Neuro ICU, Staff lounge
"Please tell me, Mr. Ackerman, how do you know the deceased?" Inspector Addison asked after she took a seat across the table from Jason and Claudia.

"You may answer that, Jason," Claudia said.

"His name is Calvin Garrison. He was a corporal in the army. He was a patient on the ward I was assigned to when I was a corpsman."

"Why was he at your home?"

"Go ahead, Jason," Claudia nodded. "You can answer that."

"He told me he had come there to kill me."

"Do you know why?"

Claudia nodded to Jason.

"He said it was because I was the one who ruined his life and his career."

"Why would he say that?"

"You don't have to answer that, Jason," Claudia cautioned.

"No, Claudia. I'll answer it. I have nothing to hide. He said that it was because of me that he was put under scrutiny and was then accused of being a homosexual and given a dishonorable discharge."

"How was it you caused him to be put under scrutiny?"

Jason waited for Claudia to say something. She whispered in his ear, "Go ahead and answer. I won't interrupt unless I don't like the direction her questions take."

"There was a trial," Jason went on. "He'd accused me of sexually assaulting him while I was giving him a bed bath."

"Did you?"

"No. You can contact the army. They'll have a record of the trial. It was proven that he was the one who wanted sex from me and every other corpsman and nurse who bathed him, not the other way around."

"I don't have those records available to me right now," the inspector said, "and it isn't likely I could get ahold of them any time soon, let alone at all. So let's say you're telling the truth. What happened in the barn?"

"I went out to milk Heather like I do every evening. He was waiting for me and ambushed me."

"Heather?"

"My nanny goat."

"How did he ambush you?"

"He'd turned off the master circuit breaker in the barn. The light didn't turn on when I flipped the switch. I thought the bulb had burned out, so I used the flashlight I keep in my coat pocket to find my way to the next switch to turn on the other lights. I had a feeling that something wasn't right, but I didn't know what. Nellie and Sarah and Heather and Jasper were pacing in their stalls, and they didn't come to greet me. I told myself it was because I was using the flashlight or from an earlier lightning strike, but I was wrong."

"Who are Nellie, Sarah, and Jasper?"

"My donkeys and billy goat. It was very dark. On my way to the next light switch, I heard the door close behind me. Then all the lights came on. I couldn't see for a minute. Then he said, 'Hello there, Corpsman. Long time no see.'"

"Then what happened?"

"When I turned around, he hit me in the jaw with the butt of his M16. See the bruise? See my tongue?" Jason showed the inspector his cuts and bruises.

"I yelled 'coz I was startled, but he told me to shut up. He said if I made a sound my friends wouldn't live to see the sunrise. That he was just there for me. I didn't recognize him. That's when he said that I hurt his feelings, especially after an intimate moment we almost shared back when we were in the service? He said that he sure remembered me. I had no idea who he was. That's when he said that I ruined his life and his career. He told me to look at him, so I did, real hard. Then I suddenly recognized him.

"He said he wasn't a fag. That he didn't—sorry, ma'am—that he didn't let guys fuck him up the ass and that he doesn't suck other guy's dicks, that when they see his cock—sorry ma'am, that's what he said—that they can't get enough of it. He said that they come after him all the time, and that—sorry, ma'am—that when they offer him a tight little ass or a warm mouth, who was he to, and I quote, 'turn down a good nut bust'.

"Then he told me that he didn't need my approval when I told him I didn't judge him. He got this real mean, lecherous look in his eyes. Then he called me a faggot and told me that he wanted to sample what I had."

Claudia squeezed Jason's hand under the table to show her support perhaps as much as to reassure herself.

"I pleaded with him not to do that, ma'am. That it would be rape. He told me it didn't matter, that I'd be dead in a few minutes. Then he said he'd make a deal with me. If I didn't put up a fuss, he'd leave my animals and friends alone and that maybe he'd even let me live if I made it worth his while. Then he unzipped his fly and pulled out his penis and swung it around to show it to me. He said, and I quote, 'It's tougher when they squirm.' He told me that I wanted it while he pointed the barrel of the rifle at my head. He told me to show him a good time while he, sorry ma'am, 'pounded my ass'.

"Then he pushed me over to the work table with the barrel pressed into my back and told me to strip. While he tied me down over the table he propped the barrel against the back of my neck. He told me how he'd come all the way across the country and searched for me for months after he'd seen me on TV in a news report about Aaron, but I don't ever remember being on TV. He said he searched and searched for me, but he couldn't find me.

"Then he said he finally got a break when he saw another news story two days ago about Aaron having to leave the Bighorns when they showed the same footage that showed me getting out of the chopper. He said that it was then that he saw the name of the company that delivers my supplies on the chopper's tail. That's how he tracked me down. He hid in the chopper when they came back yesterday to deliver more supplies and Aaron's belongings.

"He spread my legs apart as wide as the table legs and tied my ankles to the legs so that I couldn't close them. I was completely naked, ma'am."

Jason unbuttoned the cuffs of his sleeves. "These are the abrasions and burns the ropes made around my wrists." Then Jason untied his boots and pulled off his socks. "This is what the ropes did to my ankles."

Claudia began to cry. "Sorry. Sorry, Jason." She shook as she tried to pull herself together.

"Then I heard him unbuckle his belt and unzip his fly. Then he pulled down his pants. He grabbed me at the shoulders. As he leaned in, he raked his fingernails down my back. It burned. Then he grabbed me around the waist with his hands and started to push his dick—sorry, ma'am, his penis—against my anus."

Jason stood up and turned away from the inspector to unbutton his shirt. He lowered it to below his waist. "I can't reach it, but can you see my back? Those are his scratches and the burns the ropes made there, too. That's when Aaron came in through the back door from the woodshed.

"Garrison yelled, 'what the fuck,' and I felt his fingers dig into my groin." Jason shrugged his shirt off his arms and let it fall to the floor. Then he unbuttoned and unzipped his jeans. He turned to face the inspector and lowered them in the front, just revealing his pubic hair to show the inspector his wounds. "As he pulled away, his fingernails left scratch marks over my hips and part of my butt cheeks." Jason turned back around and lowered the back of his jeans to reveal the top of his buttocks.

As Jason continued to speak, he put his clothes, socks, and shoes back on. "When Aaron saw what he was doing, he screamed my name and charged at Garrison. Then I felt Garrison's weight shift as he reached for his rifle. That's when I pushed backward into his groin with all my strength. It didn't seem like I moved much because of how tight he had me tied to the table, but it must have been enough because he screamed. Then he yelled—sorry ma'am—'My cock! My cock! What did you do to my cock? It's bent! It's bent! You fucking faggot! You broke my cock!'

"I turned my head to see what happened. He was bent over holding his penis and screaming in pain, but he still had a hold of his rifle. He started to come up and pointed the barrel at Aaron. Then I heard a repetition of cracks as the rifle fired. There must have been over two dozen rounds expelled. Pieces of wood started flying all over the place in an arc, and I heard glass shattering.

Then the dirt was flying in front of Aaron's feet.

"The next thing I knew, Big John flew at him—oh, sorry, Big John is my rooster. Big John attacked his face. I could hear Garrison screaming so I'm sure John got him good. Then, at the same time, Aaron dove for him. Plowed right into his legs and tackled him just as Jasper came charging out of his stall. Aaron hit him low, and Japer hit him high. I saw a chunk of Jasper's horn get blown off by a round, but I didn't know how bad it was. He almost died, ma'am.

"When Jasper crashed into Garrison, into his side I mean, he became airborne. That must be just after Aaron hit the post, 'coz he let go. Then Sarah reared up in her stall and hit him in the clavicle with her front right hoof. I heard it crack. At almost the same time, Nellie spun around, reared up on her front legs and kicked out, striking him with her left rear hoof in the temple. I saw blood and what looked like brain splatter into the air. Then his head struck the post, and he crumbled into a pile on the floor. He wasn't moving. When I looked back at Aaron, he was down. He didn't get up when I called his name.

"I don't remember leaving Heather and Jasper's gate open. I was sure I'd closed it. The next thing I knew, Rod and Jack came charging into the barn. I told Jack to untie me so I could get to Aaron, and I told Rod to go help Aaron until I was free. I looked down at Garrison while Jack untied me. His head was caved in, and he wasn't moving. Brain matter was bulging at the hole on the side of his skull where Nellie kicked him, and blood was oozing out. That's when I knew he was dead."

****

Administrative Wing, Office of the CEO

"That poor man," Simone whispered from behind her desk.

Penelope's shoulders shook as tears slipped from the corners of her eyes.

"Penelope, are you all right?"

"He was so kind to me. So kind. He forgave me. He didn't have to do that. He didn't. How could anyone do something like that to such a kind man?"

Simone reached out and took Penelope's hand. "Penelope, he must never know we witnessed this. I'm so sorry that I've done this. I'm so sorry that I did. Oh, that poor, dear, sweet man."

Simone reached over and turned off the monitor.

Chapter Twenty-Five
The Worst Kind of News

Neuro ICU, Staff lounge

Inspector Addison continued. "Tell me what happened next." Her portable phone rang. She held up her finger. "Hold on a minute, please, Mr. Ackerman."

"Yes? Who's this."

"Go on."

For two minutes, Inspector Addison listened and spoke briefly in one- and two-word sentences.

"I see. Yes. Thank you."

Claudia's phone rang. She forwarded the call to voicemail and put the phone on vibrate.

"Mr. Ackerman, that was the trooper at your home. It appears he's found overwhelming, corroborating evidence that supports your statements and the statements of the other witnesses are also corroborative.

"The lead slug of a bullet was removed from the goat's horn by the veterinarian there while she was examining it and treating it. She's turned it over to us."

"It's Jasper. His name is Jasper. It was Jasper's horn," Jason said.

Claudia's phone began to vibrate. She forwarded the call to voicemail again.

"Yes. Jasper. Sorry."

"It looks like Jasper must have broken through the latch on the gate to get at Mr. Garrison," the inspector continued. "The gate was shattered where the latch used to be from the inside."

"Did she say how he's doing, the vet I mean?" Jason asked. "He saved my life and Aaron's life. He's a hero."

"No, I have no information on him. I'm sorry. I

truly am, but you should also know that two forest rangers are also on the scene. They led the trooper to what is believed to have been a camouflaged hideout and evidence was collected from it. There was also evidence found in the hold of a helicopter that was on the helipad when they arrived. That evidence appears to match evidence collected from the hideout and the barn."

Claudia's phone vibrated again, and again she forwarded it to voicemail.

"Everything is pointing to suggest your claim that the stalker, Garrison, stowed away on the helicopter and made his way onto a bluff that overlooks your home. Clothing and supplies found at the scene match the description of items stolen from a sporting goods store the night before last. It appears that at some point in time, Garrison gained access to your property via a rope, thrown over the stockade wall, and lay in wait for you in the barn. There's something else."

"What's that?" Jason asked.

"The coroner arrived on the scene twenty minutes ago."

Claudia's phone vibrated again. She answered it.

"Hold on, I'm with Jason," she said into the phone. "Sorry," she directed to the inspector, "will you wait a minute?"

"Yes," Inspector Addison answered. "I'll wait."

"Go on, Rod."

"No. No!"

"Yes. Yes, I'll tell him."

"Thanks. Good bye."

When Claudia hung up and looked at the inspector, the color had drained from her face.

Jason became worried. "What's wrong, Claudia? What's happened to Jasper?"

The inspector held up her finger to Claudia and

continued. "Mr. Ackerman, when the coroner examined the body, he found a pulse. As of ten minutes ago, Mr. Garrison was still alive."

Jason started to breathe heavily. He turned pale, then dusky. The edges of his vision darkened.

"Mr. Ackerman, are you all right?" The inspector stood up and began to walk around the table.

"I don't feel well," Jason whispered.

"Jason? Jason what's wrong?" Claudia grabbed Jason's shoulders as he lowered his head to the table.

"Nurse! Nurse!" Claudia began to yell.

"Inspector," Jason gasped, "please, please do not tell Aaron that Garrison's still alive. Not unless you absolutely have to."

Inspector Addison walked to the doorway and called out, "We need some help in here!"

Chapter Twenty-Six
An Unexplained Lump

5:12 PM
Room N-615

Chief Inspector Cassandra Addison and Trooper Byron Stringer stood against the wall of Aaron's room, watching.

"Mr. Ackerman ... Jason ... please. I must insist that you allow us take you to the ED so that we can examine you properly!" Dr. Chandler demanded.

"Jason," Dr. Spencer added more calmly, "the ED has all the staff, equipment, and diagnostic tools that are needed to perform a comprehensive examination on you. The Neuro ICU does not, and we shouldn't be doing this in Mr. Jaeger's room. Now please, listen to Dr. Chandler."

"I feel much better after the orange juice." Jason answered from the chair behind the desk. "My blood sugar just dropped, that's all."

Braden shook his head and mouthed "No," as he showed Dr. Spencer the glucometer.

"I haven't slept in ... I can't remember when I last slept, and I haven't eaten since breakfast and that was only toast."

"I'm sorry, Jason, but that's not quite correct," Dr. Chandler answered. "You ate with us in the conference room at lunchtime, remember?"

"And your blood sugar was eighty-nine when Braden took it before he gave you the orange juice," Dr. Spencer added.

"Jason," Aaron said from his bed, "please go to the ED and let them take care of you."

"What's happened?" Ms. Jones asked as she rushed into Aaron's room.

"Everything's under control, Simone," Dr. Spencer assured her. "Jason had a little dizzy spell. We just want to take him to the ED so we can check him out to be sure he's okay."

"I'll call ahead." Simone immediately dialed her phone to Dr. Gladstone. "Sylvia," she said, "clear a primary ED treatment room. We're bringing Mr. Jason Ackerman down right now. He's had a fainting spell of some kind. Yvonne and Phyllis are examining him right now." Then she called Penelope. "Penelope, we're heading to the ED with Jason. He's had some kind of event."

"Jason, you were short of breath when I got to you," Braden said as he squatted down next to him, "and you were a little cyanotic. Your Pulse Ox was eighty-nine. From what I could hear over your shirt your breath sounds were diminished on the right. Please let us take care of you properly."

"Jason, may I listen to your lungs?" Dr. Spencer asked.

"Okay, if it will make you feel better." Jason unbuttoned his shirt and removed it. Everyone in the room gasped.

Braden touched his shoulder, gently. "Jason, what happened to your back?"

"Those are rope burns from when Garrison had me tied to the table, and the scrapes are from where he dug his fingernails in. They're nothing. I'm fine! I'm fine!"

"Good God, Jason," Aaron said as he climbed out of his bed and leaned over him, avoiding touching his back. "You're not fine! I never saw these! Why didn't you tell me? Please go to the ED and let them take care of you. At least let them bandage those wounds."

"I'm not leaving you, Aaron."

"Jason, I'm fine, really. I'll never rest until I know you're all right. Now go with them, please."

"Everyone, be quiet," Dr. Spencer ordered as she placed her stethoscope over the lower lobe of Jason's right lung, "Jason, take in some deep breaths. Again, please. Again, please. Just keep taking deep breaths through your mouth until I tell you to stop," she ordered as she moved her stethoscope from one lung field to the other at the front and back of Jason's chest.

"Jason, I can't hear any breath sounds in your right lung at all. Jason, sit up and look at me, straight on."

Jason sat up.

"Jason, your trachea is deviated to the left. You said there was gunfire when Aaron was injured. Is there any chance you were shot?"

"No way. I'd have felt it," Jason answered, annoyed.

"Jason. Look at me," Dr. Spencer ordered. "How many fingers am I holding up?"

"Three."

"What is today's date?"

"December 23."

"What big holiday is nearly here?"

"Christmas?"

"Okay, everyone who doesn't need to be in here, out of the room. Now!" Dr. Spencer commanded.

Dr. Spencer closely inspected Jason's chest. "Jason, there's an unexplained lump that doesn't belong here next to your scapula, sorry, your shoulder blade."

"I know what the scapula is, Doctor," Jason answered.

Dr. Spencer continued to scrutinize every inch of Jason's chest and back, looking for an entrance wound. "Braden, lift his right arm for me." As Braden held

Jason's arm in the air, Dr. Spencer palpated Jason's right axilla. Then she began to percuss over the lower half of Jason's right lung, receiving a dull thud each time she tapped.

"Jason, take in a deep breath," Dr. Spencer ordered. A barely perceptible sucking noise could be heard as Jason inhaled. "Mister, you're going to the ED this very minute, and that's final."

"What? What is it? What did you find?" Jason asked.

"Jason," Dr. Spencer began, "you've been shot. You have a bullet hole under your right armpit with a sucking chest wound. I believe it's from the bullet that's now lodged just under the skin on your back. Putting it all together, I believe you have a tension pneumothorax or hemopneumothorax."

"What's that?" Aaron asked loudly.

"Aaron, it's air or air and blood in his chest cavity that isn't in his lung," Dr. Spencer answered. "His right lung has collapsed."

Chief Inspector Addison and trooper Stringer looked at each other. Inspector Addison called headquarters to advise them that there was another victim from the incident at the cabin.

Things began to move very quickly in Aaron's room. Braden brought in a wheelchair and a portable oxygen tank with a partial rebreather mask, and Dr. Spencer called Dr. Gladstone. "Sylvia, forget a primary treatment room. We need a trauma bay cleared right away."

"A trauma bay! What the hell's happened?"

"Yes, it's Jason Ackerman. He has a sucking chest wound with what's probably a tension hemopneumothorax."

"He must have caught a bullet."

"That's right. It's on the right, and he's decompensating."

"Makes sense. It's been nearly twenty-four hours. I'm surprised he's lasted this long. What's his sat?"

"That's right, his Pulse Ox is 89 on room air."

"Definitely decompensating. Better get him on some O₂."

"Yes, we're putting oxygen on him as I speak."

"Better get a move on. The Neuro ICU isn't the place to be treating him. I'll notify CT."

"Right."

"Are you heading down now?"

"Yes, that's right."

"We'll be ready. Surgery's already in the department. I'm going to tell them to hang around. We'll get a chest X-ray on him first. If he's stable we'll send him over for a CT angio to find the bleeder."

"Great. We'll see you in less than five."

Dr. Spencer looked at Jason. "Jason, they've got a surgical team standing by. First, you'll have a chest X-ray done to confirm my suspicions. If it's positive, you're probably going to need a chest tube and depending on what the CT angio shows, they may need to go in there to find that bleeder."

"Braden," Aaron pleaded, "please go with Jason. I don't need you here. Please take care of him. Please take care of my Jason!"

"I will, Aaron," Braden said. "I promise, I will."

Chapter Twenty-Seven
Unwanted Attention

5:21 PM
Hinnen Valley, final story on the local evening news
"We're bringing you this late breaking story. Aaron Jaeger is back in the news once again. As you may recall, Jaeger, the new, young quarterback from the Nevada Bighorns made headline news for several weeks this past September following the plane crash that took the life of his trainer, Nathan Taggart.

"The last report we received was that the Idaho state police, the forest service and Hinnen Valley coroner, Dr. Theodoric Adler have responded to the site of a homicide at a residence where Jaeger was found after being injured during the homicide. The residence is located in a secluded, privately held tract of land in the Bear River Mountains.

"There are no roads in the area, and the only access to the site is by helicopter. Jaeger is currently being treated at Hinnen Valley Medical Center for injuries he sustained during the homicide. Details are sketchy, but it is now believed to be the same residence he was taken to for treatment after he was found following the plane crash.

"We just reported several days ago that Jaeger was recently released from his three-year contract with the Bighorns for his inability to fulfill the requirements of quarterback after incompletely recovering from the injuries he sustained in that tragic plane crash.

"Queries to the Nevada Bighorns organization have gone unanswered. When contacted by telephone, Jaeger's former coach, Hank Thompson, said he's had no contact with Jaeger since he was let go from the team and can offer no further information on him.

"That's all the information we have at the moment. A news crew has been dispatched to Hinnen Valley Medical Center for news on Jaeger's condition, and we're attempting to access the site of the homicide to learn more about the police investigation.

"Stay tuned to Channel 18 news for further breaking news on this story as it unfolds."

****

5:39 PM
Room N-615

Simone Jones and Penelope Whitley returned to Aaron's room minutes after the local evening news broadcast ended.

"Mr. Jaeger, I'm afraid we have a situation," Simone began.

"What's wrong?" Aaron asked, "What's happened to Jason?"

"Jason is doing okay. They're taking good care of him in the ED, but it appears the news media has gotten a hold of the story about the incident at the cabin and that you are currently being treated in our facility. We expect they'll arrive at the hospital any minute now."

Claudia and Winston came into Aaron's room just as Simone finished. "So you saw it, too?" Claudia interjected.

"Yes, we did," Simone answered, "but we're handling it."

"I can't be any clearer, Ms. Jones, when I tell you how important Mr. Ackerman's privacy is to him," Claudia said, advancing toward her. "That must remain paramount."

"No, Claudia," Aaron said. "Jason's life is paramount! Fuck everything else right now!"

"I understand your concerns, Aaron," Claudia said in a placating voice, "but I have my orders from

Jason. They go back to the very beginning of our relationship."

"What's all the commotion?" Dr. Chandler said in soft but determined voice. I don't want him," she emphasized, pointing at Aaron, "upset. We have to keep Aaron's blood and intracranial pressures down."

"Dr. Chandler, everyone, please take a breath," Simone said. "This is a very tenuous situation at best. I know everyone has their priorities, but can we all agree that we all have Aaron and Jason's best interests at heart? We each have a job to do, and we should be mindful that sometimes, in our performances of our jobs, there may lie conflict. What we need to do is also be mindful of those conflicts and try to take them into consideration before we act."

"Yes, Ms. Jones. I can agree to that, but please know this, my allegiance and priority lie with Jason and Aaron. No one else."

"Well, if that's the case, Miss…" Dr. Chandler asked.

"Duncan!"

"Well if that's the case, Miss Duncan," Dr. Chandler continued firmly, "please know that this confrontation is not good for Aaron. Look at his blood pressure right now. It's 187/ 97."

"I suggest you all regroup out of Aaron's presence, if this all so high and mightily important. Otherwise I'm going to have to order you all to leave."

"I'll be heading downstairs to deal with the media," Penelope said. "You have nothing to worry about, Mr. Jaeger. We just wanted to advise you of what's happening."

"Can I see Jason?"

"No, not yet," Simone answered. "As of five minutes ago he was still being evaluated, but I promise, I will inform you the moment I know what they've done for him. I promise. In the meantime, I'm stationing a security guard outside your room, and a security guard is being posted outside of the Neuro ICU, so that no one can disturb you. Understand?"

"Well, that's more like it," Claudia said.

"Claudia, please!" Aaron had had just about enough of Claudia Duncan for the moment. "Be silent!"

"Ms. Jones, thank you. And both of you, Miss Whitley, you too, please call me Aaron. I don't know why I didn't clear that up earlier."

"And please call me Simone."

"And me Penelope."

"Thanks, Simone. Thanks, Penelope."

Okay," Simone said as she patted Aaron's arm, "I'll be in touch as soon as there's anything to tell you.
****
6:01 PM
ER Room 15
"Hey, I think I recognize him. Isn't he the guy who came in with Aaron Jaeger when he was found in the mountains back in October?" said a camera man for Channel 18 from the doorway of his wife's room.

"Leave it, Frank. You're always looking for the next big news story. What about my migraine?"

"Your migraine, your migraine. It's always your migraine."

"Here's your breaking story, asshole!" she yelled, "My fucking head is exploding! Why don't you film that!"

Frank had already lifted his pocket video camera and was recording Jason as he was wheeled out of the ED to the CT Scanner. When Jason was out of sight, Frank called Chuck Jackson as he was pulling out from the News 18 parking lot on his way to Hinnen Valley

Medical Center.

"Hey, Chuck. I think I've got an angle on the Aaron Jaeger story."

Chapter Twenty-Eight
Profound Decompensation

6:15 PM
Emergency Department

"Put him in Trauma Room One," Dr. Gladstone directed to the flight crew. "Hello, Dr. Adler. Well this is a first. A live one! What can you tell me?"

"Hello, Sylvia. You're not kidding. Approximately forty-year-old male suffering from head trauma and hypothermia. My initial findings were an open fracture of the right temple extending into the frontal bone. There was brain matter bulging from the wound, and it's contaminated with hay and animal feces. Bleeding had stopped, probably tamponaded itself from brain swelling.

"His pupils were blown, but I thought I saw him take a breath so I felt for a pulse. It was thready at about one-sixty per minute. I didn't have a sphygmomanometer with me, but then I've never needed one in my line of work. He's also got a fractured right clavicle and multiple puncture wounds and lacerations about his face, hands, and arms. There's also several fractured ribs at the right, lateral chest and a huge ecchymotic area on the right flank that extends up into the ribs. Finally, he has a fractured penis. There's no good reason he should still be alive, but there he is anyway."

"Thank you so much, Dr. Adler. If he makes it past the ER, he'll be treated by neurosurgery and urology. Can I get you anything? A cup of coffee? Something to eat? Whatever you need, my staff will get it for you immediately."

"A cup of coffee would be great if you can really manage it, and something sweet, like a honeybun or donut if there's anything like that around."

"We'll get right on that for you."

"If I may add, Dr. Gladstone, your flight crew is one top notch outfit. I'm very impressed by their actions. Very impressed indeed."

"Thank you for saying so. We're all very proud of them and the work they do under some often really nasty circumstances."

****

6:17 PM
CT room

As Jason was moved from the CT scanner back to the ED stretcher, he grabbed his chest and tried to sit up. "Something's wrong! I feel weird!" He started panting. "I can't breathe! I can't breathe!" He fell forward, almost falling off the stretcher as he gasped for air, but Braden caught him. Jason was turning blue. His trachea was pushed even further to the left. He slumped over on the stretcher.

While Braden turned the oxygen all the way up, Bryce, the ED nurse, raised the head of the stretcher into a sitting position. Then they both ran, pushing and pulling the stretcher the twenty yards it took them to get back into the ED. When they blasted through the double doors, Bryce called out, "I've got a Code Blue. Code Blue, Trauma Room Three!"

All hell broke loose.

****

6:19 PM
ER Room 15

Frank had been waiting for something to happen, and his patience paid off. He caught the whole thing. He uploaded the footage to Channel 18 News Headquarters. Then Chuck Jackson's camera man downloaded it into his laptop.

****

147

6:21 PM
Trauma Room 3

"I want three milligrams of Etomidate in him now. That's three point zero milligrams understand, Bryce?" Dr. Gladstone said. "Follow that with sixty milligrams of succinylcholine. Again, that's sixty, six zero milligrams of succinylcholine. The moment he's under, I'll intubate."

"Got it," Bryce said as he turned to prepare the drugs.

"Someone give me a number eight ET tube and a 10-cc syringe," she called out as she checked the laryngoscope's lightbulb.

"I'm sorry, Dr. Gladstone," Dr. Phineas Baum, the chief surgical resident, said, "but I can't wait for that. I'm putting this chest tube in him right now."

Dr. Baum leaned over Jason's cyanotic face. "Mr. Ackerman, I'm sorry, but I have to put a tube into the right side of your chest. This can't wait, and it's going to hurt like a mother."

"Understand … can't breathe," Jason gasped behind the oxygen mask. "Do it … do it."

As Braden lifted Jason's right arm over his head with his right hand to expose Jason's chest for the procedure, he picked up the chest tube with his gloved left hand. Dr. Baum poured providone iodine over the side of Jason's chest and scrubbed it with a wad of 4x4 gauze pads saturated with the same. Then he picked up a syringe. "Mr. Ackerman, you're going to feel some burning, then some pressure, and you're going to hear a loud pop, starting now."

Immediately, he injected 10 milligrams of Xylocaine into the skin as he moved the needle around the site where he would insert the chest tube. With a scalpel, he made a two and one-half inch incision just anterior to the mid axillary lines at the 5th intercostal space. With Kelly forceps he performed a blunt dissection between the fifth and sixth ribs in towards the chest cavity, spreading the forceps open to make the hole bigger.

Once he was satisfied, he grasped the forceps with both hands and using his body weight, lunged forward against the opening. Suddenly there was a loud pop, followed by a rush of air and blood from the wound.

"Jesus fucking Christ!" Jason yelled as he wrenched his right arm free from Braden and swung his left arm towards Dr. Baum. "Fuck that hurts!"

Braden grabbed his arm again and held it securely.

"Mr. Ackerman, hold still!" Dr. Baum yelled as he inserted his gloved, right index finger into the hole to ensure that he was cleanly all the way in to his chest cavity. "I'm almost done."

"Ow! Motherfucker!" Jason yelled as he saw stars. He lifted his head and shook it to try to clear his mind.

Dr. Baum took the chest tube from Braden and began to slide and twist it into Jason's chest in an upwards and backwards direction towards his shoulder blade.

"I'm sorry, Doctor," Jason said. "I couldn't help it."

"We just lost his IV," Bryce yelled.

"I want another line in him, now," Dr. Gladstone ordered. "Move it! As soon as the drugs are in him, put in a second large bore line."

"Yes, Doctor," Bryce answered, "Right away."

"Mr. Ackerman," Dr. Gladstone said. "Please hold still. You just yanked out your IV line."

"I'm sorry. I couldn't help it."

"I know, I know," she said, patting his shoulder, "Just try to hold still."

As Dr. Baum sutured the chest tube into place, Braden released Jason's arm and attached the chest tube to the underwater seal drainage system and then turned up the suction module on the wall until the system started to bubble. Immediately blood and bubbles began to flow out of Jason's chest. Within seconds, Jason's color began to turn back to the normal pink.

"I can breathe!" he exclaimed after a minute. "Oh my God! I can breathe!"

"Let's get a portable chest X-ray," Dr. Baum ordered. "Dr. Gladstone, you may want to hold off on that sedation. I don't think he's going to need it, at least for the immediate future. Look at him. His color's turning back to normal."

"Let's hold off on the sedation for the time being, Bryce," she said. "We'll wait to see what the X-ray looks like."

"Right, Doctor," Bryce answered opening the IV catheter package, "I'll still get those two lines in."

Bryce scrubbed Jason's arm with antiseptic. "Little prick, Jason," he said.

"You're wrong about that," Jason answered with a smile, "It's a big prick," he whispered, loudly. Then he started to laugh.

Bryce blushed and then inserted the IV.

"Ow!" Jason said as he winced at the pain. Then pain shot from his chest tube site, between his ribs. The more it hurt, the more he laughed.

"Ow! It's not huge. Ow! Ouch!" Then Jason giggled. "But it is big."

"Braggart," Bryce whispered under his breath, as he secured the IV catheter into place.

The room fell silent as everyone turned to look at

Bryce. He blushed even redder.
   Then Trauma Room Three erupted in laughter.

Chapter Twenty-Nine
Two for the OR

6:30 PM
Hinnen Valley Medical Center, main entrance

"Good evening, sir, I'm Penelope Whitley the administrator on duty. How can I help you?"

"We're going to film this, Miss Whitley," Chuck Jackson said as the news camera's light came on.

"This is Chuck Jackson reporting from Hinnen Valley Medical Center. I'm here with administrator, Penelope Whitley. So, Miss Whitley, we understand that Aaron Jaeger was brought here this morning for treatment after a homicide at a private residence with no public access. How is he doing, and what are his injuries?"

"I'm sorry, Mr. Jackson, is it? I have no information for you on an Aaron Jaeger, and as you know, HIPPA regulations prevent…"

"We know he's here, Miss Whitley."

"As I was saying, HIPPA regulations prevent a healthcare provider from revealing any information on any patient without the patient's expressed consent. I can confirm that Mr. Jaeger was here this past October, but I believe you covered that story already."

"Miss Whitley, we've heard the preliminary police reports. We know he's here."

"I'm not aware of any police report, Mr. Jackson."

"You're stalling, Miss Whitley. The people have a right to know. They have a right to the news."

"Not that I am aware of, Mr. Jackson. Nothing supersedes HIPPA regulations."

"Well then, who is this man, Miss Whitley?" Chuck pointed to a video monitor. The same footage was simultaneously transmitted to Channel 18's viewers. "This man accompanied Aaron Jaeger to this hospital in October in a private helicopter. Is he the man who found Aaron Jaeger? We never learned his name, and we were never able to find him after that footage was shot."

For the briefest of moments, Penelope's breath caught. "I'm sorry, Mr. Jackson. I can't comment…"

"Miss Whitley, look here," Chuck said, pointing again to the monitor. "Our viewers can see that this is the same man who was being treated in your Emergency Department less than ten minutes ago. What is Code Blue? Can you hear that? It says Code Blue Trauma Bay Three. Was a Code Blue called for this man? Isn't this the same man who was with Aaron Jaeger in October?"

When Penelope saw Jason being wheeled on an ER stretcher gasping for breath she inhaled sharply. "I'm sorry, Mr. Jackson. I don't know, and I can't comment on speculation."

"Miss Whitley, why did you just jump? You obviously know who he is."

"I'm sorry, Mr. Jackson, I was reacting to the fact that you've illegally made a video recording of a patient. You've violated his right to privacy and HIPPA regulations."

"Who said we recorded it, Miss Whitley? We received this footage from an anonymous source who sent it to our newsroom."

"Who is Jason Ackerman? It that Jason Ackerman? What is the relationship between Jason Ackerman and Aaron Jaeger? Will you confirm or deny that Aaron Jaeger is a patient in this hospital? Will you confirm or deny that Jason Ackerman is a patient in this hospital? Those names are on the police report. The police report is that Aaron Jaeger was transported to this hospital."

"I'm sorry, Mr. Jackson. I cannot confirm anything. This interview is over."

Chuck Jackson's interview with Penelope Whitley was broadcast within thirty minutes by numerous national and local television networks around the country.

****

6:35 PM
OR Room 2

"Here we go, ladies and gentlemen." Dr. Johann Richter, Chief of Neurosurgery, began. "We need to keep this poor bastard alive long enough for urology to see him. Now, let's see how much of this debris we can get cleaned out."

"Suction," he said in a calm voice.

"Forceps." Still calm.

"Damn, he's got a bleeder." Sweat began to form on Dr. Richter's forehead. "Blot me, please."

"Hand me a clamp."

"Another one."

"Vascular clips and keep them coming, and have the fibrin foam ready!"

****

6:37 PM
Trauma Room 3

Mr. Ackerman," Dr. Baum said. "This is a consent for surgery. It gives us permission to go into your chest in the operating room to find and stop the bleeding that is occurring there. From the CT angio, we know exactly where the bleeding is coming from and which artery was hit by the bullet, but we may find other damage that will need to be repaired. You have a nick to one of the anterior intercostal branch arteries. It's comes off of the internal thoracic artery. This consent allows us to perform that surgery. Do you have any questions?"

"No, Doctor, I've performed or assisted with this surgery myself. I trust you."

Dr. Baum handed the consent form and a pen to Jason. After he signed it, Jason turned to Braden. "Braden, you've got to go be with Aaron. He's gonna freak when he finds out I'm in surgery."

"I'll take care of him, Jason, I promise, but I'm going to go with you to the OR first. Then I'll go right up to stay with Aaron."

****

6:45 PM
OR Room 1

It's me, Mr. Ackerman, Dr. Baum," he said behind his surgical mask. We're going to get started right away. This is Dr. George Tunisia. He's the chief of thoracic surgery and my attending. I'll be assisting him with your surgery."

"Hello, Mr. Ackerman," Dr. Tunisia said in his rich, native accent. "It's nice to meet you, though I wish it was under more favorable circumstances. You're going to be going to sleep in just a few moments. The anesthetist is going to place a mask over your face, and you'll just drift off."

"I know, Doctor," Jason said. "I've done this surgery a few times myself."

"Very good, Mr. Ackerman," he said as he raised his eyebrows. "Perhaps one day we can have a nice sit down and talk about your experiences."

"I look forward to it. You have very kind eyes, Doctor. I trust you. I'm ready now."

"Thank you, Mr. Ackerman. I'll see you on the other side."

"Yes, Doctor. I'll see you on the other side."

"Hi, Mr. Ackerman. I'm Judy. This is the mask that Dr. Tunisia told you about." she said as she placed it over his face. "I want you to breathe normally and count backwards from one-hundred. Okay?"

"Okay."

"One-hundred."

"Ninety-nine."

"Ninety-eight."

"Ninety-seven."

"Ninety-six."

"Nine … ty-fi."

"Nine … ty … f…"

"Nine…"

Chapter Thirty
Aaron in Charge

6:47 PM
Room N-615

"How are you feeling, Aaron?" Sonya, Aaron's Neuro ICU nurse, asked.

"I'm worried about Jason. Nobody's told me anything for a while."

"I'm sure they'll tell you something when they have something to tell you. Now, how are you?"

"I'm okay. No more dizziness."

"Great. I have your medications here that the doctors have ordered for you. Is it okay if I give them to you?"

"Yeah, sure. Thanks."

After Sonya administered Aaron's medications intravenously, she left the room and closed the door behind her. She nodded to the group assembled right outside Aaron's room. "He got all two milligrams of lorazepam, Dr. Chandler."

"Thanks, Sonya," Dr. Chandler answered.

A moment later the group entered Aaron's room. "Aaron," Dr. Spencer began as she walked in with Dr. Chandler, Claudia, Winston, and Simone Jones, "I want you to know that Jason is doing okay. I want you to know that first."

"What's happened?" Aaron shouted. "Why the hell are all of you in here? Is Jason dead? Oh my God! He's dead, isn't he?"

"No, Aaron. Jason is not dead. I promise you," she went on. "However, his treatment has been a little more complicated than we had hoped."

"Complicated! What do you mean, complicated? What complications?"

"Aaron, please trust the doctor," Claudia said calmly, though she was visibly shaking.

"Claudia, I've only just met you today!" Aaron shouted. "Don't tell me what to do. I don't know you! I don't know any of you! So don't tell me who to trust. Got it. Now I'll say it again! Why are all of you ganging up on me in here?"

"Aaron, you know me," Dr. Spencer said. "Do you remember? I took care of you when you were here this past October."

"I only saw you for a few minutes at a time. Where's Braden? I want Braden! I know him. I trust him! What's happened to Jason?" Aaron shouted.

"Aaron, please try to calm down. Stress is not good for your head injury," Dr. Chandler said.

"Braden is with Jason," Claudia added. "Remember, you asked him to go with Jason."

"Oh, God. I feel funny," Aaron said as he leaned back on the bed.

"Sonya," Dr. Chandler called from the door, "Call down to the ED and get Braden Darby up here right away."

****

6:55 PM

"Aaron, I'm here, buddy," Braden said as he put his hand on Aaron's shoulder.

"Braden, I'm not right in my head. Why am I not right in my head? I can't think straight."

"Aaron, they've given you a little lorazepam. It's to calm you down."

"Okay, I'm calm. I'm calm! What's happened to Jason?"

Dr. Chandler mouthed, "Go ahead," to Braden.

"Aaron, I need you to listen to me, okay?" Aaron nodded. "Jason is fine. He's okay now, really, he is. Dr.

Spencer was right. There was a piece of bullet in his back. They're taking it out right now, and they've put a tube into his chest to drain the blood that the bullet caused to pool in the bottom of his lung. That's why he was short of breath. There was also extra air in his chest between his lung and his chest wall. It's called a hemopneumothorax, but listen to me. They had to take him to the OR to fix him because there was a small blood vessel that the bullet nicked, and it was bleeding very, very slowly. That's why he was able to go for as long as he did before he became short of breath.

"The bullet went into his chest through his armpit and made a small hole in his lung on its way to the artery before it nicked it. The surgeons are going in to clip the artery to stop it from bleeding anymore."

"You swear to me he's alive," Aaron pleaded.

"Yes, Aaron, I swear it to you. I just left him in the OR," Braden said. "Jason is alive, and he's going to be okay now."

"When can I see him?"

"Not for a while. He'll be going to the recovery room after they've finished with his surgery. They're still working on him right now. They're checking him from stem to stern to be sure he doesn't have any other hidden injuries."

"Where's the bullet?" Aaron asked. "I want to see it."

"The bullet was immediately given to the police. That inspector went into the OR with the surgeons, and they gave it right to her when they took it out of him."

"How come?"

"Because it's evidence."

"Oh, okay. That makes sense."

"Aaron?" Claudia moved up to the side of Aaron's bed. "There's some things I need to discuss with you, some legal things. Do you think you're up to it?"

Drs. Spencer and Chandler and Simone Jones stepped out of the room.

"Yeah, I'm feeling better now that I know Jason's okay."

"Right before the meeting that Jason called today with all the people who are taking care of you, he made out a new will. He's named you his primary beneficiary. He also signed papers giving you control over his estate if he should become incapacitated, and he's given you durable power of attorney over his estate and his medical care. Because Jason is unconscious right now, you're in charge of everything. Jason ordered many changes to be made at the cabin for both your sakes. It's a lot to go through, and I think it's okay if I don't go into it all too deeply right now, but I need to know if you want us to continue with his orders."

"Yes, most definitely. If Jason thought they were important, then they are. Keep doing whatever he wanted."

"Very good. We'll keep going, but let me tell you this, he's beefing up security because of the shooting. He's hired a security firm to guard the grounds contained within the stockade. He's ordered modular housing to be installed for the security people and for any other staff that might be needed in the short term and also for any future meetings that you'll be having to get your project off the ground. I think that's the gist of everything. Any questions?"

"Yes. Is Simone Jones here?"

"She stepped outside to give you and me some privacy."

"Will you get her for me, please?"

"Sure." Claudia walked to the door and signaled for Simone to come in.

"Yes, Aaron," Simone asked. "What do you need?"

"Where's Jason going to go after he gets out of the Operating Room?"

"He'll go the Recovery Room and then to the surgical ICU."

"Where's that?"

"It's the critical care unit right next door, why?"

"Because I want to be moved there into the same room with him. I need you to make this happen, Simone."

"Mr. Jaeger," Dr. Chandler chimed in from the doorway as she entered. "I don't think that's a good idea right now. You're only recovering yourself from a second head injury."

"I don't care, Dr. Chandler. Simone, is there any logistical reason why you couldn't make this happen?"

"None that I can think of, Aaron."

"Dr. Chandler. Is there anything that Jason's ICU can't do for me?"

"It wouldn't be the best place for you, Aaron."

"That's not what I asked. There must have been surgical patients who also had head injuries in that unit. Right?"

Dr. Chandler pressed her lips together. "Yes. However, I do not recommend it."

"Thank you for your honesty, Dr. Chandler. Simone, I want you to make this happen. I don't care what it costs. If you need to move staff around to make it happen, do it. If you need to bring in extra staff then do it, and pay them well. And I want my bed connected to his. You can put our beds right up against each other, 'coz I want to be able to touch him.

"I give you my word that I will not do anything to interfere with his care, but he needs to know that I'm there, and I want to be the first face he sees when he wakes up. Understand?"

"Yes, Aaron. I'll make it happen."

"And there's one more thing. I want Braden to be there with us. I want Braden to be with us as long as we're here."

"Yes, Aaron." Simone nodded. "I'll see to it."

****

Room S-644

In less than an hour, Aaron had been moved to Jason's room in the SICU, but their beds hadn't been connected. That would happen after they moved Jason from the Recovery Room stretcher.

Because Jason would need the monitor in the room, Sonya brought a portable monitor from the Neuro ICU for Aaron that sat on a cart next to his bed.

Aaron waited and waited for any news on Jason. As the hours passed, he began to think that his insistence on being with Jason might not have been the best decision. The last thing he wanted to do was jeopardize Jason's recovery. Then he fell asleep.

Section Four
Post-op

Chapter Thirty-One
Only a Fragment

8:25 PM
Room S-644

"Mr. Jaeger, I'm Dr. Phineas Baum. I'm the chief surgical resident. I put in Mr. Ackerman's chest tube in the ER, and I assisted Dr. Tunisia, the chief of thoracic surgery in his surgery. I wanted to give you an update on him. Right now, he's been moved to the Recovery Room. He'll be there for a couple hours, and then he'll be moved here."

"Thank you, Doctor. It's been so long. I was worried."

"I'm sorry about that. I understand you were briefed on what we had to do in the OR to stop his bleeding."

"Yes, sir."

"We were able to make a smaller incision than normal because we didn't have to explore the wound to find the bullet. We knew exactly where his bleeding was coming from because we used IV contrast when we did his CT scan. Mr. Ackerman was very lucky. We believe his injuries weren't any worse than they were because it was only a fragment of a bullet that entered his chest cavity. The bullet probably broke apart when it struck something else. The fragment must have ricocheted so its velocity wasn't as high and its mass was smaller than a full-sized bullet would have been if it had been fired directly into him. I can stop if this is upsetting you."

"No, Doctor, please continue. I want to know everything. I can take it."

"There is a three-inch incision below his right collar bone and another smaller one on his back next to his shoulder blade where we took out the bullet fragment. We repaired the damaged muscles as best as we could, but I really don't think he'll have any major problems. He was in really good physical shape, and that will work to his advantage as he recovers."

"Doctor, you have no idea just how hard he works. He's a real outdoorsman."

"That's going to be a big help to him in the coming days. He has a tube in his chest to keep his lung inflated while he heals. It's attached to a device that makes bubbling noises. It will be connected with a long tube to the suction unit on the wall behind his bed. He's going to be very groggy for a while after he gets here, so please don't think there's something wrong if he doesn't respond to you."

"I hope my being in here with him is okay. I don't want to put him at risk."

"Well, to be honest with you it's a first for me, but it's not unusual for family members to stay with ICU patients for days at a time. You're just the first I know of who is also a patient in the hospital. Just be sure to allow the nurses and other staff members to do their jobs. We can't have his care being interfered with in any way. Though his recovery should go without a hitch, our expectations are based on a tried and true process of care, and that care can't be interrupted. Do you understand what I'm saying?"

"Yes, Doctor. I won't get in the way. I promise you that."

"Thank you. There's one more thing."

"Yes?"

"He's going to be on a ventilator at least until tomorrow sometime if not for a couple of days. He has a tube down his throat so he won't be able to talk to you. We may have to keep him sedated if he fights the tube too much. Some patients have trouble tolerating a ventilator because they can feel like they're choking and they can't completely control their breathing. We put them on the machine and sedate them to allow their bodies to rest while they heal, and the ventilator does all the work of breathing for them. If that's the case, he may be unconscious for most of the time while the tube is in his throat. I just want you to know all this before he gets here."

"Thank you, Doctor, for taking the time to talk to me. It was very kind of you."

"You're welcome, Mr. Jaeger. Do you have any questions for me?"

"No, but please, call me Aaron."

"Very good, Aaron. As I said, he should be here in a couple of hours. I'm on call tonight so I might stop in to check on him, but I'll definitely check on him before I go off duty in the morning."

"Thanks again, Dr. Baum."

****

11:15 PM

Jason was accompanied by two recovery room nurses, one of whom was breathing for him with a bag valve mask. When he was wheeled into the room, Aaron woke up. Sonya put her hand on Aaron's arm when he tried to get up and go to Jason. Immediately, Drs. Chandler and Spencer came in to monitor how Aaron reacted, and Jason's SICU nurse, Reggie, came in behind them.

Aaron started to cry when he saw Jason. "He isn't breathing, is he? Thank God he's out of it. I'm okay, doctors, really, I'm okay," he said, waving them away. "It's just hard to see him like that."

"Aaron," Dr. Spencer said in a comforting voice, "this is all normal. You have to understand that because of your request to be in here with Jason, you're going to see things that most family members would never see because we usually ask them to step out of the room when we do certain things to their loved ones.

"Yes, Dr. Spencer. I understand that."

"Aaron," Dr. Chandler added, "if this becomes too much for you to bear, we can always move you back to the Neuro ICU."

"No, Dr. Chandler. I can do this. He took care of me for five weeks at the cabin, and he had to do things for me that I could never have imagined a person would have to do for someone else. I can do this for Jason. I can do this for him."

"Please remember, Aaron," she went on, "you're a patient, too. You also have to think of yourself. You won't be much good to Jason if you become so affected by all of this that it makes you ill or puts too much strain on you. Remember your brain has taken two very bad hits since September. When you get upset it raises your blood pressure, and that will increase the pressure in your brain. Do you understand me?"

"Yes, thank you, Dr. Chandler. I'll behave, and anyway, I'm stronger than I look, believe me."

"Maybe it would be helpful if you allowed us to medicate you. You seemed to tolerate the lorazepam pretty well."

"I don't think I'll need it, Dr. Chandler. And anyway, that stuff made me too foggy. I want to be clear and present for Jason when he wakes up."

"We didn't give you too big of a dose, Aaron. Perhaps, with a smaller dose, it would just take the edge off."

"I'll make you a deal," Aaron said. "I promise

you, if it starts to get to be too much for me, I'll let you know and then you can give it to me."

"Deal." Dr. Chandler offered her hand, and Aaron shook it.

The moment Jason was in his bed and hooked up to the ventilator, Aaron asked if he could touch him.

"Can you give me a couple minutes, Mr. Jaeger?" Reggie asked. "I need to check him over so I can establish a baseline so we know his initial parameters. We'll compare him to those as the night progresses."

"Yes, sure. I'm sorry. I didn't mean to interfere."

"You're not interfering at all right now, but believe me, if I thought you were, I would tell you. I understand that you're going to be in here with him, but he's my patient. You're not, and my only concern is for him right now. Does that make sense to you?"

"Yes, of course," Aaron answered. "I want that. I want someone to only be concerned about him. I know I can't do anything for him right now."

"Sonya is here for you. If you need something, she'll take care of it."

"We're going to go now," Dr. Spencer said for herself and Dr. Chandler. "We'll see you in the morning unless you need us before then. I'll be in the hospital all night, but Dr. Chandler will be going home. We're just a phone call away if you need us."

"Thank you, both of you. You've been great. Thank you so much for taking care of Jason and me."

"Good night, Aaron," they said as they walked away.

Once Reggie had Jason settled, he invited Aaron to come to his bedside. "He might not be able to hear you, Mr. Jaeger. He's pretty sedated right now."

"Please call me Aaron, and that's okay. I'll be here for him whether he can hear me or not. Jason, I'm here. It's Aaron," he said as he took Jason's hand. "I'm here, my love. You're in the ICU. You had surgery, but you're doing fine." Jason's hand squeezed Aaron's. "He squeezed my hand! He squeezed my hand! He knows it's me!"

Reggie came to the bedside just in time to see Jason briefly opened his eyes. He tried to turn his head, but it barely moved at all.

"I'm here, my love. I'm here," Aaron said as he leaned over and kissed Jason's forehead.

"Aaron," Jason mouthed. His eyes fluttered for a moment, and then he fell back into darkness.

"Where's Braden?" Aaron asked.

"I believe he's gone home, Aaron," Sonya answered.

"I thought he was going to be here with us."

"I'm sorry. I didn't realize you didn't know that, Aaron," Sonya went on. "Please, try to understand. Braden was here for over twenty hours. He came in for his regular shift at seven last night. He left to go home to get some sleep sometime after nine this evening."

"Oh, wow," Aaron said, "that never occurred to me. He must have been dead tired. Of course, you all have your own lives. That was a selfish thing for me to assume."

"It is true that we have our own lives, but when we're here, our only focus is on our patients. Never forget that. You're not being selfish at all. It's obvious you love Mr. Ackerman, and it's understandable that you only want the best for him."

"When do you go home, Sonya?"

"My shift started at three this afternoon. I'll be here until three in the morning. Then another nurse will take over for me."

"When are you here until, Reggie?"

"My shift just started. I'll be here until eleven tomorrow morning."

"I think I should let Jason rest now," Aaron said as he kissed Jason on the forehead again, "and maybe I should try to get some shuteye, too."

"That sounds like a real good idea, Aaron," Sonya said. Would you like us to push your beds together now?"

"No, not now. I don't want to disturb him, and anyway, there aren't any body pillows. That's what Jason did for me when I was injured. He'd pack body pillows between us so he wouldn't bump me. I'll have to ask Claudia to see if she can find some in the morning."

As Aaron lay down on his bed, he said to them. "Do you guys want to know something that just occurred to me?"

"What's that?" Sonya answered.

"I'm listening," Reggie said.

"What you said about how many hours Braden was here, your long hours, and how hard I see you both work to care for us. It makes me think about everything Jason did for me. That man took care of me twenty-four hours a day for five weeks straight. He cooked my meals, fed me, bathed me, treated my wounds, emptied my bedpans and urinals, and kept me from losing my mind. He rescued me from a tree, twenty feet off the ground, took care of the cabin and the animals, and he did it all alone with no one to help him.

"I never knew anyone could do all that, and yet, he never complained, not once. He never let it show just how hard he had to work to keep me alive. All I ever saw was a sparkle in the eyes of a man who cared deeply about another human being."

"That's called love, Aaron," Reggie said.

****

169

"Oh, Aaron. That feels so weird, but it's so, so good. How are you doing that inside my cock?"

"It's my magic tongue, baby. I'm sliding it in and out of your piss slit, all the way to your prostate. Feel the tingle? Feel the burn?"

"Yes, it's wonderful, but it hurts, too."

"I'm going to make you come from the inside."

"Yes, Aaron. Make me come."

"I want to come, too, Ackerman. Here, take my cock deep into your throat. That's it. That's it. Now deeper. Yes, deeper. Now breathe through my cock while I fuck your throat. You can do it. Breathe just long enough until I come."

"It's too much, Aaron. I can't breathe. I can't breathe. You're choking me, Aaron. You're choking me!"

"If I'm choking you, Ackerman, how can you talk?"

"I can't breathe, Aaron. I can't breathe!"

"That's right, faggot. You're not going to ever breathe again! You're mine, faggot. You're mine!"

"Aaron, why are you saying that?"

"Aaron? Who the fuck is Aaron? You idiot! No, faggot, it's me, your old pal."

"Garrison!"

"That's right, faggot. Now take my load. Are you ready for it? Here it comes!"

"Aaron, help me. Help me! I'm drowning!"

Chapter Thirty-Two
I'll Do Anything

December 24, 2009, 6:50 AM

Aaron woke to whispering.

"Yes, I've had to sedate him twice for bucking the vent. He had one really nasty spell where I suctioned him for copious amounts of mucous. He was flailing all over the place, but I finally got him calmed down. After that initial suctioning there was one episode that returned a moderate amount of bloody mucous. Since then, I've gotten only scant amounts of white mucous from his endotracheal tube with an occasional rust colored streak. I don't believe that's from traumatic suctioning though. His lungs are clear from the apices to the bases anteriorly and posteriorly and the chest tube dressing has a moderate amount of bloody drainage, but that hasn't advanced since my initial assessment when he arrived.

"Yes, his vitals have remained stable throughout the night. He did come to briefly when his partner called his name right after I got him settled in, but that's it. He's had two-hundred milliliters out from the chest tube since he arrived in the SICU at 11:15 PM, but it's been mostly serosanguinous with a few thready clots.

"His infraclavicular dressing is the original one from surgery. It's still dry, but there's about three centimeters of drainage on the posterior scapular dressing. I thought I'd wait until you arrived to change them so you could see for yourself. That way he'd only have to be disturbed once."

"Okay, I'll see you in about fifteen."

"Who was that?" Aaron asked Reggie as he sat up in bed, cross-legged.

"That was Dr. Baum. He'll be here in a few minutes to check on Jason before he goes off duty."

"What was all that you were saying to him?"

"I was telling him how Jason's night was."

"Oh. Jason's the medical person. He'd understand what all those words mean, but I only know football. Can you explain it to me so I understand?"

"Sure, Aaron, I told Dr. Baum that Jason was only awake for a moment when you talked to him last night. His vital signs have remained stable since he arrived in the SICU. He's had about seven ounces of a serum-blood mixture from his chest tube, and the dressing there hasn't had any new drainage since he's been here. The dressing below his collar bone looks real good, and it hasn't had enough drainage for it to come through. The dressing on his back has about a fifty-cent piece size patch of blood. He lungs are clear from top to bottom and front to back. I got a lot of mucous out of him the first time I suctioned him. That was to be expected. Since then I got some bloody mucous only once, and after that only very little mucous. I did have to sedate him twice through the night because he was fighting the ventilator."

"So is that good or bad?"

"Oh, it's good," Reggie explained. "It's very, very good. The doctors will make a decision about when his breathing tube will come out after they evaluate him. They'll be making rounds some time this morning."

"Thank you, Reggie. Did Dr. Baum come in the middle of the night? He said he might."

"Yes, he did. He was here briefly, but Jason was quiet. He didn't want to wake you just to tell you he was here."

"Thank you. Where's Sonya?"

"Remember, she went off at three. Your new nurse is Sylvester. They also didn't want to wake you just to introduce him. He went down to get a cup of

coffee a little while ago. I told him I'd cover until he got
back, which should be any minute now."

"Thanks. Where can I go to take a leak?"

"You can use the bathroom right there." Reggie
pointed to the door. "The monitor cable will reach.
Remember, you're on intake and output until further
notice. Use the urinal that's in there so Sylvester can
measure it, and be sure to wash your hands when you're
finished."

"Will do."

After Aaron finished, he washed his hands and
then went to Jason's bed and took his hand while he
watched Reggie put his stethoscope to Jason's chest.

"Good morning, Mr. Jaeger. I'm Sylvester, your
day nurse," he whispered as he walked through the door.

"How do you do," Aaron answered, extending his
hand. "Call me Aaron."

"Shh," Reggie ordered. "Hush, I'm listening."

"Thanks for not waking me when you took over
for Sonya," Aaron whispered.

Sylvester put his fingers to his lips, reinforcing
his order to Aaron to stop speaking.

"Okay, go ahead," Reggie said once he finished.

"Thanks," Aaron said again. "I didn't realize how
much I needed to sleep. Oh, shit! I wasn't supposed to
sleep too much. I have that EEG to do."

"You didn't, and we figured it was best not to
wake you," Sylvester continued. "So, you're Mr.
Ackerman's partner?"

"Yes, I am. Oh, I nearly filled the urinal to the
top. It's in the bathroom. Reggie said you needed to
measure it."

"Thanks. I'll take care of that in a moment. I
think it's great that you're here for Mr. Ackerman, but
try to keep in mind that some of this might be disturbing.

We send most family members out of the room when we do certain procedures, like what Reggie's about to do."

"What's that?" Aaron asked pointing to a small fluid-filled plastic packet in Reggie's hand.

"It's saline, salt water. I'm going to push it down into his lungs," Reggie answered. "It's going to make him cough, and that'll help to break up some of the mucous I'm hearing down there. You might want to look away. A lot of family members find the sight and sound of it a bit gross."

"I think I'll be okay." Aaron didn't react when Reggie squeeze the saline down the endotracheal tube, but the moment Jason started to retch and cough, he got queasy. Reggie pressed a button on the ventilator that forced a big breath into Jason's lungs, then he pushed the catheter its full length down the tube. Jason's eyes opened, and tears formed in them as his body heaved up off the mattress. Aaron immediately turned away from the bed and bent over, dry heaving, just as Dr. Chandler walked in.

"Mr. Jaeger! Aaron!" Dr. Chandler said sternly. "I told you yesterday not to raise your blood pressure!"

"Sorry, Aaron. I tried to warn you," Sylvester said, handing Aaron a washcloth.

"I'm okay. It just happened so fast," Aaron said, wiping his mouth. "Guess my stomach's empty. I didn't puke."

"You may not have vomited, but you certainly retched!" Dr. Chandler's voice went up an octave. "Sylvester, get me a blood pressure right now."

"Back into bed," Sylvester began to say.

"No, while he's standing, right now!" Dr. Chandler stood with her arms crossed in front of her.

"It's 170/95, Dr. Chandler."

"See, Aaron. It just went through the roof!" Dr.

Chandler exclaimed. "Back to bed. I want to examine you."

From the stimulation of Reggie's suctioning and all the loud voices in the room, Jason was wide awake. Instinctively, he reached for his ET tube. "No!" exclaimed Reggie, just in time as he grabbed for Jason's hand. "Sylvester, help me!"

Sylvester jumped to the other side of the bed and together they held Jason's arms down to the mattress. "Someone grab me a milligram of lorazepam!" Reggie shouted out to the nurses' station.

A middle-aged doctor who Aaron didn't know walked in. "What's all the ruckus about?"

"He just tried to extubate himself, Dr. Fleischmann. I just suctioned out a good sized mucous plug. Then he had a coughing spell."

"Let me have a look first, before we go ahead and sedate him. Maybe he's trying to tell us he's ready to come off the ventilator."

"Good morning, Mr. Ackerman," he said leaning over the bedrail." I'm Dr. Fleischmann. I'm a pulmonologist or lung doctor. It's my job to evaluate your breathing."

"No!" Jason mouthed. "No more drugs!"

"I hear you loud and clear, Mr. Ackerman. I'm here to determine whether you're strong enough to breathe on your own yet or if you still need some time on the ventilator to recover. Your chest and lungs have been through quite a bit these last twelve hours."

"Get this fucking tube out of me!" Jason mouthed.

"I couldn't agree more, Mr. Ackerman, but all in good time. The sooner we can wean you off the machine, the less chance your lungs and chest muscles will become complacent and the less chance you'll develop complications."

"I'll do anything!" Jason mouthed. "Anything!"

"Good. Then hold still while I listen for a moment and then I'd like to hear from your nurse about how your lungs have been overnight. Can you promise me you'll keep your hands off the tube for a few minutes?"

"Yes! Yes! Anything!" Jason mouthed.

"Okay, boys. Let him go."

"Mr. Ackerman," Dr. Fleischmann said as he leaned over and looked into Jason's eyes, "I'm taking your word now. Please don't disappoint me."

"I won't," Jason mouthed. "I promise!"

"Cancel that lorazepam," Reggie said from the door to the other SICU nurses at the station.

"What's going on, Reggie?" Dr. Baum asked as he walked to Jason's room.

"Dr. Fleischmann beat you to him. He's evaluating Jason to see if he can extubate him."

"Well, I don't have any problem with that if he thinks Mr. Ackerman is ready. When can I get in there? I'm about to go off duty."

"Give us five?"

"Okay, I'll go check on another patient."

It took all of Jason's willpower to not grab for the tube and pull it out, but he managed while Dr. Fleischmann listened to his lungs.

"So tell me, Reggie, how's his pulmonary toilet been overnight?"

"Real good, Doctor. I've gotten very little white mucous out with a couple rust streaks now and then, even with saline, that was until just a minute ago. That's when I got the plug with aggressive toileting. That's been it since 11:15 PM last night. The most was a copious amount of bloody mucous when he arrived from recovery."

"Very good."

"Mr. Ackerman," Dr. Fleischmann said, leaning over the railing again, "I'll make you a deal."

"What's that?" Jason mouthed.

"Agree to keep your hands off the tube for the next fifteen minutes while we take you off the ventilator and hook you up to a tube of humidified oxygen, and I won't sedate you. It's called a T-piece. You'll be breathing all on your own. If you don't tire yourself out, we'll put you back on the ventilator for thirty minutes, and then we'll put you back on the T-piece for another fifteen minutes. If you can do all of that, and you're still feeling strong, I'll take that tube out myself. If not, I'm going to keep you on the ventilator until at least this evening."

"You're on!" Jason mouthed, wide eyed.

"Great. I'll see you in sixty minutes."

"Dr. Fleischmann, is there any reason Dr. Baum can't take a look at Jason while he's weaning? He's about to go off duty, but he wanted to check on him before he left."

"I don't see any reason why not. He isn't going to do any procedures, is he?"

"None that I know of. He just wants to check him over, I guess so he can report off on his condition to the next surgical resident on rotation and to his attending, Dr. Tunisia."

"That's fine. It shouldn't interfere with what we're going to do."

Reggie disconnected Jason from the ventilator and attached the T-piece, a length of corrugated blue tubing with an extra short blue piece that extended beyond the ET tube. It had mist coming out of the end. "This is the T-piece, Mr. Ackerman. You're on your own right now."

"Call me Jason," he mouthed.

"Very good, Jason. Oh, here's Dr. Baum."

"Hello, Mr. Ackerman. I'm Dr. Baum. I don't know if you remember me or not, but we met in the ED last night under less than ideal circumstances. I know everything was moving pretty fast. I'd like to check your surgical sites if that's all right with you."

"Go ahead," Jason mouthed.

****

While Drs. Fleischmann and Baum evaluated Jason, Dr. Chandler gave Aaron the once over as well. "Well, Aaron, you've very lucky. That's all I have to say. Your neurological status looks good for the moment."

"Thank you, Dr., Chandler. I just didn't expect to see that, and the sound threw me. I'll be better the next time, but I see what you warned me about. I'll do my best to behave."

"Good." Dr. Chandler patted Aaron on the shoulder. "You can get up now if you like. I know you're probably itching to get over to him."

"Thanks, doc."

Aaron climbed from his bed and went to Jason's side while Dr. Baum was examining him. "I'm here, Jason. I'm right here. Hello, Dr. Baum."

"Aaron." Jason mouthed his name as he blinked against the tears that began to well up in his eyes. "I'm sorry. I'm so, so sorry."

"Hush now. You have nothing to be sorry for. You didn't do anything wrong. Hell, you saved my life again! I'm right here, Jason. You just breathe."

"Aaron, Garrison was here. He tried to drown me."

"I'm sorry, Jason. I didn't get that. Reggie, did you get that?"

"He said Garrison tried to drown him."

"No, Jason, Garrison wasn't here. I promise you. He can't hurt you. He's dead. It was a dream. A dream. Now breathe, My love. Breathe for both of us."

Jason did just that. He squeezed tight against Aaron's hand as he turned all his attention from the choking sensation in his throat towards his breathing. Telling him about Garrison could wait.

"Mr. Ackerman," Dr. Baum said, "I couldn't be more pleased with everything. Your incisions look great, your sutures look great, your chest tube drainage looks great. Basically, everything is great."

"Thanks, Doctor," Jason mouthed.

"I'll be off for the next twenty-four hours, but my replacement and my attending, Dr. Tunisia, will be by to see you later today. Do you remember Dr. Tunisia?"

"Of course. He has the kind eyes," Jason mouthed.

"I'll give them a full report on my findings before I leave. Do you have any questions for me?"

"No. Thank you, Doctor," Jason mouthed.

"My pleasure. Take care, both of you."

"Thank you, Doctor," Aaron added.

Chapter Thirty-Three
Now Exhale!

7:35 AM

As Jason approached the end of his first fifteen-minute T-piece evaluation, Dr. Fleischmann stuck his head back in the room. "How goes it?"

"He's doing really well, Doctor. I'm about to put him back on the vent." Reggie went to remove the T-piece and return him to the ventilator, but Jason waved him off. Dr. Fleischmann walked to the bed.

"No! I'm fine!" Jason mouthed, "I can keep going."

"Mr. Ackerman…"

"Jason," he mouthed.

"What did he say?" Dr. Fleischmann asked.

"Jason, he said Jason," Aaron answered. "He wants you to call him Jason."

"Very well, Jason, let us give you a rest for a few minutes." Dr. Fleischmann took Jason's hand. "It isn't that I don't think that you can do it or that you need to prove anything to me. It's because I need to compare your numbers off and on the ventilator. Understand?"

"I understand," Jason mouthed. "Go ahead."

As Dr. Fleischmann left, Sylvester pulled a chair next to the bed for Aaron. "Thanks, Sylvester. You guys are the best. I don't know how you know all this stuff, but you're obviously good at what you do. I want you to know how grateful I am for you both."

"That's real nice of you, Aaron, but it's what we've been trained for," Sylvester answered.

"I certainly couldn't be a professional, starting quarterback," Reggie said.

"Well, as it happens, neither can I it seems," Aaron said with a tinge of regret in his voice.

"Yeah, I heard about that," Reggie added. "That must have been real tough. Real tough, but I'm sure with your talents you'll find something that suits you."

"Jason and I just started talking about that," Aaron said as he squeezed Jason's hand, "Didn't we, love? But that's on hold right now. Everything is on hold right now."

Jason mouthed, "We'll get through this, Aaron. We'll get through it all."

****

8:20 AM

True to his word, Dr. Fleischmann returned forty-five minutes later. "So, Reggie, how did he do?"

"No hiccoughs, Dr. Fleischmann, none. His breathing was steady, and his numbers barely wavered between when he was on the vent and on the T-piece, the first time or now."

"Any diaphoresis?"

"None that I saw, Doctor."

"Heart rate?

"Steady as she goes, sir."

Dr. Fleischmann took Jason's hand. "Well, young man, you just earned yourself a reprieve. I'm going to take that tube out right now. Reggie?"

"Here's the syringe, Doctor."

"Jason, I'm going to need you to take a deep breath when I say to. Then I'm going to deflate the balloon on the end of the tube, and I'm going to tell you to exhale forcefully while I remove the tube. There's going to be some secretions at the top of your airway, above the balloon, in your trachea. Exhaling will help to blow them out. You'll probably have the urge to cough, but try to blow out all your air if you possibly can before you take in a breath. That way you won't inhale those secretions. Do you understand me?"

Jason nodded his head and mouthed, "Yes."

"Mr. Jaeger, do you want to be here for this? I understand you had a moment when Jason was being suctioned. This can be even more traumatic to watch. He'll probably turn a shade of dark purple when he starts coughing, and it's not a pretty sight."

"I'll be all right now that I know what to expect. Can I hold his hand while you do it?"

"That's up to Reggie."

"It's okay with me, Aaron," Reggie answered, "but if I tell you to back away, I'll mean it. You'll need to get out of the way so I can attend to him. Got it?"

"Yes."

After they raised the head of Jason's bed, Dr. Fleischmann said, "Here we go, Jason. Deep breath in."

Dr. Fleischmann deflated the balloon. "Now exhale hard!"

As Jason began to exhale, Dr. Fleischmann pulled out the tube. It was over in less than two seconds, and just like he predicted, Jason began to cough his guts up.

Aaron never let go during the entire coughing fit. Jason squeezed Aaron's hand so hard that it turned white and left an imprint for over an hour.

Jason's first words to Reggie were very hoarse, but direct. "Now, can we please get this fucking Foley catheter out of my dick?"

Chapter Thirty-Four
Accusations

8:45 AM
Administrative Wing, Office of the CEO

Present in Simone Jones' office were also Penelope Whitley, Dr. Phyllis Chandler, Dr. Phineas Baum, Dr. Yvonne Spencer, Claudia Duncan, and Winston Tanner.

"Thank you all for coming so early this morning," Simone Jones began. "I'm sure all of you have your plates full with your own work, so again, thank you. After taking into consideration all of last evenings events, I thought it might be a good idea for us to meet to discuss how best to handle the next twenty-four hours and beyond."

"Are you referring to the poorly handled interview with Channel 18 news?" Claudia Duncan asked. "The fact that Jason and Aaron's story got out is a real violation of their privacy, and from what I've learned about HIPPA since last night, it violates those regulations in spades."

"That was no fault of this hospital or any of its employees, Miss Duncan," Simone answered firmly, "and you know that. The reporter even told you they got that information from the police."

Claudia came right back at her. "The handling of that interview was incompetent, and the fact that the footage of Jason in the ED got out last night is proof of this institution's incompetence!"

"We have no way of preventing the news media from arriving at our doorstep," Simone responded, "nor can we control the actions of non-employees who are present in the building. We cannot search every person entering through our doors, nor can we legally confiscate anything we feel might be inappropriate."

"It's quite simple, Miss Jones. It happened on your watch, in your institution, for which you," Claudia stood up and pointed, "as its Chief Operating Officer, are responsible."

"That's enough," Dr. Chandler broke in with uncensored annoyance. "Let me make one thing clear, ladies. I have reached my absolute limit with all that's been going on while I'm trying to see to it that Aaron doesn't develop permanent brain damage. I've been a neurologist for thirty-seven years. I've worked around the country and around the world, and never once have I encountered such obstructions to proper medical care than I have these past twenty-four hours.

"Miss Duncan, you must stop interjecting inconsequential legal matters into matters of direct patient care, and Simone, I have all the respect for you in the world, but the allowances you have made at the whims of Aaron and Jason have created additional hurdles we must jump in order to care for them both.

"Jason Ackerman is not my patient, but you've caused his care to become a concern of mine because it's right up in the face of my patient, Aaron Jaeger, and it's affecting him on a clinical level. I was in with Aaron ninety minutes ago, and he experienced a visceral response to a coughing spell that Jason had, and that could have well resulted in an increase in his cerebral edema caused by a rise in his intracranial pressure.

"He is a dear, sweet, kind young man who is obviously head-over-heels in love, but he's clearly not suited to be present in the critical care setting of his partner because of his sensitivity to those sorts of things. Had he not been present, he would not have had such a severe and potentially catastrophic reaction. A whirlpool has been created here, Simone, that I have no control over, and we may well find ourselves unable to navigate out of it."

Simone and Claudia sat stone faced as if they were schoolgirls who had been called to the principal's office for pulling each other's hair.

"If I may," Dr. Spencer began.

"Sorry, Yvonne, but I'm not finished. Miss Duncan, for you to accuse Penelope of incompetence for the way she handled that reporter last night was a shot to the balls, sorry, but that's what it was. If it had been me, I'd have slugged that son-of-a-bitch, Chuck Jackson, right in the choppers. Now I'm finished."

"Dr. Chandler, you're correct in what you've said about how Aaron and Jason are reacting to the care required to treat each other's injuries," Simone answered, "but unfortunately the horse has already run away from the barn. It's too late to close that door. My concern now is how do we contain what's already in motion?"

"Look, everyone. I'm sorry, but I'm dead tired," Dr. Baum began, "I've been here for over twenty-four hours. I've taken five patients to surgery and answered numerous emergency pages throughout the house and in the ED. I don't know how much I have to offer here, but I can tell you that none of what I've heard so far has affected the medical status or the care received so far by Mr. Ackerman.

"Quite frankly, he's my only concern. Yes, Mr. Jaeger's presence in the room with Mr. Ackerman is odd, but from what I've witnessed firsthand, his presence has not only not hindered Mr. Ackerman's wellbeing, it has been beneficial to his recovery."

"It's my turn to add my two cents," Dr. Spencer began. "I've had very little time with Jason, but I've had quite a bit of time getting to know Aaron, even if he doesn't remember it at the present. When he was here three months ago, his focus was on his recovery, but it was not only to return to football.

"Though he never said it directly, it was very clear to me that Aaron was intent on maintaining a relationship with Jason. I did not know why that was at the time, and it didn't quite fit with the reason he alluded to, which was that Jason saved his life. Now that I understand they are in a loving relationship it makes much more sense to me, but that really shouldn't matter to any of us. What should matter is that they have both made it clear that they are committed to one another, whatever the reason, and they have told us outright, or demonstrated to us they need to be together right now.

"I am not aware of anything they have done that has hindered each other's care, and before you say it, Phyllis, yes, I know, there've been a few ripples, but Aaron is doing well. We've made allowances hundreds of times for family members to remain present in the critical care units in the past. That's enough for me. That's it. I'm finished."

"Penelope, would you like to say something?" Simone asked.

"Only this," Penelope began. "In recent months, I have done a lot of thinking about how patients and their families are forced to navigate the maze we call the healthcare system. It can be a scary thing, particularly to those who've never had to do it before, and particularly from the other side of the bed.

"As Dr. Spencer put it so very eloquently, we have been presented with two people who are committed to each other and want and need to be together. We have the means to accommodate them. Why should we not?"

"Mr. Tanner?" Simone asked, "I've heard very little from you these past twenty-four hours. Do you have anything to add?"

"Yes. Thank you. I've known Jason for, gosh, how long as it been? For more than fifteen years now. He saved my life in Iraq on the battlefield, and he visited me before I was shipped stateside to recover. He didn't have to do that, but he did.

"He was kind to me, a stranger, and he kept in touch with me after he returned stateside. When he found out I was going into finance after I left the service he was very happy for me. After he won the lottery, he told me I was the first person he thought of to manage his portfolio. I've never forgotten any of those things.

"For the past eleven years, I've been his financial manager, and except for a few social niceties, our relationship has been a professional one, but I've always thought of him as a friend. During those years it was very obvious to me just how lonely he was. I don't mean just alone. He was *lonely*, and I don't think he even realized it. That was until he found Aaron.

"He loves Aaron, and he wants to make a life with him. I'm damn well sure going to do everything within my power to see that that happens. And that's all I have to say about it."

"Thank you one and all for your comments and recommendations." Simone looked over her notes from the meeting. "Here's what I believe our plan should be as we move forward. Number one, we must protect Jason and Aaron from anything that might distract them from recovering, but we must do so carefully because, as evidenced, they have the potential to sacrifice their own wellbeing for each other's.

"Number two, because Jason and Aaron have made unlimited resources available to us, which will enable us to provide them with whatever they want while they are here, we are going to do just that."

Though Dr. Chandler raised her hand to speak,

Simone waved her down and continued. "With the caveat that it does not honestly, honestly now, jeopardize their welfare. Are we all in agreement?"

Everyone present nodded or stated they agreed.

"Good, one more thing, and I caution you all that the following is privileged information. It has been brought to my attention that the assailant who attacked Jason and Aaron has been brought to our doors for treatment. I include you, Miss Duncan, and you, Mr. Tanner, in this out of respect for how it might affect Jason and Aaron. You will have to deal with this information at some point, to some degree, and though I cannot say why, it is clear to me that you will likely learn this anyway, shortly.

"Though I cannot prevent you Miss Duncan, or you, Mr. Tanner, from revealing this to either of them, I can with my own staff. Not only does HIPPA prevail on this matter, I fear this knowledge may have a negative impact on Jason, or Aaron, or both of them.

"We will cooperate with the authorities in whatever way they require of us, but we will not otherwise volunteer any information on his status. Do I make myself clear?"

They all, including Claudia and Winston, agreed.

"Oh, I'm sorry, there was one final thing. Aaron made it known last night that he needed body pillows. I have dispatched my assistant to pick up several immediately. She should be back shortly."

Chapter Thirty-Five
There's Been a Development

9:10 AM
Room S-644

"Good morning to both of you," Simone said as she knocked on Jason and Aaron's doorframe. "May I come in?"

"Yes," Jason croaked.

"Good morning, Simone," Aaron said with a big smile as he leaned away from Jason and rolled over to his bed.

"How are you this morning?" Jason croaked again.

"Jason asked me to apologize to anyone coming in this morning. His voice is still very hoarse," Aaron said as he stood up to embrace Simone. "He just had the tube taken out of his throat a little while ago."

"Oh, goodness, I understand," she said after returning Aaron's hug. "Please, Jason, don't speak and thank you for asking. I'm just fine, and I don't expect you to answer this, but what is more important is how you are feeling."

"He's much better now that he's had the throat tube and catheter taken out," Aaron answered for him.

"I heard from a little birdie that you needed something," Simone continued, "so I hope you don't mind that I've taken care of it for you."

"What did we need?" Jason whispered.

Simone walked back to the doorway and reached out beyond it. Then she pulled in a stretcher loaded with body pillows.

"Oh, wow!" Aaron exclaimed.

"Why?" Jason croaked. "Aaron, what's this?"

"I mentioned to Sonya last night that I couldn't

lie on the bed next to you without body pillows because that's what you did for me in the cabin so you wouldn't bump me. I was afraid that I could do the same thing to you while I was asleep so I told her I was going to ask Claudia to see if she could find some for us."

"Yes," Simone added. "Sonya left me a voice mail to tell me. I had my assistant stop on her way in to the hospital to pick them up. Are they the right size?"

"They're perfect. Thank you so much, Simone," Aaron said as he walked over and hugged her again.

"There's six of them here. If you need more, just let me know. I also had her pick up eighteen pillow cases for them so that you'd always have fresh ones, and don't worry, we'll take care of laundering them. I'll just slip a few of them into cases right now."

"Ah, Miss Jones," Reggie said as he walked in. "I saw you come in. May I suggest that we put a barrier between the pillows and cases. If the pillows become soiled with blood or something else, we'll never be able to clean them. Otherwise we could go through them all in a single day. They're not standard hospital issue so they're not made with waterproof fabric. After Sonya told me, I thought about it. These large, disposable bags we use to cover the ventilators after they've been cleaned should work just fine," he said, placing a stack of the bags on the stretcher.

"Cool," Aaron said. "That's what was on Jason's ventilator when they wheeled it in. They look like giant, clear trash bags."

"That describes them perfectly, Aaron," Reggie answered.

"Here, let me give you a hand with those," Sylvester said to Simone and Reggie as he came into the room.

****

10:00 AM
Surgical Intensive Care Unit

"Hello, miss, I'm Chief Inspector Cassandra Addison with the Idaho State Police. I'm here on official business. I need to see Jason Ackerman and Aaron Jaeger. I understand they're both in this unit."

"I'll call Mr. Ackerman's nurse." Sabrina, the unit clerk, picked up the phone and dialed Reggie's hospital-issued, portable phone. "Reggie, there's an inspector here with the state police. She wants to see Mr. Ackerman and Mr. Jaeger."

"Stall her, Sabrina. Have her wait there. I'll be out in a few minutes."

"Mr. Ackerman's nurse will be right out," Sabrina said. "He's doing a procedure at the moment. Would you like to have a seat in our lounge?"

"No, thank you. I'll go and see Mr. Jaeger then."

"Um, ma'am, they're in the same room."

"I beg your pardon?"

"They're in the same room, ma'am."

"They're in the same room? But they're both patients, correct? Isn't that a little odd?"

"Ma'am, I don't make the rules. Would you like to have a seat in our lounge?"

"I'm fine standing. I'll wait right here."

After Reggie hung up with Sabrina, he redialed. "Miss Jones," he said softly into the mouthpiece, "there's an inspector here from the state police to talk to Jason and Aaron."

****

Administrative Wing, Office of the CEO

"I'll be right up," Simone said. She hung up and called Claudia, Drs. Chandler, Spencer, and Fleischmann, Dr. George Tunisia, Chief of Thoracic Surgery, and Penelope and instructed them all to meet her in the SICU.

****

10:07 AM
Surgical Intensive Care Unit
"Good morning, Chief Inspector Addison. What brings you here this morning?" Simone asked, walking up to the nurses' station, extending her hand.

"I have to hand it to you, Ms. Jones," Inspector Addison answered as she stared in Sabrina's direction while shaking hands. "Your staff is very good at their jobs. If I didn't know any better, I'd think I'm being stalled."

"Stalled? No. Never, but thank you for complimenting our staff. I'm very proud of each and every one of them. So you're here today for…" Simone asked again.

"I'm here on official police business, Miss Jones. I need to speak with Mr. Ackerman and Mr. Jaeger."

"Has anyone told their nurses?"

"I believe that's already been done. Mr. Ackerman is in the middle of a procedure. I asked to see Mr. Jaeger, but I was told they're sharing a room. Is that correct?"

"Yes, special circumstances. Would you like to have a seat in our staff lounge? It's much more comfortable than standing here at the nurses' station."

"No thank you. As I've already said, I'm fine waiting right here."

****

10:08 AM
Room S-644
"Hello, Mr. Ackerman, I'm Dr. Tunisia. I'm the Chief of Thoracic Surgery. Do you remember meeting me last night?

"Yes, Doctor," Jason croaked.

Aaron sat up from cradling Jason.

"My chief resident, Dr. Baum, filled me in on your progress, and his assessment of you this morning. How are you feeling?"

"Other than a scratchy throat, a sore urethra, and a throbbing prostate, I'm feeling good, except for the tugging between my ribs," Jason whisper-croaked.

"Hello, Doctor. I'm Aaron, Jason's partner," he said, extending his hand. "He's decided to whisper. It doesn't hurt as much when he talks."

After Dr. Tunisia shook hands, he continued. "Yes, that chest tube will likely stay in for a few more days. Your throat should feel better soon and as for the other things, well, they should clear up quickly, but I sympathize. Those tubes do tend to irritate. We may be able to take you off the chest tube suction soon, if your drainage tapers off, which I suspect, based on your remarkable progress so far, may be tomorrow, but I'm not making that a firm promise yet."

"That's great. When can I get out of here? And please, call me Jason."

"I think you're jumping the gun a bit, Jason. Most patients who've had thoracic surgery are in the hospital for at least seven to ten days. You were shot, so I'd lean towards the upper end of those two numbers, regardless of how you might feel. How about you let me listen to your chest for a minute. Do you think you can sit up for me?"

"Yeah."

"I'll help," Aaron offered.

"Um, why don't you let me do that, Aaron?" Reggie said. "And anyway, I just saw Dr. Chandler walk onto the unit. She has to be here to see you since you're our only neuro patient."

"Deep breaths now, Jason," Dr. Tunisia said as he

placed his stethoscope to Jason's chest.

****

10:14 AM

While Dr. Tunisia was examining Jason, Dr. Chandler came in with Dr. Spencer at her side and then closed the door behind her. "Hello again, Aaron. Are you feeling any better since earlier this morning?"

"I'm great, doctor," Aaron said as he saw Dr. Fleischmann walk past the door. "What's really going on, Doctor? There's four of you here right now."

A moment later, Claudia and Winston entered the room with Dr. Fleischmann.

"Claudia, what's going on?" Aaron asked with a little trepidation in his voice.

"Good morning, Aaron. Good morning, Jason," Claudia began. "How was your night?"

"Give, Claudia," Jason whispered. "What's up?"

"Well guys, that inspector from the state police is here to talk to both of you, again."

"Aaron, listen to me," Dr. Chandler began. "There's been a development in the investigation the police are conducting."

"Yes?"

"Aaron, I want you to listen to me now," Dr. Chandler continued. "Everything is fine. You're in no danger whatsoever."

"Aaron, baby," Jason whispered, "the bastard's alive. He didn't die."

"Fuck!" Aaron yelled. "I'll kill the son-of-a-bitch! Where is he? I'll fucking kill him!"

"You'll do no such thing, Mr. Jaeger," Chief Inspector Addison said from the doorway with Simone and Penelope on her heels. "He's in police custody at the present time. He's under my protection. Do you understand me, Mr. Jaeger?"

"I'd like to see you try and stop me!" Aaron yelled, as he lunged towards her.

"Aaron, do you remember what you promised me?" Dr. Chandler asked stepping between them and pressing her hand against his chest. Aaron couldn't stop quickly enough and pushed her backwards several steps as he advanced. He towered over her, seething. Dr. Chandler looked at Sylvester, who pulled the syringe out of his pocket.

"I don't care! I'm gonna kill that motherfucker. Look at what he's done to Jason! That fucking bastard! That fucking bastard!"

"Aaron, if you don't stop this this very minute, I'm going to have you sedated!" Dr. Chandler retorted. "I'm not kidding about that."

"Mr. Jaeger." Inspector Addison stepped next to Dr. Chandler, standing nearly chest to chest with him, bracing her body and gripping her hips with her hands. "You listen to me, Mr. Jaeger. All indications are he's brain dead. He's not expected to last out the day. Do you understand me, Mr. Jaeger? He's not expected to last out the day. There's nothing for you to do. He's dead already."

Aaron's shoulders fell as crumbled in on himself and began to cry. "That bastard! What he did to my Jason. He'll rot in hell for that. He'll burn in hell for all eternity!"

"Come on, big guy," Inspector Addison said as she patted Aaron's shoulder. "Why don't you have a seat and calm down. He's a dead man, Aaron. He's a dead man. There's nothing left for you to do."

"Jason," Aaron sobbed. He crawled on the bed next to Jason and wept.

Chapter Thirty-Six
On a Loop

10:40 AM

"Aaron, would you be willing to identify him for us?" Inspector Addison asked. "I don't believe Jason could safely travel to his room right now."

Dr. Tunisia confirmed the inspector's statement by shaking his head, "No."

"Yes, I'll do it," Aaron answered.

"Thank you. So this is how it's going to go. "We'll walk to his room, all of us together."

"No," Dr. Chandler said firmly. "He'll be wheeled to the room."

"Very well. Then you'll look through the glass. You will not try to enter the room, do you understand me?"

"Yes, Inspector, I will not do anything to him."

"You will then tell me whether he is the man you saw attacking your partner, Jason Ackerman. That's it. That's all of it."

"Yes, Inspector."

"Good. Let's go."

Aaron walked to Jason and kissed him on the lips. Jason pulled him down and hugged him. "I'll be right here when you get back."

****

10:45 AM
Neuro Intensive Care Unit

It was an entourage. Sylvester, followed by Drs. Chandler and Spencer, Claudia, Simone, and Penelope, and Chief Inspector Addison, wheeled Aaron to room N-610. Two state troopers stood guard, one in the room and the other outside the door. "Mr. Jaeger, is this the man you saw attacking your partner, Jason Ackerman? Yes or no?"

Aaron looked closely at the bandaged face. He tried and tried to remember what he's seen in the matter of only a few seconds. "Is this the man, Mr. Jaeger?"

After several moments, all the rage, all the pain, all the revenge slipped from Aaron as if they were grains of sand in his open palm. Aaron answered. "Inspector, I don't know. I can't be sure. I can't tell you what you want to hear, but I believe you when you say this is the man from the barn. This man's face is so swollen, and his head is wrapped up. He looks nothing like the man I saw that night. The man I saw was a beast. He was thick in the face. His eyes were evil, and he had long, stringy hair. Ma'am, I don't know. I just don't know."

"Thank you, Aaron. That's all I need from you."

"I can keep looking, ma'am."

"No, that won't be necessary. Thank you for trying."

Dr. Chandler remained behind.

****

10:55 AM

Room S-644

Inspector Addison held her phone tightly in her hand. "Mr. Ackerman, I know you've been through a lot, but I must ask you whether you feel up to identifying the man who was recovered from your barn last evening. I have his image here on my phone. It was taken just a few moments ago."

"Yes, Inspector. I can look at it."

Jason stared at the image of the man who tried to rape him, who threatened to kill his beloved Aaron and his friends, Rod and Jack, who'd shot Jasper, and who, nearly nineteen years ago, accused him of the most heinous of crimes.

"Yes, Inspector Addison. That is Calvin Garrison,

whom I first met as a corporal in the Unites States Army on January 17, 1991. He is the man who tried to rape me and threatened to kill me, Aaron, Rod, and Jack in my barn two days ago."

****

10:58 AM
Room N-610

From the moment he was kicked in the head by Nellie and Sarah, deep in the recesses of Calvin's mind the same scenario played on a loop:

Motionless. Baby across my lap, locked and loaded, itching to see action.

Unfinished business.

"Enjoy your dinner. It'll be your last."

"Hello there, Corpsman. Long time no see."

"Don't make a sound. I'm just here for you."

"You hurt my feelings, Corpsman."

"Remember that intimate moment we almost shared?"

"You ruined my life and my career!"

"Bingo!"

"Because of you, I was ruined. It's all your fault!"

"I'm no fag!"

"Who am I to turn down a good nut bust?"

"What the fuck does it matter?"

"Show me a good time, Ackerman."

"Show me a good time while I'm pounding your ass."

"It's tougher when they squirm."

"You want it, don't you? Don't you!"

"What the fuck!"

"My cock! My cock!"

"You fucking faggot! You broke my cock!"

Squeeze the trigger!

Kill the faggot!

Kill the faggot!
Kill!
Kill!
Kill!
"My face!"
"Pain!"
A flash!

****

11:00 AM
Room S-644
"Good morning, guys! How was your night?"
"Braden," Jason whispered as he opened his eyes.
"Braden," Aaron said, as he lifted his arm from Jason's side.

The tension and sadness in the room was overwhelming as Braden walked to Jason's bedside. From the looks on their faces, he realized something was wrong.

"What's happened?" What's happened to you two?" He put one hand on Jason's shoulder and the other on Aaron's back. "What in the world has happened?"

Reggie, Sylvester, and Zaim, Jason's new nurse, quietly came into the room.

"Jason," Reggie said softly, "I'll be leaving now. Zaim is taking over. Take care of yourselves, both of you. I'll keep you in my thoughts."

"Do you need anything, Jason?" Zaim asked quietly.

Jason shook his head and mouthed, "No."

"We'll leave you guys alone," Zaim whispered, "but don't hesitate to call if you need anything. Anything at all."

"We'll be right outside, Aaron," Sylvester said. Aaron nodded and then cradled himself against Jason's left side.

Sylvester nodded back. Before he followed Zaim out, he whispered to Braden, "Don't bother yourself with anything, Braden. You just focus on helping them. Zaim and I will take care of everything else."

****

11:05 AM
Room N-610

"He's completely herniated," Dr. Chandler said out loud to everyone in room N-610.

"What does that mean, Doctor?" Inspector Addison asked.

"It means that he was developing a cerebellar tonsillar herniation. We identified cerebral edema on his first CT scan and feared he was heading in that direction. His most recent CT indicated it was imminent, even though we've been giving him the appropriate drugs and treatments to decrease the swelling. We knew full well that all the drugs in the world weren't going to do squat, but we gave them anyway.

"The damage to his brain from the initial injury was just too extensive and had gone on for too long without treatment. We've been monitoring Aaron for the same kind of swelling because of his head injury."

"Yes, Doctor, but you still haven't told me what that means."

"I'm sorry, Inspector, I forget sometimes that all people aren't physicians. It means that his cerebrum, the main brain, the part that make you you and me me and his cerebellum or hindbrain, the part that controls balance, equilibrium, coordination, muscle movement and tone have been shifted by the swelling so much, that they've pressed against his reptilian or primitive brain, the brain that controls breathing, heart rate, blood pressure and so on, basically squishing it and cutting off its blood supply. There's nothing more to be done."

"I'm sorry, Doctor," Inspector Addison said, "but you must try. He is a ward of the state and under my guardianship."

"I understand, Inspector, but there really is nothing to be done. I don't believe he will survive the hour."

"Try anyway, Doctor."

"Very well, Inspector."

****

11:10 AM

The loop that had played over and over again in Calvin Garrison's brain faded to black.

Overhead the operator paged, "Code Blue, room N-610. Code Blue, room N-610. Code Blue, room N-610."

****

11:28 AM

Room N-610, bedside

"Stop compressions," Dr. Chandler ordered as she shined a flashlight into the former Corporal Calvin Garrison's eyes to check his pupils. Next, she placed her fingers against the carotid artery in his neck as she watched the wall clock for sixty seconds while simultaneously listening to his chest with her stethoscope. As she leaned away and returned the stethoscope to her lab coat, she announced to the room, "Pupils fixed and dilated, absent carotid pulse, silent chest with no breath or heart sounds. Time of death, 11:29 AM."

Chapter Thirty-Seven
Conrad

2:15 PM
Administrative Wing, Office of the CEO

"How can I help you sir? I'm Simone Jones, Chief Operating Officer of Hinnen Valley Medical Center," she asked as she walked around her desk. "You can remain just outside the door, but leave it open," she directed to a security guard.

"Good afternoon, miss?"

"It's Ms., but that's okay. What can I do for you? I was told you wanted to see one of our patients."

"Yes, Ms. Jones, I'm Conrad Tolbert. I'm an old friend of Jason Ackerman. I was a physician in the Emergency Department where he worked after he was discharged from the army. I saw Jason on a news broadcast where I was vacationing for the holidays. I heard what they'd said about a homicide, and he looked hypoxic in the video so I dropped everything and headed here. On my way, I checked in with my service. They said I'd received multiple messages from Claudia Duncan. I know she's Jason's attorney."

"Do you have any identification with you, Doctor?"

"ID? Well, yes. What on earth has happened to Jason? All the extra security just seems so out of sorts."

"I'm sorry, Doctor, but before I can do or say anything, I need to see some form of identification."

"Here's my driver's license and my medical license wallet card."

"Thank you, Doctor." Simone looked at the documents and then handed it back. "You're on the list of approved visitors, but I had to be certain it was you. I can tell you now that this has been a very difficult experience for Jason and his partner, Aaron."

"Partner? Do you mean partner as in a life-partner? Jason's found someone? That's wonderful! I haven't heard from him since the summer, so this must all be recent."

"I'm not aware of the specifics, and it's none of my business, but yes, I believe from what's been said to me, it is recent."

"So, can I see him now?"

"Yes, of course. I'll escort you there myself."

****

2:30 PM
Room S-644

"Excuse me, Aaron, Jason," Simone said as she knocked on the doorway. "There's someone here to see you, Jason."

"Hello there, my boy," Conrad said as he walked into the room. "I came the moment I heard."

"Conrad!" Jason whispered hoarsely. "It's really you!"

****

3:07 PM

A spit and polish volunteer escort with carrot-red hair and apple-red lipstick announced herself while she read from a paper as she walked into the room, pushing a wheelchair.

"Mr. Jaeger, I'm Dorothy. We've got to get you down for your EEG right away. I've been told they're holding the machine for you right now and not to dawdle."

Dorothy stopped in her tracks. A confused look appeared on her face, as she raised her head from the paper in her hand. "I'm sorry, I don't understand," she said noting the two male patients lying next to each other on the two hospital beds that were pushed together.

"Hi, Dorothy," Braden said as he hurried in, followed by Sylvester. "What brings you up here this afternoon?"

Sylvester walked to Aaron's bed.

"Can't they do it up here?" Aaron said to Sylvester before Braden could continue. "We've had a hell of a day, and it's only half over."

"I'm sorry, I'm confused," Dorothy said, "I don't know anything about that, sir. I only have my orders, but is one of you Mr. Jaeger?"

Conrad got up from the chair next to the bed. "I'll just excuse myself and go have a look at your charts while this gets sorted out."

Dorothy turned to Braden. "I'm supposed to get a Mr. Jaeger down for his EEG, but I don't understand. Did I come to the wrong room? Is one of these men Mr. Jaeger?"

"Special circumstances, Dorothy," Sylvester answered, and then he turned to Aaron. "Aaron, Sonya is coming on now. I'll be going off duty as soon as I've given her report so if I don't see you before I leave, I want you to know that I'll be back at 3 AM. You take care of yourself and do what they ask of you, okay?

"Yes, Sylvester, I promise to be good."

"Good." Sylvester patted Aaron's shoulder. "I'll see you later then."

Sylvester turned to Dorothy. "May I speak with you out in the hall for a moment?"

After Sylvester explained the circumstances surrounding Aaron and Jason's special arrangement, Dorothy returned to the room a minute later, still a little bewildered, but she covered it well.

"Braden, I'm supposed to transport Mr. Jaeger down for his EEG. My orders are to get him down there right away." Dorothy opened the foot pedals and locked the wheels. "Now if you will, Mr. Jaeger."

"Um, Dorothy, let's wait just a moment so I can check with Dr. Chandler. She was on the unit a little while ago, and she never mentioned anything about Aaron going for an EEG this afternoon. I'll be right back."

"Okay, Braden, but I'm going to have to call the department and tell them there's going to be a delay. They're not going to be happy about it, seeing as they're holding the machine."

****

3:12 PM

"Aaron," Braden said as he reentered the room. "Dr. Chandler is coming right up, but she doesn't want to delay your EEG any longer. She said she'll explain when she gets here."

"Just go with them, Aaron," Jason whispered. "I'll be fine."

Dorothy moved the wheelchair next to Aaron's bed and grasped his arm as he stood up. Aaron towered over the five foot zero inch Dorothy. He chuckled. "Do you really think you could catch me if I fall?"

"I'm stronger than I look, Mr. Jaeger," Dorothy said with a smile and a twinkle in her eye, "and besides, it's hospital policy."

"Aaron, stop giving this nice lady a hard time and cooperate." Jason managed to force the words out, but there was also a tinge of annoyance in them.

"I don't like leaving you alone, Jason," he answered. "And I'm sorry, Miss Dorothy, I meant no disrespect."

"None taken," she answered as she buckled his seatbelt and unlocked the wheels.

"Oh, I'm glad I caught you," Dr. Chandler said from the doorway with Zaim, and Sonya behind her.

"Aaron, we talked about your EEG yesterday. Because of that business with the state police, I had to have the test rescheduled and now is the time to go. Do you understand?"

"Yes, Doctor. I just don't feel comfortable leaving Jason alone."

"Jason will be just fine. Look at all the people in here right now. He's got Braden and these two critical-care nurses. I think they can handle him without your supervision for the next few hours."

"A few hours?" Aaron lifted his feet off the wheelchair's pedals and braced them against the floor. "You said it would take only one hour."

"Yes, Aaron, I did, but they have to get you to the department, prep your head, explain the test and review the instructions with you, do the test, disconnect you from the machine, clean you up, and then bring you back here. It'll take about two hours, but it'll be over before you know it. Now be a good team player and go with the volunteer."

"Yes, ma'am."

"Can he go unmonitored, Dr. Chandler?" Braden asked. "I could put a telemetry module on him if you like."

"You go right ahead and do that, but I think he'll be fine."

After Braden had attached the leads for the module and checked to be sure it was working Aaron looked up at Dorothy. "Can we race?"

"Vroom, vroom," she mimicked with a smile on her face, "Now hold on to your hat." As they rolled through the ICU's doors and disappeared down the hall, Dorothy made sounds like tires squealing. It was the first time Aaron had smiled in the past forty-eight, and then he laughed.

"He laughed," Jason croaked to the room. "My Aaron laughed!"

****

3:45 PM
EEG Lab

"Okay, Mr. Jaeger," the EEG tech said through the intercom from the observation room. "I'm going to turn the lights down. Like I told you, please close your eyes now."

After obtaining multiple baseline readings, the tech's voice came over the speaker again. "Mr. Jaeger."

Aaron was softly snoring.

"Um, Mr. Jaeger, please wake up."

"I'm awake! I'm awake!"

"Good, now open your eyes and look at the monitor over the exam table. Please do the math calculation and give me the answer."

"Seven plus six is thirteen."

"And the next?"

"Fourteen minus six is eight."

"Very good, Mr. Jaeger. Now please read the paragraph."

"While walking to the mailbox, Sarah noticed shrill chirping coming from a tree above her head. She realized the sound she heard came from baby birds. The cardinal's eggs were hatching…"

Chapter Thirty-Eight
When Aaron Smiles

6:05 PM
Room S-644

Dorothy made the screeching sound of brakes as Aaron's wheelchair came to a stop. Aaron's smile extended from ear to ear.

"You light up the room when you smile," Jason whispered, smiling himself.

"Welcome back, my boy," Conrad said. "We've been talking about nothing but you since you left."

"I guess that's a good thing?" Aaron answered. "I had a nice nap during my EEG, Jason. They were very nice to me."

"Glad to hear it," Jason whispered.

"Now here you go, Aaron," Dorothy said, resting her hand on Aaron's shoulder as she leaned over to lock the brakes. Aaron began to climb out of the wheelchair, but he was held back by the seatbelt. "Just a minute, Aaron. Let me unbuckle you."

After Aaron was sitting on the side of the bed, he said, while taking Dorothy's hand. "Thank you, my lady. You were a wonderful driver." He smiled into her eyes and leaned down to kiss the back of her hand.

"My pleasure, kind sir." Dorothy curtsied, then blushed and smiled wistfully. Her face radiated warmth, and her eyes glowed with understanding. "I wish you all the best, Aaron, all the best, and you, too, Mr. Ackerman." Then she unlocked the brakes and pushed the wheelchair out of the room.

"So I guess you know all about me, Conrad," Aaron said as he lifted Jason's hand and kissed his palm.

"Oh, my boy, I'm sure there's much more to learn, but I know enough to know for sure that Jason has found his soulmate. I'm grateful, Aaron, really grateful that the two of you found one another. Now I know I won't have to worry about him anymore."

"I think you've got it backwards, Conrad," Aaron answered, squeezing Jason's hand, "We didn't find one another. Jason is the one who found me and then saved me." He drew Jason's palm to his cheek and closed his eyes briefly.

"There's more than one way to be saved, Aaron." Conrad patted Aaron's shoulder. "Now that Aaron's back, Jason, let's talk about the future. What do you need me to do?"

"I'm not at a hundred percent yet, Conrad," he croaked, "and I'm still a bit fuzzy, but I do know now that I want you to be part of our future, whatever that may become. Aaron," Jason whispered, "would you tell Conrad about Nathan's Promise? I need to rest my voice."

"Hello, Aaron," Braden said as he carried in his dinner tray. "This just arrived from the kitchen for you. Are you hungry?"

"Starved. What is it?"

"Surf and turf. Lobster tail and filet mignon with béarnaise and asparagus with hollandaise," he said, removing the sterling silver, domed cover. "There's also a real baked potato—not nuked, baked—and there's steamed yellow squash with an Italian dressing and carrot cake for dessert. Interested?"

"I'll wait until Jason's dinner arrives. Does the smell of this bother you, Jason?"

Jason's words were clipped. "No. I ate. Clear liquids, then soft. Yum. Meat. Potatoes. Carrots. All pureed and mashed. Then tapioca pudding."

"Okay, Braden," Aaron answered, "The truth is, I'd be happy with a bowl of Jason's chicken soup right now, but sure, the food sounds great. I wasn't supposed to eat too many of those French sauces when I was on the team, but I do like them."

"You go ahead and eat, my boy," Conrad said. "You can fill me in on Nathan's Promise later.

"Okay, I'll eat it now 'coz it's hot, but as soon as I'm finished, I need to take a shower. Then we can talk about Nathan's Promise."

****

7:30 PM

While Aaron was explaining Nathan's Promise to Conrad, Claudia and Winston came into the room. "You must be Dr. Tolbert. I'm Claudia Duncan, Jason and Aaron's attorney, and this is Winston Tanner, their financial manager."

"Nice to meet you both," Conrad answered, shaking their hands. "I'm just being briefed on this project of theirs by Aaron here, this Nathan's Promise, and Jason says he wants me involved. It sounds like they're going to need a lot of help pulling the whole thing off."

"Yes, sir, they will," Winston answered. "I've heard a lot about you over the years from Jason, and I think you could be a real asset to the whole operation, that is, if you're interested."

"If Jason needs me, I'm there. I have no further commitments so I just need someone to tell me where to unpack my bag, and I'm ready to go."

"That's great, Dr. Tolbert," Winston said.

"Please, it's Conrad. I've been keeping myself busy these past, some fifteen years by volunteering at various clinics around the country and the globe, going wherever I'm needed, but I'm ready to put down some roots. That is if you really think this is something that's going to take a few years to reach fruition."

"I'm sorry, Conrad," Jason said, his voice still quite hoarse, "for not making myself more clear. I want you as the medical director for the whole organization. Can you do it? Are you willing to do it?"

"Sounds interesting, Jason, but give me some time to learn about what it's going to involve. I want to be sure I'm up to the task before I say yes. I wouldn't want to do a poor job for you if I'm not. Regardless, anything you need in the short term, I'll be happy to help, but I'll need to know a whole lot more about this rehab center before I'll know whether I can be effective."

"The thing is, Conrad," Aaron said, "we don't know just yet. We were just beginning to formulate our plans when Jason was attacked." Aaron paused and swallowed as his memories of seeing Jason tied naked to the table in the barn returned. "Sorry." His eyes began to tear, but he wiped them away.

Aaron cleared his throat. "I think for just the next few weeks, I'd like to ask that you just hang around, talk to everyone involved. Jason told me you were the director of an ER. We're going to need so much just for ourselves right now, even before we begin to formulate our plans for Nathan's Promise. We have no idea where we're even going to start."

"I have an idea," Claudia said. "Why don't I put Conrad in touch with Rod and Jack? Maybe have them fly him up there so he can see what you have and what the terrain is like. I think Conrad could be very helpful to them. They're just breaking ground with everything so now would be the time to get him involved."

"Great idea, Claudia," Aaron said. "We'll leave it to all of you to put it in motion, but I want you to keep me in the loop."

The conversation continued, but after a few more minutes, Braden could tell that both Jason and Aaron were becoming fatigued.

"Okay, everyone," he announced, "that's enough for tonight. They've both been through hell today, and it's time for them to get some rest."

"Good idea, Braden," Conrad said. "I'll find a place where I can talk a little more with Claudia and Winston and then I'll go check into my hotel. We can get started with whatever we come up with bright and early tomorrow morning."

"Doctor," Claudia said. "You won't need a hotel. When I found out you were here, I made arrangements with Simone Jones, the hospital's CEO. A suite has been prepared for you upstairs on the seventh floor, next to Winston's and mine. It's all been arranged. That way you won't be wasting precious time with unnecessary travel back and forth to the hospital."

"Then it's settled. I'll talk again with you boys tomorrow. Now get some rest." Conrad patted them both on the shoulders and then left with Claudia and Winston.

After they'd left, Braden lowered the room lights and pulled the curtain around the beds. "How about a little massage to help you guys drift off to sleep?" Braden asked them. "I'm also a licensed therapist."

"Oh my God," Aaron sighed, "a massage. I could sure use one. How about you, Jason?"

"Sure. Do you think it would help? At this point, I'll try anything to help me relax."

"Yes, I do, Jason," Braden said.

"Start with Jason, Braden," Aaron said, "He needs it way more than me."

"What do I do, Braden?" Jason asked.

"Just lie there and let me know if I do anything that's uncomfortable, but I'm definitely going to avoid your surgical sites for the time being. Are there any other areas you want me to avoid?"

"Not that I can think of, Braden, but I'll let you know."

"Are you ticklish?" Braden asked.

"No. Not at all."

"Okay, it would work better if you were lying on your back and your belly, but I want you to be comfortable. I can do it with you like you are, propped partway on your side. I just won't be able to work all the areas as well."

"I'll can roll onto my back. Just take the pillows away."

"I think instead I'll go get Zaim to help me position you and pull the beds apart. I'll be right back."

Chapter Thirty-Nine
Braden's Hands of Gold

7:47 PM

Within just a few moments, Jason began to sigh under the ministrations of Braden's skilled hands while Zaim held onto the chest tube and supported him, turned almost all the way onto his right side, while Braden massaged his back, avoiding the abrasions and scratches, his right shoulder, and below the dressing near his right scapula. When Zaim noticed tears begin to fall down his cheeks, he pointed them out to Braden. Braden stopped.

"Am I hurting you, Jason?"

Jason didn't answer at first. Then, he finally whispered, "No, Braden, not at all. You've got hands of gold. It's wonderful what you're doing. I've never felt anything like this before. Every place you touch me, I feel like my body is melting. It's like I have been bound tight by ropes, but now they're falling away. There's no more tension. It's wonderful, Braden. Thank you."

"Okay, I'll keep going then, but stop me if I do anything that hurts or that you don't like."

"Is it okay if I touch him while you work, Braden?" Aaron asked.

"I don't see why not, Aaron, but I'd suggest you just hold his hand. That way you won't block me or Zaim."

"Sure, sure, whatever you say." Aaron walked around the bed and took Jason's hand.

As Zaim slowly rolled Jason onto his back, Braden moved to his chest.

Zaim leaned over and whispered, "Whatever you're doing, Braden, keep it up. His heart rate and blood pressure are way down, and his breathing has slowed considerably. Even the narcotics we've been giving him haven't relaxed him this much."

Braden nodded as he scooped some massage cream into his hands and began to gently work it into Jason's well-developed pecs, avoiding the surgical wound at his right upper chest.

Jason moaned and signed. "Oh, oh, so good, Braden. So very good. Thank you."

"You don't have to thank me, Jason."

"Yes, I do. You have no idea what's happening, what you're doing for me."

Through Braden's touch and the residual narcotics that were still in his system, Jason began let go of all the emotions and memories he'd kept under tight control. As Braden continued, Jason began to access the deepest of his buried pains. Years of torment and hidden disappointments, regrets, and guilts were freed from their bonds, and he began to weep.

"Jason, are you all right?" Aaron asked.

"Yes, Aaron. So much pain. So much pain I've held inside. Don't stop, Braden."

Braden had seen this before. Before he became a nurse, Braden had worked full-time in a five-person massage therapy office. Occasionally, he would have a client on his table who would begin to weep. After their sessions, they would admit to him their buried memories, that they'd become unearthed, and that the healing effects of his technique were more than physical.

Braden recognized that Jason was now in a very vulnerable emotional state and knew he would have to proceed carefully. There was a possibility that when he moved to below Jason's waist, Jason may react in a way that was not intended to happen. He would watch closely and stop if things started moving in that direction.

Braden scooped up more of the cream and began to work in into Jason's extensively developed abdominal muscles. He watched the sheet that covered his groin for any reaction, but none ever developed.

When Jason began to sigh again, Braden spoke up. "Jason, I think that this has become an emotional experience for you as much as a physical one."

His tears now drying, Jason answered. "Yes, Braden. How did you know?"

"It's happened to a lot of people, especially when they're very vulnerable as you are now and have experienced a lot of pain, as you have. I want to be sure that you're still okay."

"Yes, Braden, I'm fine."

"Then I'll keep going."

Braden moved to Jason's legs, being sure to avoid the abrasions and rope burns around his ankles. With long sure strokes, he massaged deep into the muscles of Jason's calves, first one, then the other.

When Jason began to murmur softly, Aaron caressed his face while he whispered into his ear. A smile spread across Jason's face, and he turned his face towards Aaron. Aaron nuzzled Jason's neck and kissed him softly on the cheeks and forehead.

By the time Braden had finished Jason's calves, Jason was snoring softly. Aaron looked down at Braden and mouthed, "keep going," so he began to work Jason's thighs, beginning by gently and slowly running his hands up and down their lengths to spread out the lubricating cream. As the muscles relaxed he grasped and lifted each muscle group and began to knead them.

Jason exhaled slowly as the muscles slid from Braden's grip when he released them. After Braden began to massage Jason's feet, Zaim commented on Jason's eye movements under his lids. "He's in REM sleep now, Braden," Zaim whispered. "Your technique is incredible."

Braden finished by massaging Jason's hands. Beginning with the left, he massaged cream around and in between each finger and used his thumbs to press deeply into the muscles of his palm so effectively that he could feel the bones of Jason's hand move slightly beneath them when the muscles began to relax. When soft moans began to rise from deep within Jason's chest, Braden knew he had achieved his goal, total relaxation.

After walking around the bed to do Jason's right hand, Braden lowered it to the bed and then pulled the sheet up over him.

Aaron smiled and nodded at him, mouthing the words, "Thank you."

"I'm good now, Zaim. Thanks for your help."

"Any time, Braden," he whispered. "You should teach that to all the nurses in the hospital. It would sure cut down on the amount of narcotics and sleep meds we'd have to administer."

"Maybe I'll talk to the VP of nursing about it. We'll see."

Zaim walked around the curtain and then closed the door behind him. Braden looked at Aaron. "Your turn, big guy. Why don't you lie down on your bed and let me have a go at you?"

"Thanks, Braden," Aaron whispered. "I would love a massage, if you're still up to it."

"Absolutely. Lie on your belly and scoot over to the left edge of the bed. I'll give you a massage that will focus mostly on your back in order to help you to relax enough so that you can fall asleep. How does that sound?"

"Sounds great. Thanks."

After carrying the jar of massage cream and a few towels to Aaron's bed, Braden began. With slow, strong strokes, he glided up and down Aaron's back, shoulders, and waist, kneading, lifting, and pressing his muscles into submission. Aaron became so relaxed that his left arm dropped from the bed and hung down the side. His breathing slowed, and a puddle of drool began to form on the bedsheet.

When Braden focused his hands around the lowest part of the lumbar region of Aaron's back and across the top of Aaron's buttocks, Aaron began to sigh. "Are you okay, Aaron?"

"Yes, Braden. Thanks. It just feels real good. Your hands. They're like magic."

Braden moved on to Aaron's thighs and then after finishing with his calves, he asked, "Aaron, are you ticklish in the feet?"

"A little, but it's never happened when the trainers were working them. They were using too much pressure. It's only when someone's trying to tickle me that it happens."

"Okay, then I'll do them, too. It can be very relaxing."

As Braden began to press into the soles of Aaron's feet, Aaron vocalized what he was feeling.

"Oh. Oh. Oh my God, Braden, that's so good. Oh, my God, it's wonderful."

"Just close your eyes, Aaron. Maybe you'll fall asleep."

By the time he'd finished, Aaron was snoring softly. Braden gently shook his shoulder. "Aaron, wake up and roll onto your back so I can finish."

"Mmmm, Braden. I'm so relaxed. Can't I stay like this?"

"No, sorry, big guy. Sonya and I are gonna need to access your IV through the night, and we won't be able to reach it with you on your belly."

"Okay, I'm moving."

Once Aaron was on his back, Braden began to massage his hands like he had done Jason's.

"Aren't you going to do my pecs and abdominals?"

"They're something I normally do with one of my therapeutic massages, but my goal with you is to get you to sleep." Braden answered as he noted the bulge at Aaron's groin. It appeared to be growing second by second. He was not prepared to deal with the consequences if they occurred. "Do you really need them done, Aaron?" he asked, as his voice squeaked a little. He cleared his throat.

"No, not really, but it would be nice."

"How about we save them for next time?" he answered, relieved that Aaron wasn't pushing for it.

"Okay."

By the time Braden had finished, Aaron was fast asleep. As he moved from behind the curtain to leave the room, Sonya was opening the door to come in.

"I don't know what you did, Braden," she whispered, "but all his vitals are down to the low normals."

"Yeah," he answered, "I don't think he'll need any sedatives tonight. He's out cold. Would you mind helping me push the beds back together?"

"Not at all."

****

When Braden and Sonya returned a while later, they found Aaron with his left arm and leg draped over top of Jason, with a body pillow between them, his right arm behind his neck, and his face nuzzled against Jason's cheek. Jason's left hand was draped over Aaron's biceps and his right hand rested in the crook above his forearm. The two of them were sleeping peacefully in an embrace of the purest form of love that either Braden or Sonya had witnessed in a very long time.

Chapter Forty
Just Tired

December 25, 2009, 7:55 AM

"Good morning, you two," Conrad said as he walked into the room. "How was your night?"

"It was great, Conrad," Aaron said. "Jason and I slept like babies after Braden's massages. I can't remember the last time I slept so good."

"Right," Jason said with a hoarse voice.

"You're sounding a tad bit better there, Jason," Conrad said. "How's the throat?"

"A little better. Thanks."

"Winston and Claudia will be here in a few minutes. They were going to stop by Ms. Jones's office before coming down to see you. Something about providing meals and refreshments for meetings we'll be having."

"Good," Jason whispered. "Wait, isn't it Christmas?"

"Yes, it is."

"Simone is here? Today?"

"Yes. Apparently, Miss Jones has made it clear that she's available whenever we need her."

"She doesn't have to do that."

"Not my business, Jason."

"Did you speak with Rod or Jack?" Aaron asked.

"Yes, Aaron, last night, briefly. I'll be flying up there tomorrow morning. Rod said he'd be spending today with his sister."

"That's right. He did say that. God, that seems like months ago."

"Time has a way of becoming distorted at times like this, Jason."

"I guess." Jason stared off into space.

"You still with me, Jason?" Conrad asked.

"Yes. Sure. Sorry."

"So anyway, Claudia has hired a service to supply us with a car or van service, depending on how many people will need transportation. They'll be available around the clock to schlep us back and forth to the airport or around town."

"That was smart. Any word on progress up there?" Jason whispered. "Sorry, my voice is failing."

"That's okay. I really don't know much of what's being done, Jason. Claudia said she'd brief you this morning."

"I can't wait to get out of here. I'm getting antsy, but I'm still so tired, like someone's sucked the life-force out or me."

"Jason, my boy," Conrad said, "you've just had major thoracic surgery. You'll not be going anywhere for a while yet, but I don't hear your underwater seal chest drainage bubbling. When did they turn it off?"

"Just this morning, Conrad," Aaron answered for him. "He's on trial right now to see how he does. Dr. Baum turned off the suction when he made his rounds, first thing this morning. He said they'll decide when the chest tube will come out, depending on whether he remains stable with it off."

"Then you're moving in the right direction, Jason, but remember, I'm here only as a friend and advisor and as an advocate if need be right now. I'm not part of your treatment team."

"I know, Conrad, I just feel like something's off."

"Well you two are certainly looking better," Winston said as he and Claudia walked in together, with Simone right behind.

"Feel better, some," Jason whispered.

"Jason," Claudia began. "Simone has arranged

for the hospital to take care of meeting space, meals, and refreshments for us while we're here. A suite on the seventh floor is being converted as we speak. She's been bending over backwards to be accommodating. It's going to be a big help."

"It's the least I can do," Simone said.

"Thank you, Simone," Aaron answered for Jason, "and thank you for coming in on Christmas Day."

"It's nothing, Aaron, really."

"Here's what's happened so far," Claudia continued. "Rod has hired a company that produces pre-fab buildings to provide the housing units and the construction company they subcontract with on a regular basis to install them and do all the electric, heating, and plumbing connections. They supply units for vacation resorts. They're like one story cottages. He's also contacted the architect and construction company that built your cabin and the other structures on your property to be there to help them to get everything hooked up. Do you think you both will be up to a meeting with everyone so they can present their plans sometime after you're transferred out of the ICU?"

"I think so," Jason whispered.

Aaron nodded.

"Excuse me," Conrad interrupted. "I think you should run anything like that by their treatment teams before you schedule anything, Claudia. Jason's has just had major surgery, and Aaron is recovering from a severe concussion. All the best intentions aside, those kinds of meetings can be very taxing. Everyone involved should be mindful of their limitations before they're asked to attend any such meetings."

"Point taken, Conrad," Claudia said.

"Claudia," Jason whispered as he raised the head of his bed and pushed himself up, "Conrad's right, and we've already been over this. I trust those I've put in charge to get done what needs to get done."

"Jason," Braden said as he moved to the bed while looking at the monitor and then feeling his radial pulse, "are you okay? Your heart rate has nearly doubled."

"I'm okay, Braden." Jason waved him away. "I'm just tired."

He turned back to Claudia. "Have Rod come here tomorrow when he flies down to pick up Conrad. Aaron and I'll give instructions to you and Winston, and Conrad and Rod then. Don't count on me for any long meetings. You can work it out amongst yourselves either down here or up there, it's up to you. If Aaron's up to attending that's fine, but for right now, I'm focusing on healing and getting the hell out of here A-SAP. I'm done talking." Jason closed his eyes and lowered the head of his bed.

"I think we have our answer, Winston said.

"If Jason hadn't spoken up," Conrad said, "I would have. I'm sorry, Claudia, but I don't think either of you understand just how significant his surgery was or what his recovery is going to be like. He's not going to be the same Jason with the same drive you've known for years. Not for quite some time yet."

With that, everyone said their goodbyes and then left the room.

Chapter Forty-One
Pulmonary Consolidation

December 26, 2009, 9:25 AM

"Hello, Jason, Aaron," Rod said as he walked into their room. Claudia, Winston, Conrad, and Simone followed. "Are you strong enough to talk?"

"Sure, Rod."

"Tell me what you want, and I'll get it done."

"You know how to do this," Jason said, slowly, "I want housing for ... I want ten housing units, including enough for security. If you think ... if you think more will be needed, get them. I want an ... I want an office for me and Aaron ... and I want a large ... meeting room." Jason stopped to catch his breath.

"I want as much as possible to be solar ... with propane ... for cooking and as a backup ... for hot water." Jason stopped again. "Braden ... please turn up my ... oxygen."

Braden came to Jason's side. "Jason, you need to stop. Let me listen to your lungs."

"No! Sorry, Braden, I didn't mean ... I didn't mean to shout. I've got to get this ... get this done."

"Okay, Jason," Braden increased the flow. "It's up."

After a moment, he began again. "If we're going to need a bigger generator get it ...and enough diesel to keep it running for ... for a month at a time. I want ... I want someone in the house to run it ... and cook for me and Aaron ... and for all the staff ... think up to thirty ... thirty people and everything that that many ... that many people will need to live ... to live up there the whole time. I'm gonna need ... we're gonna need a personal ... personal assistant, like a valet for us, personally ... and a secretary for our office ... office work, too. Try to get people … people for Aaron and me to interview after we're out … out of here."

"Jason," Braden said, "take a break for a minute. You're tiring yourself out, your sat is dropping, and you're turning dusky. I need to listen to your lungs" He opened a non-rebreather oxygen mask and replaced Jason's nasal cannula with it, turning the flow up to fifteen liters.

"Okay, Braden. In a minute."

"Jason, what's wrong?" Aaron asked as he scooted to his knees on the bed and hovered over him."

"I'm so tired," Jason answered.

Claudia started to tear up. "Oh my God, Conrad," she whispered, grabbing his arm. "You were right."

Tears began to spill from Aaron's eyes. "I'm okay, Aaron," Jason whispered, as he patted his arm, "really."

"Jason, I could have lost you." Aaron began to cry. Through his tears he said, "Something's wrong. Tell me. That bullet … had it been off by a fraction … a fraction of an inch … it could have … it could have killed you." He moved tight up against Jason's side, "Oh, my Jason. I love you. I love you, Jason. I love you. Always."

"And I love you, Aaron," Jason said, patting his arm again.

By then, everyone in the room had tears in their eyes.

"Excuse me," Simone said, as she shook her head to clear it. Then she hurried to the nurses' station and snapped her fingers. "Sylvester, Reggie, get in there!" she said with intention. "Sabrina, page Dr. Fleischmann, STAT!" Then she grabbed a tissue and turned and walked towards the staff lounge. "I need a minute."

Sylvester and Reggie hurried into the room.

Braden shook his head at them and mouthed, "He's de-sating." Then he said aloud, "He was down to 91 on nasal at eight liters. I've got him up to 93 on a non-rebreather at fifteen."

"That's it," Sylvester said.

"This meeting is over," Reggie added.

"Everyone out." Sylvester pointed towards the door. "Everyone out! Now!"

Jason had the final word. "You all know what to do."

Overhead the operator paged, "Dr. Fleischmann STAT, Room S-644. Dr. Fleischmann STAT, Room S-644. Dr. Fleischmann STAT, Room S-644."

Reggie listened to all of Jason's lung fields with his stethoscope. "You got this for a minute?" he said to Braden and Sylvester. They nodded. "He's got no breath sounds in the right base, and he's diminished in the left. I'm paging Doctor Baum, too. Either his hemopneumothorax is back or he's developing pneumonia."

Conrad shook free of Claudia's grasp and hurried to Jason's bedside. "Let me borrow your stethoscope, Braden," he said as he lifted it from his shoulders, not waiting for an answer. Conrad listened to Jason's chest, nodded his head several times, and then percussed over all of Jason's lung fields. "I believe Reggie's right. He's going to need a STAT chest X-ray."

Overhead the operator paged, "Dr. Baum STAT, Room S-644. Dr. Baum STAT, Room S-644. Dr. Baum STAT, Room S-644."

****

December 27, 2009, 8:20 AM

"Hello, Aaron," Dr. Chandler said as she came to the bed.

Aaron mouthed, "Hi," then brought his index

finger to his lips. "He's sleeping," he mouthed again.

Dr. Chandler pointed to the door, indicating for Aaron to follow her. After he met her outside of the SICU room she walked him to the nurses' station and offered him a chair. "I'm sorry to hear about Jason. How's he doing? How are you doing?"

"According to Dr. Fleischmann, 'as to be expected'," he said with air quotes, "but I'm not exactly sure what that really means."

"It means exactly what he said. Look, Aaron, Jason isn't my patient, but you are, so whatever affects you, I'm concerned about, so I've made Jason my business."

"What do you mean?"

"It means that all of us on the medical staff are concerned about the both of you. Not only because of the fact that you've presented us with some challenges along the way…"

"Yeah, I'm sorry about that," Aaron offered. "Both of us in the room together must have created some real headaches for you all."

"Aaron, that's not what I was getting at. We've learned something from the two of you that we seem to have forgotten somewhere along the way, and that is that family and love are just as important to the wellbeing of patients as all of the medical care we can provide as physicians and the contraptions we hook you up to put together."

"Well, yeah."

"Well and simply put, Aaron. While I'm not directly involved in Jason's medical care, the team of us have decided to share information with each other about the both of you. What Dr. Fleischmann meant is that while Jason is very sick with pneumonia, he's doing okay. He's not back on the ventilator. That's saying a lot.

Just let him get all the rest he can."

"I will, Dr. Chandler. I promise."

"Good. Now for some good news. Your EEG is perfectly normal. There's no evidence of any functional abnormalities, which means we have no evidence that your brain was damaged by the impact when you struck your head in the barn, or even when you fell out of the sky, back in September."

"That's great, Doctor."

"Yes, it is, but that doesn't mean you're completely scot-free. You'll need to be careful from now on. We don't know enough yet about the long-term effects of repeated concussions. There's new evidence that suggests they can have a cumulative effect so I'm advising you to behave and not take any chances, and by that I mean for the rest of your life."

"I will, Doctor."

"Glad to hear it. Now get back in there and take care of your man." Then she smiled a huge smile.

Aaron leaned forward in his chair, wrapped his arms around her, and lifted her into a hug.

"Okay, Aaron. Put me down. You're going to give me a nosebleed all the way up here."

Aaron kissed her on the cheek and then lowered her to the floor. "You're the best, Dr. Chandler."

Section Five
The Road to Recovery

Chapter Forty-Two
Whatever It Takes

December 29, 2009, 8:15 AM
Suite 709, Jason and Aaron's new room

"Good morning, Jason. How are you feeling?"

"I'm feeling better, Dr. Tunisia. Not one-hundred percent, but better."

"I'm glad to hear it. You really skirted a bullet, no pun intended, on that one. I'm glad we didn't have to put you back on the ventilator or hook your chest tube back up to wall suction. How does the site feel, now that the tube's out?"

"It's sore, but at least it's out."

"I'm glad to hear it. How about you let me have a look and listen? Braden, give me a hand sitting him up."

"Uh huh, deep breath now," Dr. Tunisia said as he listened to the base of Jason's right lung. "Hmm … yes … uh huh. Another now please."

"Okay, Braden, let's ease him back down."

"How do I sound, Doctor?"

"Like you've still got some junk in there. I'm sure Dr. Fleischmann is going to continue your chest PT for a while yet."

"I'd bet on it," Braden added.

"Good. Well that's it for me, Jason."

"Thank you, Dr. Tunisia."

Dr. Tunisia hesitated.

"Is there something wrong, Doctor?" Jason asked.

"No. Nothing wrong, but if you have a moment, I have a question about something I wanted to clear up, that is if you're up to it. It's just a curiosity really."

"What's that?"

"Do you remember Judy, the anesthetist who put you to sleep?"

"Yes, why?"

"During your surgery, she noticed an indentation in your skull, in the occipital region. We've documented it in your medical record for accuracy's sake, but I'm wondering what caused it."

"When I was a kid, I fell through the floor of a haymow in an old barn and broke a few bones on the way down. I crashed through a wall that separated some stalls and that flipped me over. I landed with my head against an anvil, or so I'm told. I was knocked unconscious, so I don't remember it. I do remember falling though."

Aaron jumped up. "Oh my God, Jason. You never told me about that!"

"It wasn't important, Aaron. That was a long time ago. God, more than twenty years ago now."

"But still, you could have told me."

"I'm sure it would have eventually come up, Aaron. Remember, I was taking care of you. We've only just gotten back together. It wasn't a priority, and I don't think about it that often."

"I'm sorry," Dr. Tunisia interrupted. "A haymow?"

"Yeah, sorry. That's what we called it. It's a hayloft."

"Oh, I see. Did anything else happen to you?"

"Yes. I had a fractured left ulna and radius and right femur. I had an ORIF for the arm, and I was in skeletal traction for the femur for eight weeks. I'm so hairy that you can't see the scars unless you look real close. I also went into cardiac arrest on the way to the hospital, but they got me back, obviously."

"Cardiac arrest! Jason, your heart stopped?"

"Yes, Aaron, but I'm fine. I was sixteen at the time. I got a clean bill of health after it all."

"Oh my God, Jason!"

"Aaron, baby, I'm fine. I'm fine, really."

"Was there any residual damage?" Dr. Tunisia continued. "Any aftereffects from the head injury, like seizures? Persistent headaches? Anything?"

"No. Nothing. Never."

"Well thank you for telling me. That's quite a story. I'll be sure to add that information to your medical record. We did note the limb fractures and hardware on your CT scan, so now I think your medical record is complete."

After Dr. Tunisia left, Aaron climbed into bed with Jason and just held him.

****

9:45 AM

Claudia, Winston, Rod, and two other men in business suits heard dull thuds coming from room 709 as they approached the open door. When they entered, they found Jason positioned on his belly, facing the foot of the bed, with his chest draped over the knee gatch, set to its maximum, elevating his partially exposed buttocks high into the air. An oxygen mask was over his face, providing a bronchodilator treatment.

With his hips flexed at ninety degrees, and another pillow under his chest, he was shaped like an upside down, letter V. Braden was percussing over his ribs with his cupped hands.

Clup, thud, clup, thud, clup, thud, clup, thud, clup, thud.

"Almost sounds like horse hooves on cobblestones," Rod said. A big toothy grin appeared on his face. "Now, if I only had a camera for that tushy of yours."

"You wish!" Jason started to laugh. Then he turned red, and his eyes bugged out. Suddenly, he coughed up a huge wad of green mucous. "Disgusting." he said as he lifted the misting oxygen mask from his face. He spit into a tissue and closed it, depositing it into a paper bag that was taped to the footboard.

Claudia's turned away as the color drained from face. She turned nearly the same shade of green as she walked back out into the hallway. The other two men followed her.

"You're doing great, but there's a lot more where that came from," Braden said, not breaking the momentum of his *clup, thud, clup, thud, clup, thud.* "Keep it up!"

"I know," Jason answered, "but it's still disgusting." He coughed again into another tissue and then dropped it in the paper bag.

Conrad listened over Jason's chest with a stethoscope. "Better," he said, nodding, "Not great, not normal, but better."

With Aaron's help, Braden turned Jason almost all the way onto his side, elevating his right ribs and bending him in an awkward position.

"Welcome to the pretzel factory," Aaron said with a smile. As he held Jason in position, Braden began again, *Clup, thud, clup, thud, clup, thud, clup, thud.* Jason winced.

"I'm sorry," Braden said. "I know that hurts your chest-tube site."

Jason nodded. "It's okay. Keep going. Whatever it takes."

"That's the attitude, my boy," Conrad said, "I'd never have guessed that you'd be out on a floor three days after coming down with pneumonia and just five days after a thoracotomy."

"Two and a half days after pneumonia," Aaron bragged. "We were up here last night. You don't know my Jason like I know my Jason."

"Fair enough, Aaron. Fair enough," Conrad answered.

"Aaron, don't go boasting on my behalf," Jason said through the mask. "I don't want you to go and jinx me."

"I won't, Jason."

Jason turned red again as another coughing spell overtook him. "Disgusting," he said as he deposited another tissue.

"I'll be another five minutes," Braden said to the Winston and Rod. "Why don't you guys come back then?"

****

"Okay, you can come back in," Aaron said from the doorway. After they all returned, a man Jason didn't know stepped forward.

"Mr. Ackerman, Mr. Jaeger, I'm Jessie Kruger, owner and president of Kruger Luxury Pre-fab," he said extending his hand, "We're supplying the cottages for your mountain estate."

"Hello," they said. "Nice to meet you."

"You might remember Tobias Jacobson, Jr., Mr. Ackerman, from Jacobson Construction, the company that built your home. He's taking over the company operations from his father, Tobias, Sr."

"Yes, I do," Jason answered in recognition, as he reached for the offered hand. "Yes, I do. How've you been, Toby?" A flashback of the young, virile Toby, returned to Jason. He closed his eyes for a moment and remembered their camping trip in the canyon above the site where his home was being built. During that week,

Jason had introduced Toby to the pleasures of man on man sex. Toby was a quick study for he gave as good as he got.

Jason opened his eyes to Toby's smile.

"I still remember the sting from the sunburn I got when we went camping that week in the mountains," Toby said as he winked. He extended the middle finger of his right hand and caressed Jason's palm while they shook hands, recreating the secret handshake they had used from years before to signal a desire for sex.

Jason placed his left hand over Toby's right as he continued to shake it. Then he drew Toby in close and whispered, "As I remember it, you got stung from more than a sunburn, but that was a long time ago."

"I know, Jason," Toby whispered back as he caressed Jason's cheek with his own, "but I'll never forget the summer you made a man out of me, and I've never stopped trimming my pubes, like you taught me."

As Toby leaned away, his eyes twinkled.

Jason said aloud, "Toby, this is Aaron Jaeger, my partner."

"How do you do, Mr. Jacobson," Aaron said, shaking his hand. "It's a pleasure to meet you."

"And you as well, Mr. Jaeger."

"Please, it's Aaron."

"And please call me Toby."

"How's your father, Toby?" Jason asked.

"Like Jessie said, he's retiring, slowly, but he still comes into the office every day. I've taken over most of the daily operations. My son, August, has a real aptitude for the business. Dad and I are hoping he'll want to continue in our footsteps. He comes to all of our construction sites, but he's still about ten years away from joining a crew."

"A son, Toby!" Jason exclaimed. "That's

wonderful!"

"Yeah, thanks, Jason. I have another son, and two daughters. My wife, Sydney, and I are expecting our fifth in about three months. We're hoping for a girl."

"Good lord, Toby, that's quite a family you're building there!" Jason exclaimed. "I'm so happy for you."

"Well, I am in the construction business."

Jason laughed, and everyone else chuckled at the joke.

Jessie Kruger cleared his throat. "Mr. Ackerman, I apologize for interrupting, but we were instructed to limit our meeting time with you, seeing as you're still in the hospital." He looked at Claudia, who nodded her head.

"Go on," she mouthed.

"Would you like us to get down to business?"

"Yes, sorry, Mr. Kruger," Jason said. "It's just that I haven't seen Toby for over ten years, and please call me Jason and Aaron, Aaron. We're pretty informal."

"Sure, sure, and you can call me Jessie."

"Why don't we move to the suite next door," Aaron offered, "It's been set up as a conference room.
                    ****

After everyone had taken a seat at the table, Jason continued, "Before we begin, I've asked Claudia Duncan, our attorney and Winston Tanner, our financial manager to explain a few things first. When we're finished, Winston will cut down payment checks for you both."

"Thank you, Jason," Claudia began. "Jason and Aaron will be finalizing the formation of a corporation during the next week or so, the name to be determined. In the interim, we'll be conducting business for Jason and Aaron as a non-business entity, but we expect this all to be concluded soon. Does anyone have a problem with that?"

Jessie and Toby answered in unison, "No."

"Good. Winston?"

"Thank you, Claudia. The down payment checks will be drawn against Jason and Aaron's private funds. Are you both comfortable with this arrangement?"

"Certainly," Jessie said.

"Of course," Toby added.

"Now that that's settled," Aaron said, "what do you have to show us, Jessie?"

"Bring them on in, boys," he said as he walked to the door. A moment later two workmen entered, carrying five wooden models on short planks of wood.

"As you can see," Jessie continued, as he lifted the roof off one of the models, "you can view the standard floor plans, as they are currently designed, from above. That'll give you a better idea of their layout. Again, they can all be customized. Rod said you wanted ten of them."

"That was our initial thought," Aaron said. "Okay everyone, let's all have a look."

****

11:30 AM

After a little more than an hour, Jason spoke up. "Well it looks like we were on target, Jessie. We will take the ten units we've discussed. You can begin construction immediately, and just in time. I think I hear lunch arriving. I've ordered a buffet. I hope everyone can stay."

Chapter Forty-Three
Memories

Seventh floor elevator bank

As they stood waiting for the elevator to take them down to the ground floor, a smile spread across Rod's face as he rubbed his hand across his chin. He'd always wondered about the young Toby and Jason. Toby had seemed to hang on Jason's every word, back in the day. Nor did the caress of Toby's cheek when they shook hands go unnoticed. It only served to confirm his suspicions.

Back when he was airlifting supplies up to the construction site that eventually became Jason's home and compound, Jason had had dalliances with more than a few of the men up there, and he and Jack knew that all too well.

"So you remember Jason from back in the day, do you?" he asked Toby.

"Why yes, Rod. Of course I remember him," Toby answered, feigning innocence. "I was learning the ropes back then. He was incredibly kind to me. Even took me camping up in the canyon, high above the construction site for an entire week. I had a great time. One of the best of my life, and I'll never forget it."

"Jason was incredibly kind and generous to a lot of us that summer," Rod said, his eyes saying more.

"I've never known anyone else like him," Toby answered as he looked into Rod's eyes. "He showed me tremendous kindness many times that summer."

A wistful look came over Rod's face, and then he smiled. When Toby recognized the sentiment, his own face revealed his understanding. "Then we can both be grateful for having known him."

"My boy," Rod added, "you've said a mouthful."

Toby leaned forward and whispered to Rod, "It was more than a mouthful."

Rod barked a loud laugh and slapped his thigh. He began to laugh so loud and so hard that tears began to fall from his eyes.

"Did I miss something?" Jessie Kruger asked.

"Not at all, Jessie," Rod answered, after he regained his composure. "That was a long time ago. I guess you had to experience that summer to really understand it." Then he became serious. "But you will learn in the coming weeks that Jason Ackerman is one of the kindest and most generous men you will ever have the good fortune to meet. That I can tell you for sure."

"Hear, hear," Toby added, as he raised his hand and patted Rod's shoulder.

****

"Um, Jason?"

"Yes, Aaron."

"That look on your face when you closed your eyes, when you met Toby. What did that mean?"

"I was just remembering him from before."

"You mean ... you and him? You, ah..."

"Yes, Aaron. We had a thing, but that was a long time ago. He was young. I was young. It was hot. We were half naked most of the time. I was horny. He was horny."

"Do I need to worry?"

"Oh, Aaron! God no! I love you and only you."

"I think he remembered, too."

"I know he did. We had a summer together, Aaron. One unforgettable, once-in-a-lifetime summer together, but that's all. Didn't you ever mess around? I was so young back then, and I felt free from the world for the first time in my life. I was discovering what being gay and freedom felt like. That's all."

"And you haven't been with him since?"

"No, Aaron. Today is the first time I've laid eyes on him since that summer."

"And those feelings, they haven't returned?"

"Aaron! No, baby. What are you afraid of?"

"Jason, I just got you back. I don't want to lose you again."

"Aaron, you're not going to lose me. Nathan wasn't your only lover, was he?"

"No, Jason, but after I met Nathan, there was no one else."

"Did you ever run into any of the guys form your past who you took to bed, after you met Nathan?"

"Yeah, I did, but I didn't feel anything for them."

"And after I met you, I've had feelings for no one else but you."

"Like you don't have feelings for Rod and Jack?"

"Exactly, Aaron. They're my friends, not my lovers."

"How many guys were you with up there? I mean back then?"

"A handful. How many guys were you with before Nathan?"

Aaron blushed. "Dozens."

"So you see, you've had dozens of guys. I had a handful that summer. Probably a couple dozen over my lifetime, just like you, and you're not thinking about going back to any of them, are you?"

"No. Thank you, Jason. Thank you."

"You have nothing to worry about, Aaron. Now come here and lie down in bed with me. Even though I'm still too weak for sex, I'll try to show you how I feel, but remember, just because I can't make love to you doesn't meant that I don't want to."

"I love you, Jason."

"And I love you, Aaron."

Section Six
Going home

Chapter Forty-Four
Showing Gratitude

January 3, 2010

Ten days had passed since Jason had seen his home and a day more since their world had been nearly ripped away from them. He and Aaron had spoken briefly every day with Rod or Jack or Lars since they'd been transferred out of the SICU about the progress of the changes that were taking place within the stockade, or about the care and status of animals. During those days, Rod visited several times, bringing Jason's video camera with him. Though Aaron took the images in stride, Jason was shocked by the transformation that was taking place within the walls of the stockade. Even so, he realized that it wouldn't be until they actually saw the place that either of them would fully appreciate the effects their project would have on their lives.

As the days passed, Aaron's attitude began to change more and more. With the exception of Braden and Conrad, he'd become less the jovial, less carefree than the young man Jason had fallen in love with. Rather, he was now more focused than ever. Even the minutest detail of the reconstruction project did not pass him by. Jason's welfare was at stake, and nothing would ever jeopardize that again, not if it was within his power to prevent.

He also became very protective of Jason and focused on his needs. Aaron allowed no one to enter their suite who he did not know personally or who hadn't been vouched for by someone he'd learned to trust. Every newcomer was screened with a barrage of questions as to their qualifications and intentions towards Jason. Though it didn't happen often, if they didn't pass muster, he turned them away.

Nonetheless, both of them lauded the people who had cared for them at Hinnen Valley Medical Center, even in the smallest way, and they'd agreed that monetary gifts would be sent to them by Winston from a nondescript checking account as a way of repaying all of their kindnesses.

****

10:00 AM

After Winston returned from the bank, and under Aaron's watchful eye, Jason finally visited the dietary department to thank the staff who had tended to the luncheon he'd requested the day they arrived. On the sly, he slipped each of them a crisp, new, one-hundred-dollar bill when he shook their hands.

****

4:00 PM
Suite 709

Dr. Spencer knocked on the door and then came to the room. "Hello, Aaron. Hello, Jason. How are you both feeling?

"Tremendous!" Jason exclaimed.

"Fantastic!" Aaron added.

Both of them sat up from their matching, reclined, easy chairs.

"I'm so glad to hear it. Oh, no, please don't get up."

"No offense, Doctor, but I'm just itching to get out of here," Jason said as he stood and gave her a hug.

"None taken. I perfectly understand."

"I'll give you a moment." Braden nodded as he stood up from the sofa and then walked out the door.

"What brings you up here, Dr. Spencer?" Aaron

asked after he released her from a hug.

"I come bearing great news!"

A moment later, all the members of Jason and Aaron's treatment teams entered. Sonya, Sylvester, Reggie, Zaim, Bryce, Braden, and Dorothy the volunteer paraded in. They were followed by Conrad, Drs. Baum and Tunisia, Judy the anesthetist, Drs. Chandler and Gladstone, Drs. Emerson and Scottsdale, and even Dr. Richter, chief of neurosurgery, who had never laid hands on either of them, but was always kept in the loop. Then came the respiratory care staff, the housekeeping staff, and finally the dietary staff, who were pushing a cart with a large, decorated sheet cake, lit with a sparkler. Bring up the rear were Simone and Penelope.

Simone blew into a pitch pipe and the group started to sing.

"For they're some jolly good fellows,
For they're some jolly good fellows,
For they're some jolly good fellows,
Which nobody can deny."
"Which nobody can deny.
Which nobody can deny."
"For they're some jolly good fellows,
For they're some jolly good fellows,
For they're some jolly good fellows,
Which nobody can deny!"

After a long moment of cheering and applause, Drs. Chandler and Baum stepped forward.

"Gentlemen," they said in unison, "as of tomorrow morning, you are both officially discharged from Hinnen Valley Medical Center."

Aaron turned to Jason and picked him up and then swung him around in the air. "We're going home, Jason! We're finally going home!"

"Thank God!" Jason shouted, pumping the air

with his fist. Then he kissed Aaron.

After more cheering, everyone surrounded them to offer back pats, handshakes, and words of congratulations and encouragement.

Jason wiped tears from his eyes. "I don't know what to say, other than thank you."

"It is we who thank you, both," Simone answered. "You may not know this, Jason, Aaron, but we've all learned so much about how we practiced medicine before your stay with us, and I can tell you that we've already instituted changes in our operational policies. Because of you, we've instituted a twenty-four hour, hospital wide, visiting policy. We've begun to allow greater flexibility in family and significant other participation in patient care plans, and there are many other areas where we're making changes, and we're just getting started."

Aaron hugged her. "That's wonderful, Simone." Then he turned to the group. "Now who wants cake?"

****

5:00 PM

After everyone had left, Aaron collapsed in an easy chair. "I'm exhausted, but I'm so happy, too. Can you be both things at the same time?"

"Sure you can," Braden said. "You've been through a lot."

"I feel like a weight has been lifted off me." Then Aaron became teary-eyed. "I don't deserve it." He stood up and started to cry.

"What is it, baby?" Jason asked. "What's wrong?"

"There's nothing wrong," Aaron said through his tears. "I just can't believe it's true. We're finally going home."

"And thank God for that," Jason said as he

hugged Aaron and kissed him on the cheek.

Aaron's shoulders began to shake as he wept openly. "I've been such a prick to everyone," Aaron managed to say, "and they all came, with a cake and everything."

"No, you haven't, Aaron," Braden offered as he walked to them and patted Aaron's shoulder. "Everyone knows the horrors you've both been through, and they understand. You haven't done anything wrong."

"Really, Braden?"

"Yes, really. It's perfectly normal, and believe me when I tell you this. Your behavior was well above what's usual."

"Then you must deal with a lot of angry people," Aaron answered sniffling.

"A lot," Braden answered, offering him a tissue.

Chapter Forty-Five
A Proposition

8:30 PM

"How about a massage, guys?" Braden asked.

"You don't have to ask me twice," Aaron answered as he climbed out of his recliner. "After today, I could sure use one. Full body again?"

"If that's what you want, Aaron. Sure."

Without a shred of embarrassment, Aaron stripped out of his pajamas, grabbed a towel, and lay face down on the massage table that Braden had set up in the suite, covering his buttocks with the towel once he was down.

Braden began on Aaron's back with long, steady strokes that extended from his hips up and around his broad shoulders and then down along his sides.

"You need to insure your hands, Braden."

"Why's that, Aaron?"

"Because they're golden. You can't put a price on them."

"Why thank you, Aaron." Braden leaned in, using the knuckles on the back of his hands as he penetrated deep into the tissue fibers.

"Oh, God, just like that," Aaron moaned.

Braden began forming circles from the center, up and out to the sides and then back in again, just above the cleft between Aaron's buttocks, working his way slowly up Aaron's back until he reached his shoulders again. Then he focused on his trapezius and then deltoid muscles.

After completing his back, Braden folded the towel in half to expose Aaron's right buttock. He began to knead it using his palms and fingers from the middle to the outer sides and his fists from the middle towards the center, being sure to avoid the deep cleft that separated it from the left. Then he repeated the same strokes on the other side.

After Braden pulled the towel back up to cover him, Aaron spread his legs apart until his feet were positioned at the bottom corners of the table. As Braden moved into position to start on his legs, he cleared his throat and stopped.

"What's wrong, Braden?" Jason asked as he stood up and walked over.

"Um, I'm not sure what to do about that," he said, his face flushed and pointing to Aaron's semi-erect penis. It extended nearly a third of the way down his thighs.

"Aaron," Jason said, "you've got a … um, you're getting aroused. Braden doesn't need to see that."

"Oh, God. Sorry, Braden, I didn't even realize. I was so relaxed and then you started on my ass, I mean my butt. That must've done it."

"I'm sorry you had to see that, Braden," Jason said, again.

"It's okay, guys," Braden answered as he tried to maintain his composure. It happens." Inside, Braden was freaking out. *Oh my God. Look at his dick. It's huge. It's gigantic.*

"Braden," Jason said. "Braden," he repeated.

Braden jumped. "Yes?"

"It's not you."

"No, it's not you, Braden. It's definitely not you," Aaron added. "How do I say this? I'm a very sexual person, Braden. I guess getting the good news today really boosted my mood. When I was on the team, I used to get a hard-on all the time. The friction from my jock…"

"Aaron," Jason interrupted. "Braden doesn't need to hear that."

"Oh, sorry, Braden."

Oh my God, Braden thought. *How big does it get? All those men running around in their sweaty jockstraps...*

"Braden," Jason said. "Braden," he said, tapping Braden's arm.

Braden jumped. "Oh, sorry. Yes?"

"Braden, you don't have to continue."

As Aaron began to turn over on the massage table, the towel began to slide off him. By the time he had moved into a sitting position on the edge of the massage table, the towel had slid to the floor. His penis jumped up and began to grow. "Yeah, Braden, you don't have to finish."

"Aaron!" Jason exclaimed, "For God's sake, cover yourself!" Jason stooped to the floor, grabbed the towel, and threw it over Aaron's lap, but it had little effect in concealing his erection. It hung like a sheet thrown over a flagpole.

"Jason, we're all guys here. It's not like Braden hasn't seen another guy's penis. He's a nurse for God's sake."

Braden's face was crimson.

"Aaron, stop! Can't you see what you've done? You've embarrassed Braden."

"No, Jason," Braden said, regaining his composure. "It's me who should apologize. I know this happens sometimes. It's a reflex to physical stimulation. It happened before, when I was a massage therapist. I should have been better prepared, that's all."

"It's not your fault, Braden," Aaron said as he rearranged himself. "I guess you just woke him up. That's all."

"Aaron!" Jason exclaimed. "Just stop talking."

"It's just that caring for you guys has been like no

other assignment I've ever had," Braden said, softly. "It's like you're not just patients anymore. In the past ten days, I've come to think of you almost as friends. I'm so sorry. God, what I just said was totally inappropriate."

"Not at all, Braden," Aaron said. "Sorry, Jason, but I had to say it. Braden's been great to us."

"Thanks for that, Aaron, but I should have been better prepared." Braden shook his head. "I let my guard down. You're my patients, that's the truth of the matter."

"We understand," Jason said as he patted Braden's shoulder, "and we appreciate everything you've done for us. More than you'll ever know."

"Thanks for saying that, Jason, but still."

"No, really, but still nothing. As a matter of fact, Aaron and I were talking today. We realized we didn't know how we were going to manage without you after we go home."

"Go on, Jason," Aaron added. "Tell him."

"We have a proposition for you, Braden."

"What's that?"

"Would you be interested in coming up to the cabin with us for a week or two? Just until we're settled in and able to get around normally?"

"I don't know, Jason? I have my job here, and I wouldn't want to jeopardize that. Besides, I don't have that much vacation time left, even with what I saved from last year."

"We understand," Aaron said, "but would you be interested in helping us out if you could?"

"Yeah, I guess, but I don't see how I could make it work."

"Would it be all right with you if I made a phone call?" Jason asked. "I'm not just saying this because we want you for the next week or two, Braden. We'd both be interested in having you become part of our new company, part of the new family we're going to build, that is if you'd be interested."

"That's a lot to think about, Jason. I don't know. I have my career here."

"I don't want to pressure you at all, but we have a proposal for you to consider."

"What's that?"

"Let me make a phone call, see if we can get permission for you to come back home with us, just until we get settled in. While you're there, you can decide if you might be interested in joining our new company. There's no pressure here. If you say no, we'll drop it completely, but I can tell you, Aaron and I have been very impressed with your work and your work ethic. You're exactly the kind of person we want to include as we move forward."

"Okay, guys, you can ask, but I don't think they're going to go for it."

"Just leave it all to me," Jason said.

"And look," Aaron added, pointing to his crotch. "All this business talk made my erection disappear. Now you can finish my massage." Aaron started to laugh, and Jason laughed. Then Braden joined in.

"Okay, big guy. Lie down on the table, but no funny business."

Aaron laid down on his back and discreetly positioned the towel over himself. "I promise. No funny business on my part." He smiled a devious smile and raised his eyebrows. "But I can't promise what he'll do. He has a mind of his own sometimes."

"Aaron!" Jason exclaimed.

"Just kidding, Braden. Just kidding." Then he became serious. "No, really. Believe me, Braden, I'm not going to touch you. I'd never do that."

Braden blushed. "Okay, agreed."

Chapter Forty-Six
You're Mine

9:45 PM

As the steam began to rise in the shower, Aaron squeezed out a portion of shampoo into his hand. "I feel so good after Braden's massage." He began to lather the shampoo into Jason's hair. "I'm so relaxed."

"Mmmmm," Jason hummed as he leaned back against Aaron's chest. "That feels so nice."

"I hope he'll come with us."

"I know. Me, too." Jason's head dropped forward. "Oh, Aaron, you're giving me goosebumps."

"Just relax, baby. I love doing this for you." Aaron dug his fingertips deep into Jason's scalp. "I hope you'll let me do it after we get home."

"That would be wonderful." Jason's body started to sway from side to side. "Aaron?" he said under the stream of warm water, cascading down his back.

"Yes, my love?"

"I've asked Conrad and Braden to leave us alone for the rest of the night."

"Why's that?"

"Because," he said, as he turned around and rinsed the shampoo from his head, "I want you to make love to me."

"When?"

"Tonight."

"Tonight? Is it safe? You're just getting over pneumonia. I've been afraid to even think about it. What if…"

"You have nothing to worry about. I've already cleared it with Conrad. He says if I feel like I'm up to it then there's no reason I can't, as long as I listen to what my body tells me."

"Jason, I would love to, but remember, I've only been inside you once and that was months ago. Do you think you can take me?"

"Yes," Jason circled his right index finger around a tuft of Aaron's chest hair. "If you open me up slowly, there's no reason why I shouldn't be able to." He glided his fingers down further and then encircled Aaron's shaft with his hand. "You see, before you came back, I used the dildo."

He lowered his hand and cupped Aaron's enormous ball sack. Then he began to pat it from below, bouncing his balls up and down in the process. "Remember the dildo you were so afraid of, way back when, the one you didn't believe was bigger than you?"

Aaron moaned. "Oh, God. I mean, yes, yes, I sure do."

Jason traced the fingers of his left hand down Aaron's chest to his belly and then below, encircling Aaron's shaft again. He began to milk it, slowly. "Well I've been using it regularly."

"Really?" Aaron's voice jumped an octave. "Why?" he squeaked.

"Because it was the closest thing I had to you." Jason leaned his head against Aaron's chest and began to tremble. His voice broke. "I wanted to be ready, just in case you really did return to me."

"Oh, baby, don't cry." Aaron lifted Jason's head and tenderly kissed his mouth. "I'm here now, and I'm never going away again. Never."

Jason reached his arms around Aaron's neck and pulled him down for another kiss. He opened his mouth and moved his tongue against Aaron's teeth until he opened his mouth to received him. As their tongues began to caress each other, Jason pulled away.

"That's what I want you to do with me, Aaron.

Open me up, slowly. Caress me inside as only you can do, and claim me as you own."

Aaron lifted Jason by the buttocks. Jason wrapped his legs around Aaron's torso and began to slowly thrust his hips up and down, bringing Aaron's manhood to attention. When it was as rigid as a pillar, Jason lowered himself to the floor, released his grip, turned off the water, and turned away. As he reached for a towel, he looked over his shoulder. "Now dry yourself off. I'll meet you in bed just as soon as I've cleaned myself out."

"How are you going to…"

"Braden got me a kit."

"You're amazing, Jason."

****

"You look beautiful," Aaron said as Jason approached the bed.

"So do you. How did I get so lucky?"

"Luck had nothing to do with it, baby. You saved my life. You were kind to me, and you took care of me, and day by day, I fell more and more in love with you, and now you're stuck with me." Aaron opened his arms, and Jason climbed into them.

"I can live with that."

As they began to kiss, Aaron rolled Jason onto his back. "Now let me take care of you for a change."

"Just go slow, Aaron, and remember, just because I can't go for too long doesn't mean that I don't want to."

"Yes, baby. I'm going to take such good care of you."

"I'm all yours, Aaron."

"Yes, you're mine."

Aaron rolled to his side and began to slowly run the back of his fingertips across the thick, trimmed hair that covered Jason's chest, lingering over each nipple when he crossed them. Then he moved it up and down his belly, barely making contact, raising goosebumps. "I could do this for hours, baby, but I know I'd be pushing it, and I don't want to put too much stress on you."

"It's not that I don't want to, it's just…"

"Hush, my love, I know," he answered as he covered Jason's mouth with his own.

He ran his fingertips through the manicured lawn above Jason's growing shaft and then cupped his balls into his palm, gently squeezing and massaging them.

Jason's lips parted. As he let out a moan, Aaron drove his tongue deep inside Jason's mouth.

"Baby, I could come just like this," Jason moaned again as he pulled his mouth away.

"Is that what you want?"

"No, I want to come with you inside me."

"Then I'll make that happen."

Aaron slid himself down along the length of Jason's body until his face hovered above his shaft. He lowered his head and gently squeezed his balls as if he was testing the ripeness of an orange, just enough to bring the first drop of sweet nectar to the surface. When it appeared at the slit in the head, he flicked the tip of his tongue across it, lifting the drop as it emerged. Immediately, he encircled the reddened helmet with his mouth and began to flick his tongue around the corona and down the frenum. Then he began to suck.

Jason's body spasmed. "Oh! Oh, my! Aaron."

Aaron rose to his knees and pivoted around while moving his right thigh across Jason's chest until he straddled it. He opened his mouth as wide as he could and slid down the shaft, deep throating it until his nose became buried in Jason's balls.

Jason lifted his head and pulled Aaron's sack into his mouth as he nuzzled his nose behind it, inhaling

Aaron's musk.

Aaron sucked Jason's shaft hard as he pulled up and lingered over the crown, and then he released it for a moment. "Oh, Jason, your scent. It drives me wild."

Instinctively, Jason spread open his thighs when Aaron began to milk his shaft with his mouth. When Aaron reached down and began to circle his middle finger around Jason's hole, Jason groaned and tightened his abdominal muscles, causing his hips to roll upward. "Ow! Aaron, help me. It's pulling on my ribs."

"Where the chest tube was?"

"Yeah."

"I've got you, baby." Aaron grasped Jason's butt cheeks with his hands, spreading them apart, while he slid his mouth from the head and traced his tongue downward along the underside of Jason's shaft. When he reached his balls, he mouthed them one at a time, rolling them against his tongue. Then he moved down further, licking along the shaft of as it ran beneath the base of his pelvis until he reached Jason's clenching hole. In one long motion, he spread his tongue wide and licked along the crack from the base of Jason's cock and across the hole, until he came out the other end. Then he tightened his tongue into a lance and began to drive it against Jason's outer sphincter, jabbing and wiggling it as he went until it relented and opened itself to him.

Jason's body began to tremble and lurch in time with Aaron's advances. Guttural sounds erupted from his throat as Aaron devoured him like a predator feasting over a fresh kill. The louder Jason became, the more Aaron was driven into a feeding frenzy as he sucked and slurped and swallowed until he breached the final barrier.

Aaron pulled away and reached for a bottle of lube. He popped it open and squeezed a huge glop over his fingers.

"Aaron," Jason panted, "where did you get lube?"

"Rod brought it. Said we just might need it."

"Thank God for Rod!"

"Stop talking, baby. Just lie back and enjoy this."

Aaron wiggled his middle finger against the outer sphincter of Jason's hole at the same moment he dove down on his shaft again and began to suck, feverishly. Jason's hole puckered, but then opened as he advanced past the inner sphincter. Making small circles as he probed deeper, he massaged the muscles and coated them with the slick lube until his finger was in to the last knuckle. Then he added his index finger and began sliding them together in and out and around and around.

"God!" Jason shouted. His breathing became ragged as he gasped against the advance of Aaron's ministrations, and when he added a third finger, Jason began to pant.

"You're almost there, my love," Aaron said as he readied the fourth.

"I'm ready, Aaron. Please. I'm ready."

When Aaron had all four fingers inside him and began to caress his prostate, Jason's hips began to buck, wildly. A jet of pre-cum was ejected from the now purple head, and Aaron sucked it down his throat, greedily.

"Easy, baby. I don't want you to hurt yourself."

"I can't help it, Aaron. Not when you do that!"

"I'm sorry, I was too aggressive. I forgot…"

"Don't apologize! Not for that! Not ever!"

"Roll onto your side, baby. I'm going to take you slow. Slow and steady. Just let me do everything. I don't want you to rip open any stitches. How would I explain that to your doctors?"

"Aaron, forget the fucking stitches! They're coming out tomorrow. Now, please," Jason moaned, "make love to me."

Aaron's cock bounced with each heartbeat, aching for release. He slid his body next to Jason's, rolled him back onto his side, and encircled him in an embrace. Then he slowly slid his shaft along the cleft between Jason's butt cheeks, through his thighs, and under his balls until its head found daylight on the other side. Jason reached down and scooped up what remained of Aaron's saliva and mixed it with the pre-cum that oozed from his slit. He grasped the engorged head of Aaron's cock and began to lubricate it.

He opened his hand when Aaron held out the bottle of lube and squeezed out a generous amount into his palm. When Aaron began to thrust back and forth between Jason's thighs, Jason made a fist around the shaft. Once it was good and slick, Jason reached his hand behind him and applied the remainder of the lube to his primed and ready hole.

Aaron withdrew his shaft and guided it to the opening. Ever so gently, he pressed inward. For a moment he felt resistance, but Jason took a deep breath and then exhaled. As Jason began to release his breath, Aaron advanced and slid in the first six inches until he felt the head tap up against Jason's prostate.

Jason sucked in his breath and slid his hips back, causing Aaron's swollen head to slide past the swelling gland as he let out a soft moan. Aaron hugged him tightly and slowly advanced until all ten inches of his manhood were buried deep inside. He held there while Jason began to slide his hips forward and backwards until he felt Aaron's glans caress his prostate again and again.

"Right there, Aaron. Right there. No deeper."

"Okay, baby. I'll take it from here."

Aaron reached down with his left hand and encircled Jason's leaking shaft, pumping it in time with the thrust of his hips.

"How's that, baby?"

"Perfect," Jason moaned. "I could live in this moment for the rest of my life."

As blood flooded the floor of Jason's abdomen, both lobes of his prostate began to swell and harden, making it all the more sensitive to Aaron's glans as it flicked against it, back and forth.

"Mmmm, baby, it's like your prostate is palming the head. It's so intense, Jason, so right."

"It's better than right, Aaron. I can feel myself swelling deep inside, and I'm getting warm. The fluids are beginning to shift, and my balls are tingling."

"Me too, baby. It's so beautiful. With each pass of my cockhead I can feel your orb getting harder. I can feel it growing."

"Soon, Aaron. Soon. I'm not sure how long I can last."

"I can hold you here for a while if you like."

"No, I want to come. I need to come. Make me come, Aaron. Make me come."

Aaron slowed his pace and paused momentarily each time he withdrew and each time he thrust forward. Jason's body began to quiver, then to shake.

"I can't control it, Aaron. It's building. It's so intense. Oh, baby, it's going to happen. I can feel it."

"Good."

"Yes, Aaron, just like that. You're bringing me up. You're bring me up. It's … it's so beautiful."

"Yes, baby, me, too. Let's just let it happen when it happens."

"Oh!"

"Oh!"

"Oh, God. Yes!"

"Oh, Aaron!"

Jason's body began to shake. He couldn't control

it. He couldn't stop it. He began to grunt.

"Here it comes, baby. I'm gonna shoot!" Aaron pressed his mouth to Jason's shoulder and gently clenched his teeth down against the tensed muscles. He began to growl.

"Aaron! Oh, God! Aaron!"

Jason's eyes rolled back in his head. Aaron wrapped his arms around him in a bearhug as he thrust one last time.

"Now, Aaron! Now!" Jason's cock erupted in a stream of two week, pent-up, man-spunk as his body rocked and quaked and shuddered while guttural, animalistic sounds escaped from his throat.

Aaron held on tight. He wrapped his legs around Jason's and pressed his hips forward, impaling his shaft to its hilt, into Jason's depths, as the first wave of cum painted Jason's colon white.

The back of Jason's head slammed into Aaron's chest as all the muscles in his body tensed at once, turning his skin a deep purple and raising the veins on his arms, legs, face and neck. His mouth opened in a silent cry.

Aaron pulled back and then thrust in again, then again, and again in time with each contraction of his prostate, driving his seed into the recesses of Jason's depths.

When it was over, both of them collapsed, spent, their love and their lust realized. They woke the following morning, still cradled in the same embrace.

Chapter Forty-Seven
Discharged

January 4, 2010

Since Jason had given them instructions the day they had arrived at Hinnen Valley Medical Center, Claudia and Winston spent the days devising a business plan to ensure that Nathan's Promise would become a reality. Jason and Aaron finally settled on a combination of their names to reflect their new company and they signed incorporation papers for Jaron Enterprises, L.L.C., the morning of their discharge from the hospital.

****

11:45 AM

Aaron had a particularly hard time saying goodbye to Dr. Chandler. She'd become like a doting grandmother to him in the short time he'd been a patient at the hospital, as much to his surprise as to hers. She revealed how much she had come to care for him, too, when she began to cry when he scooped her into his arms and lifted her off the ground and hugged her goodbye on the hospital's helipad.

Both Jason and Aaron promised to return as ordered for their follow-up appointments with the specialists who had treated them. They also promised to visit with Simone and Penelope either in the city or to have them flown up to the cabin, for they had developed a great fondness for them and a tremendous appreciation for the way they'd championed them.

Chapter Forty-Eight
I'm With My Love, and oh, How I'll Love Him

12:29 PM

The moment Big Daddy lifted off the hospital's helipad, the last of the tension and worry that Aaron had carried the entire time they were in the hospital, slipped away. "I can't wait to see it, Jason. Are you excited?"

"Excited isn't the word I'd use, Aaron, but I'm glad to see you returning to your old self. Resolved is more what I'm feeling. Everything's going to be different now. Our old life, the life I had hoped for will never be for us. We didn't have even forty-eight hours, did we?"

"No, love, we didn't, but we did have that first night."

"That was a fantasy, Aaron," Jason said as he laced his fingers through Aaron's. "But that's not as important as us being together now, whatever this is going to become." Jason lifted the back of Aaron's hand to his mouth and kissed it. "We'll be together. That's all that's important."

"That's a great outlook," Conrad said.

"Yeah, guys," Braden added, "that's all in the past. Focus on the future you're going to build."

Big Daddy climbed as he approached the ridge. "Any moment now, guys," Rod said into his headset. Aaron, Braden, and Conrad leaned over their armrests to peer out the large window in Big Daddy's cargo hold door.

As they crested the peak, the stockade came into view. Jason sat motionless, as he stared silently at what used to be his home. He barely recognized the place.

"Wow," was all he could manage to say.

Aaron squeezed his hand, stunned. "I had no idea."

Rod listened through his headset to the conversation behind him as they began their descent. He'd known it was going to be a shock to them both, but he'd followed Jason's instructions to the T. They were going to be safe now, at least as safe as anyone could be, and that's what was most important.

"Guys," he said to them, "I know this isn't the future you'd planned or wanted, but it is a future, think about that. If things had gone differently—if the bullet that hit you, Jason, if it had taken a lethal trajectory, if it was a bullet that had struck Aaron in the head and not the post—you might not be going home at all."

Jason shook his head, shook out all the bad thoughts, and turned to look into Aaron's eyes. "Rod's right, Aaron. What the hell am I thinking? We're together. Whatever it may be. However it must be. Wherever it will be, all that's important is that I'm with my love, and oh, how I'll love him."

"Oh, Jason, yes. Whatever. However. Wherever. I'm with my love, and oh how I'm going to love him."

Aaron leaned in for a kiss, and Jason gave it to him.

Touchdown.

To be continued...

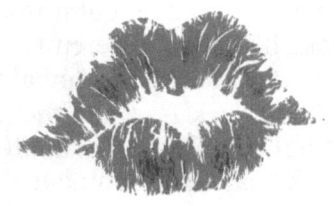

EVERNIGHT PUBLISHING ®

www.evernightpublishing.com